THE MOON TO ME

Praise for Ana Hartnett

Coasting and Crashing

"*Coasting and Crashing* is a slam dunk for fans of watching loveable disasters slowly figure it all out and find love. It's especially satisfying if you were one of those high achieving kids who showed early academic or athletic talents and subsequently had a world of pressure placed upon your shoulders. Even if you weren't or have no idea how basketball works, it's still a great romance worthy of your time."—*The Lesbrary*

Comes in Waves

"I thoroughly enjoyed this. It is the first of her books that I have read, and I shall no doubt now want to read more."—*This Lesbian Is Reading*

Crush

"Ana Hartnett Reichardt infuses her love for wine and the winemaking process through the pages of *Crush* in such an educational yet effortless way that I was able to follow along and visualize every detail. I also couldn't help falling in love with the whole process. I highly recommend this book if you're looking for low angst and high sweetness. So grab a glass of pinot, and settle into your favorite spot to enjoy this sublime read!"—*Lesbian Review*

Catching Feelings

"I have yet to read Ana Reichardt's debut, book one in this series, *Changing Majors*. That is something I will soon rectify after reading *Catching Feelings*. *Catching Feelings* is a wonderful sophomore effort by Ana Hartnett Reichardt. The characters are so relatable and their growth both individually and as a couple, was beautifully written. I can't wait to see what comes next from this author. Her star has only begun to rise."—*Sapphic Book Review*

"From start to finish *Catching Feelings* is such a great read… It is full of sweet moments to delight, heart-stopping moments to thrill and steamy moments to make your temperature soar. Andrea and Maya have to navigate college, competitive sports, and people who want to get in the way of their friendship and eventual romance. This makes for a compelling read that keeps you turning the page and ends up wrapping you in a warm hug."—*Lesbian Review*

By the Author

Crush

Comes in Waves

The Hard Stuff

The Moon to Me

Alder Series

Changing Majors

Catching Feelings

Chasing Cypress

Coasting and Crashing

Visit us at www.boldstrokesbooks.com

THE MOON TO ME

by

Ana Hartnett

2026

THE MOON TO ME

ISBN 13: 978-1-63679-918-6

THIS TRADE PAPERBACK ORIGINAL IS PUBLISHED BY
BOLD STROKES BOOKS, INC.
P.O. BOX 249
VALLEY FALLS, NY 12185

FIRST EDITION: FEBRUARY 2026

CREDITS
EDITOR: BARBARA ANN WRIGHT
PRODUCTION DESIGN: STACIA SEAMAN
COVER DESIGN BY INKSPIRAL DESIGN

Acknowledgments

It's hard to overstate how special writing this book was to me. Exploring Eaden's grief and how it relates to her view of herself, her hope for the future, and the possibility of love was cathartic on so many levels. For a lot of us, losing a parent is, unfortunately, a familiar experience. One that tends to highlight and magnify everything else in our lives that is tender, falling short, or achy. Writing Eaden's journey through grief, and most importantly through love, was a gift. An opportunity to revisit the precarious time of my life when I lost my dad shortly after my parents' divorce, and a reminder of what he left me. How he left me. Changed for the better.

I also had the pleasure of writing Florence, a partner who gives steady support, strengthens Eaden, and resolutely stands by her as a friend through the darkest of times. Florence is a woman who has overcome her own grief and is strong enough to hold the chaos of her own world and relationships, while keeping space for Eaden's. She is a character full of light, creativity, and compassion. The joy of bringing her to life on the page is something I cherish, for I'm privileged to be inspired by someone so wonderful in my own life.

As always, I want to give a huge thanks to Bold Strokes Books for publishing my work and to my editor, Barbara Ann Wright, for helping me to better tell my stories and making me laugh all the way through my edits.

The best thing about being an author is the friends I have made in this beautiful community of writers and readers. I can't imagine my life without them. So, thank you Morgan, J, Kris, Krystina, Macon, and so many others for joining me on this journey. And to the amazing authors who have shown me grace and helped me along the way, I am so grateful for you. Georgia Beers, Melissa Brayden, and Aurora Rey, I'm looking at y'all.

Of course, a huge thank you to my mom for always supporting me. She has every one of my books stacked proudly on her coffee table. And to my family for always being there for me and putting up with me.

I want to give the biggest thanks of all to my partner, Lauren. For always seeing me through the dark and sitting with me through the storms. For being the moonlight in my midnight.

For Lauren, the moonlight in my midnight.

CHAPTER ONE

Stand straight.

I can almost feel my mother's knuckles gently prod my back. Suffering from horrid back pain herself, she was always warning me of the chaos and pain a life of poor posture could bring. Pain that lived just below the surface of her smile and cut off her embraces with a deep sigh. Pain that ultimately took her life. She didn't want that for me.

Stand straight as my world crumbles.

Standing as my world crumbles defies everything I have come to understand about physics. Instead, I fall. I fall to my knees on the soaked, spongy carpet. It makes more sense to crumble like everyone else around me. Their sadness, their guilt, their embarrassment, their anger. I'm learning they matter.

They have *mass*. They cascade. They grow. They *accelerate*.

They are forces that bring me to my knees.

This isn't the woman I want to be and certainly not the woman I was raised to be. Maybe those two facts aren't causal, and I am the painfully average woman I turned out to be. The woman who can't take charge and right the sinking ship that is my mother's funeral. There is no captain because *she* was the captain.

"Don't be an asshole, okay?"

I wasn't.

"Just don't," Sean, my older brother, repeats.

"I wasn't trying to be."

Don't be an asshole?

Sean has always been a bit patronizing, a bit dominating, a bit obsessed with his masculinity. And I have rarely challenged him. The cost risk analysis alone is enough to keep my mouth shut because no one throws a tantrum like a grown man with a wounded ego. And I'm not interested in rolling my sleeves up for something I can't change. Plus, it broke our mother's heart when we argued. Only on the rarest occasions, when he pontificates on the "the weakness of society" and gets a little too close to sounding like the president he voted for, will I merely offer an alternate view.

On the rarest occasions.

Not at her funeral. Like I said, it would break her heart. I ignore Sean's harshness and get to work next to him, though I can feel my blood pressure spike. Can hear the whooshing in my ears. The funeral service was dry, impersonal, the opposite of who our mother was. It only added to my broken heart.

I bite my lip and force myself back to the moment.

We use every napkin and a few rags provided by the horrified Olive Garden server with bright red cheeks and wide doughy eyes— yes, we're hosting my mother's funeral at Endless Breadsticks—but not even that is enough to sop up the water currently drowning the collapsed watercolor portrait of her. Words like *accident* and *poor things* pepper the whispers of our hovering family. My eyes sting under the gaze of theirs.

Ice water crawls through the knee of my pants. My breathing becomes shallow.

My control is slowly slipping. It's been a hard day.

"Eaden. I said, I got it." He leans into my shoulder to wipe the precarious spot where the glass of the frame is shattered. As water bleeds, the colors billow. My favorite image of Mom—her reading in the sunlight with a cup of tea cradled in her hands—is swiftly being ruined. Just like her funeral.

She deserves so much better than this. A palace full of mourners. A three-star Michelin restaurant. A symphony.

She deserves the moon. And my heart is imploding.

Our friend Florence painted this portrait, and the thing I love most about it is how the colors swirl and blend into not only a true representation of her physical being but a true representation of her spirit also. I'm a scientist. Worked in a lab for a decade before I followed my mom's path of teaching when I turned thirty. But even my analytical brain is dying to say *aura*. Florence captured her aura with how she pushed and pulled my mom's favorite colors across the canvas. That's why it's one of a kind. That's why I can't just print another. That's why I'm desperately trying to save it from drowning.

I need to save her.

I don't budge when Sean tries to shoulder me out of the way. "Stop," I say, my voice meek and whiny. Embarrassing. I've already lost my mother once. Now I'm letting her aura drown in an Olive Garden. This must have metaphysical implications I cannot even conceive, and I deserve every one.

Bile crests in my throat like the tide, turning my mouth bitter, then fading. It's feeling like too much. This day.

According to the official obituary, Eileen Knight Bilbo—as in "dildo" with Bs—is survived by my dad, Sean, and me. It's the only glaring lie in the three measly paragraphs of her watered-down life. She was born in St. Louis, Missouri: fact. She was a middle school science teacher: fact. She was the only diehard Cardinals fan with a soft spot for the Cubs: fact. But the three of us surviving?

Well, that's a lie.

We were in hospice before she even left us. Sean had just lost all his savings in a failed tech startup that helped him be neither less entitled nor less insufferable. Now he just feels "owed." His words. I had been dumped for the second time this year. Dodged another bullet, really. If bullets were kind, beautiful doctors beginning their fellowships in pediatric surgery in the fall. She said her schedule was about to be chaos, and though she really enjoyed dating me, it wouldn't be fair to either of us. Only, she tucks her hair behind her ear when she lies, and she wasn't lying about her schedule becoming chaos or how it wouldn't be fair to either of us. It's hard to argue my hypothesis that something about me is fatally flawed when it comes to women.

Oh, and my dad was having an affair with his personal trainer. His thirty-four-year-old personal trainer. The bile laps against my tongue again. *Same age as his youngest child.* My dad is the last man you'd expect to cheat on his wife and probably the last man you'd expect a young trainer would want to have sex with. He got caught three months before my mom's "routine" operation. But it didn't feel very routine when she died of sepsis last week.

Living.

Then dead.

Just like that, the warmth of our family vanished.

Sean hadn't been home much, busy untangling himself from the startup. When it was clear Mom was declining fast, he visited her in the hospital once. *One time.* Claimed he was too "upset" by the whole thing. Too upset to help plan the funeral. To help my dad with the logistics of her will. To notify the rest of our family of her passing. And my dad was too embarrassed and devastated to do much of anything besides show up. I'm surprised he even did that. No one knows about the affair besides me and my mom—well, just me now—yet he wears his shame in public like a winter coat draped over his mourning.

So naturally, it fell on me to pull it all together. To be calm. To plan a funeral in a week between grading finals and inputting grades for the semester. But keeping the family together was her dying wish of me. *No pressure.*

Sean sighs. "Damn it, Eaden—"

"No. Fuck this." I drop the rag on her hands, the delicate freckles on her knuckles melting together into a blur. Try not to catch her eye. She'd be so ashamed of us. Of me. I lost control when I was supposed to be strong. When I was supposed to be the glue of this family, just like her. Water trickles down my shins as I stand. With so many eyes on me, I try to look composed, but I'm pretty sure everyone just heard me cuss at my mourning brother.

I'm a grown woman. With soaked slacks. Who just made another scene at this terrible funeral. The shame makes me want to vomit.

"Relax. Flo made copies. She'll get you one." Riley, my cousin who caused this chaos and toppled the painting by having too many beers and using elaborate gestures, drops her hand on my shoulder. Another millibar of pressure threatening my collapse. Or maybe explosion. "What's wrong with you anyway? Can't you just enjoy the party?"

It takes every ounce of strength left in me not to punch her in her perfect face and chip one of those blaringly white teeth the way she chipped mine when we were ten. Give her a bloody nose like she gave me when I was eight. Never of malice but of her fragile ego. Of her need to handedly win, though I had never been real competition. She has that in common with my brother. But my mom had a soft spot for Riley, I remind myself. It only makes me want to tackle her more, even though she has three inches and twenty pounds of muscle on me.

I can hear her voice. My mom pulls me into her soft chest and whispers so only I can hear as Riley and Sean laugh about teaming up and successfully raiding the beautiful and architecturally sound fort I'd spent all afternoon building. I'm ten. "Oh, baby girl. You have quiet strength. You'll find, when you're older, it's a superpower."

I need to be strong now. But it's growing more difficult by the second. This funeral is a textbook example of entropy.

"It's my mom's funeral. Not a party," I say in the calmest voice I can manage, but my words tremble.

She sips her beer. Of course she's still drinking. "It's actually a celebration of life." She grins, clearly enjoying her little quip.

I stare. Why am I shocked by her attitude? This is Riley to her core. Riley Beckett. The fact that her mother married someone with a last name that isn't "Bilbo" may just be the thing I resent most about her.

"A celebration of life," I repeat.

But I feel like dying.

"There ya go, Eaden. You just gotta relax."

The gaze of the room is hot on my back, and I refuse to further ruin my mom's funeral with another incident.

Riley squeezes my shoulder and says, "It's what Aunt Eileen would have wanted."

I shake off her grip and walk away before I full-on cry. Or shove her. It's all too close to the surface, threatening to rip through my skin. This must be what it feels like to molt an exoskeleton. I plow through shoulder pads of blazers, brush past people I've known my entire life, to find somewhere I can breathe more—

"Ah, Eaden. There you are, dear." Uncle Rich from my dad's side stops me with a hand on my shoulder. Another millibar. "I'm so sorry. Eileen was one of the most wonderful people I've ever known. Warm and bright and smart as hell."

My eyes water. She was warm and bright and smart as hell. She was wonderful. "Thank you, Uncle Rich. She really was."

"It's such a shame what happened." He drops his chin to his barrel chest and shakes his head. "I always thought H. T. Harris was a hospital in decline. To botch such a simple procedure. I told your father to take her to Front City, but he was stubborn about it." He wipes down his whiskery gray beard as I remain quiet. "So what exactly happened in the OR? Things weren't sterile or what?"

My mouth is sticky and dry, my tongue glued to the roof of my mouth.

"You know what?" He pats my shoulder. "This is probably the last thing you want to be talking about, huh?"

I nod to his understatement of the century before I disappear to the patio to escape Riley and Sean and the rest of the family.

Riley and I grew up together, and she's supposedly my best friend. But of all the people here, she torments me the most. Especially tonight, acting so heartbroken at the service with tears streaking her face, accepting condolences as if this was *her* mother's funeral. And once her attention bucket was full, she switched to party mode at the reception. It is fully consistent with everything I know about her, to drink up every ounce of attention in the room. Our entire lives. Of course, she was the star basketball player, the star softball player, voted "Most Likely to Steal Your Girl." The last one was awarded to her by me after she swooped in and took Ashley West on a date after we'd made out in my car junior year. She didn't even like Ashley. Just had to have her because I wanted her.

But my mom saw the best in people. And though Riley is a wildly successful medical sales rep who always cheats on her amazing on-again, off-again girlfriend, Florence, my mom loved her. She gave Riley a place to feel safe when my aunt and uncle didn't handle her coming out well. They grew to accept and love her queerness, but for months, Riley was over every day and sleeping on the floor by my bedside every night. I don't know what finally changed her parents' mind about it all. Only that one day, after Riley broke into tears at our dinner table, my mom drove her back to her house, and they were gone for hours. After that, Riley slept over less, and things seemed to ease with her parents.

I typically have a vast lake of tolerance for her, but right now, it's just a dusty, decimated crater.

The breeze rustles the oak tree on the other side of the parking lot. Though it's an oddly cool night in Atlanta for late May, and the sparse strip mall lot looks almost like a dark ocean through my watery eyes, I wish I was gone. Anywhere but here. Into some gentle ether. Everyone in there has hurt me today, and I'm frustrated to the point that I wish I could cry. But what scares me the most is the realization that my shame, anger, and outright disgust of this night is no comparison to the obliterating weight of loss. Incomparable. Atoms to extinction-worthy asteroids.

What if, when all my anger fades, all that's left is something I can't face? When the only person in this life who truly sees me and loves me dies, doesn't that make me no one? Doesn't that make me nothing? Doesn't that make me utterly alone?

I lean on my elbows. The cold of the railing digging into my forearms is grounding. "Yes," I whisper. "Yes, it does."

The door creaks open, but I keep my gaze locked on the strip mall ocean, unwilling to welcome a disturbance. A gentle hand lands on the center of my back. I know it's Flo before she even speaks. No other *living* person would touch me like that. With such tender care, wanting nothing of me but to be my friend. Wanting nothing from today other than to fortify the cracks. To support Riley, me, and our family. Why she spends her love on someone like my cousin will forever baffle me. How she spends it so freely, so surely, so earnestly.

Florence drapes her arm over my shoulder as she settles against the railing next to me. "One for the books, huh?"

Her light perfume is a floral zest in the darkness of tonight, a fresh bloom adorning a grave, and I focus on the comfort of her scent to keep myself from trashing Riley in front of her. At the end of the day, Riley is my family. Plus, the thing about Florence is, she doesn't need to be told. She doesn't need to be told why I'm outside wanting to disappear into unknown ethers. She doesn't need to be told that her maybe ex-girlfriend is morally *dark* gray, and she deserves exponentially better. And she doesn't need to ask. She just understands.

I shake my head, unwilling to look at her until I'm positive the tears welling in my eyes won't fall. "I'll say."

She squeezes my shoulder, and I lean into her, letting her slightly smaller body envelop mine. A red curl tickles my cheek, and a metal button from her denim jacket digs into my arm. But it's the first time today I can rest. Breathe.

"I'm sure this funeral is exactly how you imagined it," she says, her words peppering through an obvious grin.

I smile, too. It feels like exercising for the first time in months. Foreign, tired, immensely difficult. But so deeply nourishing. "Exactly how I hoped it would go. Right down to my soaking pants and your ruined painting. Beautiful."

"Ah, see? The true marks of a lovely celebration." She rubs my shoulder, and I let our sarcastic joking be the balm over a tender burn. "I especially loved when the priest called her 'Eileen Dilbo.'"

I laugh because it's just ridiculous at this point. I laugh because it's almost as good as crying. "As if our name isn't close enough to dildo as it is."

"Hey, dildos bring a lot of joy." She shrugs. "We'll say it was a stylistic choice from Father Pete to keep things spicy."

I've only experienced a few moments of reprieve like this since my mom passed away last week. They mostly happen in the morning before school, when I can successfully flood my brain with grading exams and working. I inevitably take a couple breaks to scroll the morning news and pop in on Instagram. Florence sometimes has active stories of her current illustrations or beautiful flowers or memes about how much coffee she consumes. A few months ago, while I was bleary-eyed at five in the morning, I heart reacted to her story. Within a minute, I had a DM from @gowithflo33.

Why are you awake? Weirdo.

Since then, it's become habit to exchange a few messages in the morning while I grade and lesson plan, and Flo works on art projects and editing. She's an editor at a small children's book publisher but is finishing up her portfolio to submit to SCAD for their fall graphic design program, though the professor she's been talking to says she's a shoo-in. Illustrating covers and picture books is the dream for her, and the Savannah College of Art and Design has all the connections. Plus, she'd get to visit Savannah sometimes, her favorite city in the US, I recently learned.

"Aren't you a little old for college?" I joked with her one morning. When she didn't instantly respond, I regretted my ill-advised joke with every fiber of my being, fretting over how I could walk it back. Dying inside for offending one of my favorite people.

Then she responded, "Haven't you seen *Never Been Kissed?* This is my big moment to fall in love with a professor and ride off into the sunset. Plus, it's grad school, nerd."

It was the first time I'd ever heard her refer to wanting to date outside of Riley. I knew they weren't currently together, but I also knew the moment Riley came back to her, Flo would take her back. Wanted her back. No matter how much Riley hurt her or how many times she cheated on her.

It's kind of funny, really. I don't even have her number, but we chat almost every workday morning. Feels like we're the only people awake, then, in our own little world. I've known Flo for years. We'd always been casual friends, and we gravitated toward each other whenever she came by the house with Riley, but our friendship never extended past that until that first DM. She's living with Riley's family during her grad program because they live right next to the MARTA train that takes her to campus. And they aren't charging her rent, so she can afford tuition. But she's hinted at not feeling like she can be the most social while she's staying with them. So I suspect she's just a touch lonely, too.

We just get each other. Things don't seem so hard when it comes to her. And when she gave me, my dad, and Sean the painting of my mom, I knew she'd be my friend for a long time. That maybe Florence Davis was a little moonlight in my midnight.

"Got a light?"

I didn't even notice the door open, but there is Riley with a cigarette dangling from her lips, looking like a lesbian James Dean. A cigarette fiend when she's drunk and a beaming example of health when sober. I stare in her bloodshot eyes, feeling nothing. Or maybe everything.

"Still don't smoke, Rye. Sorry." I shrug.

"'Course you don't, Dildo."

Riley has called me Dildo more times than I can possibly remember. Sometimes, I'd ignore it when we were older. Sometimes, we'd wind up wrestling when we were younger. But the harshness of her words pushes me closer to wanting to wrestle her. The control I have over my emotions corrodes just enough to scare me.

Flo squeezes my elbow before she goes to her. "Babe. You've got yours in the center console of the car. Do you have the keys? I can grab it for you."

Riley ignores her, her gaze still trained on me. "Fucking Olive Garden, huh?"

"Excuse me?" I take a step toward her, just so I can understand better. "What do you mean?"

She pulls the cigarette from her lips and tucks it behind her ear. Her cropped, dirty blond hair just covers it. "Don't you think Aunt Eileen deserves better than this? Don't you think she was important enough, good enough, to deserve a classy, real funeral?"

"Riley." Flo tugs her arm, but Rye shakes her off.

"Deserves better than you getting wasted and ruining it by destroying the only beautiful thing about it?" My clothes feel tight, as if I may erupt and burst through the seams. "Yeah, Rye. I think my mom deserves a whole hell of a lot better than that."

I stumble backward against the railing, Riley's fist tight in the chest of my shirt. She's so fast.

"Riley, stop. Right now. This is childish and completely inappropriate," Flo pleads, but it's like she doesn't even exist to Riley.

Her breath is whiskey-soaked and sour. I don't think I know this version of her, and it scares me. I don't think Florence knows this version of her. She backs toward the door as if she's about to go get help. It's the last thing I want, to add another spectacle to this godawful night, but the way Riley stares at me has me thinking my teeth may crack tonight. But I'm not giving in to this middle school bullying.

"Get off." I push against her, though she hardly budges. "Your breath smells terrible, Rye."

"Riley. Stop it, now," Flo calls from the doors.

"She deserved better, and you failed her," Riley says through gritted teeth.

My blood is lighter fluid. My entire body ignites. Every feeling I've pushed down today explodes through the surface. All control, all analysis, is gone.

Riley turns for a split second, and I shove her hard in the chest. Cigarette flying from her ear, she stumbles back and trips over the leg of a chair. But she doesn't fall alone. She tightens her grip in my shirt and pulls me down with her.

I can basically hear Michael Buffer over our old box TV in the nineties. *Let's get ready to rumble!* And the wrestling commences. I try to get to my knees so I can escape, but she's too strong. She rolls us so she's on top, all her weight pinning me to the concrete patio. From the coolness on my knees, I'm pretty sure my slacks are ripped. For a moment, I think Riley may actually punch me in the face, a line she has never crossed. But she glances at Flo, her eyes a little wild and a lot teary. It's a really fucked-up moment to feel sorry for her and whatever demon possesses her. But I do.

Instead of punching me—which I think could've killed me with cement as the backdrop—she mashes a hand against my face like she's trying to smear my head against the ground. I feel the burn of it. Of the little sharp edges of concrete tearing into my cheek.

"She deserves better," Riley spits, hovering close.

"Fucking, get the fuck off!" I flail like a fish out of water, able to rock her off me just long enough to get to my feet.

"Fuck our trip." She stands, out of breath. "I'm not going."

I press my fingers to my cheek, and they come away red and gritty.

Flo grabs Riley's arm. Her freckled cheeks are crimson, her eyes wide. She's completely horrified. "Riley. What the hell?"

It's one of those moments where a line has obviously been crossed, but the one thing you wish for most is normalcy. I need normalcy. Or I may lose my mind. "It's fine," I say. Rye looks away. I hope it's the guilt. "We always wrestled as kids. It's fine."

"Well, you're not kids anymore. You're adult women in your thirties, and you could've seriously hurt each other." Flo lifts her arms in exasperation before she pulls her phone from her pocket. "I'm calling you a Lyft," she says to Riley, who stays silent in her brooding.

"The hell is going on out here?" Sean asks as he steps over the fallen chair. He surveys the three of us. "Christ. Can you two behave like adults for one goddamn night?"

That's it. That's my last straw. I wipe the blood from my cheek before it trickles down to stain my collar. "I'm leaving," I mutter.

"Of course you are," Sean scoffs as I walk by. "Running away from Mom's funeral. Classy."

I turn before I open the door. Riley stares at her shoes, her demon seemingly body-hopped to Sean. And Florence watches me with something like pain her eyes. This is the lowest moment of my life.

I hate Riley.

I hate Sean and my dad.

I hate my family, and I hate myself.

"Sean," I say, the formation of his name burning my face. "No one owes you a damn thing. Grow up."

And I disappear.

❖

I slam my car door and let the quiet absorb me. The Olive Garden sign glows in the night like a burning ship at sea, but I'm safe now. *Safe now.* Salty tears burn the broken skin on my face as I crumple over the steering wheel and let it flow from me, hoping the entire night and all the craziness that happened will be purged. My shoulders shake as I choke on my sobs, aspirate on my spit. I cling to my steering wheel, cling to my self-pity, unready to welcome the emptiness of what comes next.

I startle at the knock on my window.

"Eaden, my girl. Open up." It's my dad.

Half of me wants to let him be that. Let him be the buoy, the shelter, the rest. I'm so tired. But I can't. I can't because right now, I hate him, too. And to rest in him would be to forgive him. But he broke my mom's heart. And that was her last big experience in this world. A broken heart.

"No." I'm not sure if he can hear my muffled response, but he steps back when I start the engine.

I take a deep breath and drive away.

CHAPTER TWO

I nudge my cold coffee away from my laptop. If it's not steaming, I'm not drinking it. My dream electric mug sits in a gift bag, unopened under my bed upstairs, but I can't bring myself to use it. The perfect birthday gift from my mom right before her surgery the next day. I never got around to opening it. And now, well, I don't know. It may be the weird last thing I'm holding on to from before. Like, once I open it, she's really gone. I wonder what my dad is holding on to of her. Maybe a water cup on her nightstand. A hamper of dirty clothes.

The crushing weight of guilt, I hope.

The screen of my laptop dims, and I stroke the touchpad to keep it awake. Keep up the charade of me being productive this morning, but my brain jumps from sore spot to sore spot. Sean, my dad, Riley. I don't know where to put all my anger. My frustration. So I sit frozen in front of my laptop doing nothing and feeling nothing.

But not quite nothing.

It's almost like static. A white noise. Nothing's on the channel, but it's loud, taking up space, driving me just a little mad.

I take off my glasses and rub my eyes until a few lashes litter the table below. Then I microwave my coffee for the third time, convincing myself I won't let it grow cold a fourth. As the microwave hums, I slide open the drawer of bills I need to pay and take the top envelope. My stomach aches at the sight of my mom's cursive. Loopy, relaxed, unhurried. Funny how it embodies her. The letter is not to me. Even if it was, it'd probably sit in this drawer, unopened, just like the electric mug. But it still pains me that she didn't leave me a letter.

It's addressed instead to Mary Knight, my mom's aunt who still lives in Ireland. My mom tasked me with the responsibility of sending it. Well, she didn't say "send." She said "deliver." Which I took to mean just get it to Aunt Mary. But Riley convinced me she said "deliver" for a reason. Like, maybe my mom wanted me to go to Cobh to hand-deliver this letter to her favorite aunt.

"Don't be an idiot," Riley had said, the corner of her lips green from her power smoothie. "Aunt Eileen didn't even write the address. It's not meant to be mailed. She wanted us to go to Cobh."

Us? I didn't say it out loud. The truth was that I'd never been out of the country, and I was scared to go alone. So I let Riley insert herself into the trip, and she led the planning of it. It was her great-aunt, too, after all, and I didn't think I could pull something like that together so quickly. Cobh would be the final stop. But first, we'd go to Spain, France, Scotland, then finally take the ferry to Ireland. I was terrified but wildly excited.

"Don't worry. Flo speaks just enough French to get us by." Riley pointed at me. "And you're not too bad with Spanish, right?"

"Florence is coming, too?" The idea of having Florence during this three-week adventure through different countries brought me some peace. She is the calm to Riley's sometimes scary gusto.

Riley took the last sip of her smoothie and shrugged. "Well, yeah. Like I said, she speaks French."

"Are you guys even together right now?"

It was always hard keeping up with the saga of Riley and Florence's relationship. They'd broken up and gotten back together so many times, I was pretty sure Riley didn't even know if they were still together or not. Her quirked brows certainly didn't inspire confidence. Everyone knew it didn't matter if they were together, though. Riley was never faithful either way; her sleeping around was the worst kept secret. Florence had to know, but she always took Riley back. I never understood why.

"It doesn't matter if we're together. She lives with the family now. And she speaks French," she said. As if speaking French was the only qualifying factor for coming on the biggest trip of our lives. Well, of my life.

But that was before the funeral.

Now I have an unread email from Riley Beckett with *Your*

Itinerary. Not our itinerary. I take my nuked coffee and the letter back to the table and open the email.

Eaden,

    I've already paid for the accommodations and train tickets. All the confirmations are attached. I'm not going to ask you to pay me back more than your third. And Flo has already paid, too. She's still going with you. Think she's scared of you being alone.

    You still owe me half of your payment.

    Rye

I stare at the email. It's nicer than I expected. But there's no apology for her behavior at the funeral. Maybe it isn't that nice. I mean, of course I'm not paying her portion just because she threw a tantrum and doesn't want to go anymore. If I was on my own, it would be so much cheaper. I roll my eyes and catch my reflection in the computer screen. My cheek is brick brown and ugly, the scabbing covering the entire zygomatic bone.

"Oof." I touch it softly. It's tender.

I fell off a skateboard. I decide that's the story I'll tell my students today. How funny, a nerdy, thirty-four-year-old teacher trying to skateboard. Way better than Ms. B losing a fight with her cousin at her mother's funeral.

My laptop dings.

I know it's Flo. I burn my tongue on my coffee and open the Instagram tab, ignoring the quiet flutter in my stomach at seeing the little red message notification.

@gowithflo33: *How's your face?*

My scab tightens around my grin. I force myself to wait two minutes before I respond. Sip my coffee. Check the weather. Scroll NPR for current—

@eaden.bilbo: *Whatever could you be referring to?*

She responds within the minute. I imagine her, messy bun, third cup of coffee, ignoring the manuscript she woke up early to work on, messaging me instead.

Well, I'm pretty sure you left half of it smeared on the patio at Olive Garden.

I laugh, not caring that it hurts or that I'm pretty sure I'm going to reopen my wound right before the school day starts.

Ohhh, I type. *You're referring to me being cast as the new Two-Face. I gotta start carrying around a coin to determine people's fate.*

She laugh reacts to my message. *One of the best Batman villains of all time.* I wait as the dots strobe next to her name, wondering what she's typing. I have to get going soon. Want to get to school early so I can have a smooth start to the day and make sure I'm not bleeding all over my collar. Middle schoolers can be brutal. Thankfully, they seem to tolerate me, even if they do like to poke fun at me being a nerd. But I catch their smiles when something cool clicks in their brains. Like when they drop a Ping-Pong ball alongside a brick and realize that gravity exerts an equal force on everything when the objects hit the muted green carpet at the same time. Now, if they have more time to fall, then the object's mass will affect its acceleration, I can hear myself saying. "Until..."

"Until it reaches terminal velocity," my class responded in unison. I love teaching Earth Science.

Are you okay? Flo's message brings me back.

My fingers hover over the keyboard. It's funny how I always place them over *asdf-jkl;*, as if I don't just hunt and peck. Well, hunt and peck with grace. I stare at the screen until all the words and colors go fuzzy. Flo is someone who holds a lot for others. Heaviest of all, Riley's lies and her giant ego. And I don't want to be a person who adds to that weight. The truth is, I adore her, and I want to be a source of strength for her. A true friend. Someone who lightens her load.

She already knows that I'm not okay.

Yeah, I say. *Had a good night of sleep and ready to move on.*

I see her typing, but she must have deleted what she wrote because the dots disappear for a while. Then they appear again. *Hydrogen peroxide.*

H_2O_2. Are you flirting with me, Flo?

I send it before I can think better of it. My mouth goes dry as I stare at my message. Why am I such an idiot? Responding with the chemical formula? Joking about flirting with the one positive person in my life right now?

If I was flirting with you, you'd know it. And hydrogen peroxide should get the blood out of your pillowcase from sleeping with a mangled face last night.

My stomach aches with torrential butterflies drowning in a sea of caffeine. She is flirting with me just a little. *Right?* I reread her message so many times, I can't tell if she's pushing me away or pulling me closer. I shake my head and wince at the sudden stabbing pain in my cheek. What I do know is that, either way, it doesn't matter. Not only is Florence Davis dating my cousin and living with her family rent-free, she is also my friend. She is the definition of off-limits. Even if I was okay with betraying my own cousin, Florence is way too good for me. No one who I have dated has stayed, and I need her to stay. At least for a little while.

Ah right. Thank you. I'll dig my pillowcase out of the trash and try to save it, then. I have to leave in ten minutes, so I send one more message. *I gotta run. Someone's gotta teach these preteens about planet Earth, and it may as well be me.*

Just one more thing, Eaden. I know you probably wanted to go to Ireland alone this summer, and with Riley backing out, I'd understand if you wanted me to not go as well. I get it. It's a personal thing, going to visit your mom's aunt. We can figure out money, etc. I don't want you to worry about that. But if you need a friend, I think we could have a really good trip together, too. Just let me know.

She's right. I do want to go alone. There's something about solitude that I think I need, but I've been lonely my entire life. And I'm scared to be alone on this big a trip. Honestly, traveling across different countries with Flo sounds like an absolute delight to me. Plus, she knows French.

You're right. I could use a friend. And someone who speaks French.

Ouch. I see. Just using my language skills, huh?

Truthfully, I'd be honored if you came with me, Flo.

You got yourself a travel buddy, then. I got your number from Rye. I'll text you so you have mine. Can we meet up for coffee soon to go over logistics?

Sounds good to me.

Great. Now go educate our youth.

And you go tell them fairy tales. Bye Flo.

Bye Eaden.

❖

One thing I'm learning about teaching is there is never enough time to pee and never enough time to catch my breath. It is a profession of endurance. Especially when I'm not one hundred percent rested or emotionally centered, which is exactly what I am today. I yawn into my coffee mug after racing back from tending my weeping wound in the staff bathroom and pulling my hair into a bun so wayward strands don't stick in the soft scab. Even my glasses feel heavy today. But these thirteen-year-olds, they're like sharks; they can smell it on you. Whatever it is. Sadness, exhaustion, a hangover, a fight with your partner. Any of it.

So I'm in trouble with the giant scab on my face and my general air of depression. The kids know my mom passed away because having a sub for more than one day isn't very common, and I was straight up with them. But they don't know the funeral was last night, thankfully. Makes it easier to whip up a lie.

"Shit, Eaden. What the hell happened to your face?" Hakim leans in my doorway, his dark-bearded jaw hanging open. He is another eighth-grade science teacher and my best teacher friend at West Cove Middle. *Go Pirates!*

I groan. I've only had one class so far, and I'm already exhausted from answering all the questions. The kids think I got in a fight, which is exactly what happened.

Hakim walks toward my desk, his shiny bald head reflecting each light he passes. His eyes widen as he approaches. "Wasn't last night the funeral?" he whispers, a little horrified. He leans closer when I don't respond. "Clearly, we are getting a beer after school, and you're telling me why the hell you look like Harvey Dent, but what's the party line? What're you telling these little assholes?" He nods to the few students trickling in.

I can't help but crack a smile. Hakim is the warmest man, and no one cares about the students more than him. Therefore, he can get away with calling them little assholes. That's what they are. Cool, beautiful, complex little assholes. We love them.

I stand and straighten my shirt. Lean into his ear and whisper, "I tried longboarding down the hill in front of my house. Then, you know…"

He nods. "Gravity."

"Gravity." I pat his shoulder. "I'll see you at lunch."

He groans like the adorable baby he is. "Fine. I'll go back to my own classroom," he says, as if his classroom isn't literally across the hall.

A handful of the shyer students find their seats and are absorbed into their phones or their notebooks or anything that will help them avoid eye contact with other people. I've been thirteen. I get it. Then the rowdier bunch begins to file in. Conversations spill in from the hall, and students with pink cheeks from laughing begin to fill the room. I go unnoticed for about thirty seconds before one of the more rambunctious boys calls me out.

"Ms. B," he shouts from his desk. "Dang, Ms. B. What happened to your face?" He covers his mouth with a fist, and the rest of the class turns their attention to me and erupts into chatter.

I take one more fortifying sip of coffee and walk in front of the whiteboard. I've never been the most outgoing person, but I feel like I've really found my footing as a teacher. I walked in on my first day completely terrified. Terrified that the kids wouldn't like me. Wouldn't listen to me. Would make fun of me. Then Hakim walked into my classroom with a grin and a pat on the back and said, "Relax, my new friend. They're thirteen."

Now I'm bold enough to think they even like me a little. Not as much as they love Hakim, of course. Nobody can touch Mr. Abadi. But I've built a relationship with each of them to the point that I'm going to miss them when our semester ends this week.

I push my glasses up my nose and smile at my second period. "Go on. What are your best guesses?" I ask through a grin.

"You got in a fight with Jamal's mom," Brody yells from the back row.

"Shut up!" Jamal fires back. "I bet Ms. B took someone out on the soccer field with a badass slide tackle."

I chuckle at this very generous guess. "Nope. I don't play soccer, but good guess, Jamal."

"I bet you tripped on a hike," Nina, one of the more popular girls in the class, says.

"Close. But not quite," I say. "By the way, is anyone not here?" We all scan the seats. All we're doing today is going over final announcements and watching *Bill Nye the Science Guy*, so it doesn't matter that we're goofing off into class time, but I still need to take attendance.

"Colton isn't here," a small boy shouts from the corner.

"Thank you very much." I verify that Colton is the only absence and mark it on my notebook. "And for all of you curious creatures, I attempted to longboard down the hill in my neighborhood." I prop myself on the stool in front of the classroom and shrug. "It didn't go too well. You should see my knees." The lie flows effortlessly through me, and I don't feel a lick of guilt. I'm working on setting firmer boundaries in my life.

"My mom says grief makes you do crazy things," Nina says. She says it so nonchalantly, like children do sometimes. Totally unaware of the dagger she just gutted me with.

My face aches as if to emphasize her words. I'm right back at Olive Garden. My mom's portrait drowning. Riley drowning me. The hot white pain of the pavement. My fear of being empty for the rest of my life.

The whispers and fluorescent lights bring me back.

"Very true. No longboarding after thirty, folks." I clear my throat and push off the stool. "Now, sit back, relax, and prepare to have your minds blown by the great..." I point to the class and make them say his name for me.

"Bill Nye the Science Guy," they shout in almost unison. They feign a group groan, too, but I can tell they love when I play it for them. Not one of them falls asleep. Even in my class right after lunch.

"Ah, see. If you're not careful, you're gonna make me think you actually enjoy this." I pull up the episode on rocks and soil on my laptop and connect to the projector. "Brody, hit the lights, please."

The classroom goes dark, and I slide into my chair, relieved to be out of the spotlight. A wave of nausea fills my stomach as I think about the night before. How dark it was. The shame I feel. The anger I feel. I undo another button from the top of my shirt to get some air. I just want to run to my mom. Even though I'm a grown woman, she'd hold me tight, tell me everything was going to be okay. That I couldn't control Sean or Riley or Dad.

The image of her crying when she found out about the affair torches everything else in my mind, and I stifle down bile again. My throat is raw from it. I hate him for that. I'll never forgive him for that. For making her suffer through the little time she had left here.

And Sean, for being the most selfish little man I've ever known.

And Riley, for being whatever she is. The most vain and self-interested human in existence.

And the little trainer who fucked my dad. Fuck her, too.

CHAPTER THREE

S o let me get this straight." Hakim wipes his mouth with the back of his hand and slides his beer out of the way as he leans on his elbows. "Your cousin got wasted at your mom's funeral and made a scene by knocking over your mom's portrait that her girlfriend painted and—"

"Ex," I clarify. "Ex-girlfriend."

"*Maybe* ex-girlfriend."

I roll my eyes and snatch another fry from our shared basket. "Why worry about semantics when it doesn't matter either way?"

Our neighborhood Taco Mac is buzzing, everyone shaking off the week together. It's comforting to be among the hum of others. It helps to drown out my own white noise, but I can't help but dread when Hakim has to go home and I have to go back to my house alone. And sit in my storm alone.

He bows his head close to me as if telling a secret. "Then your cousin completely Hulks out on you and schmears your face on the cement? Fucking hell."

I chuckle into my pint. "*Smears* my head. You said *schmear*, like a bagel and schmear."

"Yeah, exactly. The cement is the bagel"—he holds his palms face up and raises one at a time—"and your face is the schmear." He finishes his tutorial by pretending to spread cream cheese all over his outstretched hand.

"What's that?" I plug my ear like I'm trying to hear audio coming from a headset. "Good news. The judges have accepted your use of 'schmear' for all current and future uses."

"That's fantastic news. Now I can cancel my schmear campaign I was plotting against you." His big shoulders shake as he laughs, and the old wooden booth creaks.

I laugh with him and run a hand through my hair. Feels nice to let it down after a long day. One more day until summer vacation. My first one as a teacher. As an adult, I've never had such a vast chunk of time off work, but I literally cannot imagine teaching every weekday through the entire year. It's exhausting in a way I've never experienced. Not even in my late nights at the lab, having to monitor projects in the dead of night, alone in the mostly dark buildings. Though I loved that job in a way, I had to be honest with myself that it just wasn't the best fit for me.

The isolation.

Now I work my ass off, but I'm surrounded by students, faculty, and friends. And we're all in it together.

I take a sip of lager as I think about how lucky I am to have switched jobs before my mom passed. Going into the lab alone at one in the morning, feeling the way I feel now, may have just pushed me over the metaphorical ledge. Talk about terminal velocity.

If I'm honest, I can't help but think I'm already falling.

Hakim covers my hand with his. "Day or night, I'm here for you."

I nod and wipe my burning eyes under my glasses.

"Seriously," he insists. "I know it's, like, the wildest fucking roller coaster. One minute you're mildly okay, and the next, you're about to cry in a Taco Mac."

I groan and pull my hand back to my lap. "I'm not crying."

"No judgment." He glances over his shoulder toward the army of tap handles. "I have definitely sobbed at that bar." I chuckle in disbelief. "Oh yeah. Snot and all. When Rebecca was pregnant, and I full-on freaked out about fatherhood."

"And look at you now," I say. His little boy just turned three, and from what I can tell, Hakim is an incredible dad. The kind of dad who wouldn't step out and have an affair with his personal trainer.

He takes the last sip of beer and smacks his lips. "You're gonna get there, Eaden. But in the meantime, our guest room has your name on it. Whenever you need, no questions asked."

"Hakim." I shake my head and look away from his big warm eyes.
"Yes?"

"It's just, we're new friends still. You don't know me all that well, and that's a lot to offer."

He shrugged. "I know ya. Besides, Rebecca insisted that I let you know. And now you know."

Warmth spreads in my chest. Even if I do fall off the ledge and completely lose it, I have a guest room with my name on it. And that's something. I have a friend. I'm going to miss him this summer, but at least I'll be with another friend, Flo.

"Thank you. That means everything to me."

He pushes the empty fry basket and pint glasses to the edge of the table. "Before we go, tell me more about your trip to Ireland with your cousin's maybe ex-girlfriend." He chuckles with eyes wide. "Still can't believe that's a real thing."

"Yep. It's a real thing." I blow out a deep breath. "We're going to Barcelona, Paris, Edinburgh, then a ferry to Ireland. Then, to my aunt's house."

"Are you nervous to meet her?"

I drum my fingers over the faded waxed wood of the table. "I'm nervous for everything."

"You got this." He reaches across and pats my shoulder. "It'll be good for you, taking some space from everyone. Probably a blessing that your cousin bailed."

I nod.

He raises his water glass. "To the end of the school year and to your big adventure."

The way he says "big adventure" gets my adrenaline pumping. He almost has me convinced it could be okay. Like it could be fun. And the space will definitely be good. I clink his water with mine. "Cheers."

"Cheers," he says.

The sun is still warm as it sets, and I untuck my button-down as I walk through the parking lot to my car. Things can be okay.

Maybe things can be okay.

The gate to my small townhome community creaks open with a whine, as if I've woken it from its afternoon nap. I drive carefully over the first speed bump, the most aggressive speed bump of the four, and nod at my neighbor, Christin, who's lifting kettlebells on her patio. UGA Bulldog figurines litter the front of her home, poking out of bushes, standing on the corner of the iron gate, guarding her front door. I wouldn't be surprised if there were a couple hidden in the pergola overhead.

It's one of the reasons I chose this neighborhood; I adore the individuality of spirit. Not only of my neighbors but of our homes, too. This community was built in the seventies and is a far cry from the posh townhomes sprouting up across Atlanta every day, with their monotone sleekness and tiny decks overlooking more tiny decks and a highway. I'm sure those residents would look at our neighborhood and call it shabby, but I walk through plants and refurbished patio furniture to get to my door, and the view from my back patio is a heavily wooded bike trail that takes me straight into town. The pool actually has a deep end. And the homes have some soul to them, like a bunch of different little English cottages all bundled up together.

If I ever have kids, which at this point seems far-fetched, I'd consider moving somewhere bigger. But I don't even have a hint of a partner, so for now, it's perfect. And it makes me happy.

I take a deep breath of the warm spring air before I let myself in the door and head upstairs to shower. The day is easier on me, less time alone to be with my thoughts, my pain, my anxiety. Tomorrow is the last day of school, then the days will be hard, too. But the night… nothing compares to being alone and depressed at night. Through my bathroom window, I can sense the fading sun, and I try to ignore the creeping feeling of dread gathering in my chest.

It's just another night. I'll dry off, I'll make tea, I'll watch *Bake Off* until I fall asleep on the couch, then I'll wake up again. It's going to be okay.

And I do exactly that after my shower. Since my mom's operation, I haven't been able to read or watch any show with a plot. Even *Ted Lasso* is too much for me to bear. I am, however, the world's leading expert on *The Great British Bake Off* because over the last two weeks, I've watched the six seasons available on Netflix three times. In a row. Even if I'm not watching every moment, having other voices in the house calms me.

I pour hot water over my peppermint tea and sit on the couch, ready to fall into the world of kindness and soft accents and delectable bakes, but the letter my mother wrote to her aunt taunts me from the coffee table. It's not that I'm jealous she got a letter from my mom in her last precious moments, it's that I'm...well, yeah, I'm jealous. I'm hurt. She barely had energy to spend, and she didn't spend it on me. She spent it on—I toe the letter so I can read the smooth loops of my mom's handwriting—Mary Knight.

I sink into my couch and tug the throw blanket over myself.

Jasmine, violet, orange blossom.

I know the exact scent because I bought my mom her favorite perfume every Mother's Day, and she wore it anytime she left the house. To the market, to dinner, for a walk around the park. She wore it everywhere for decades. Since I was just a little girl, though my father would buy it for her then. The scent is as much her aura as Flo's watercolor was. I tug the corner of the blanket that she must have been sitting on the last time she visited so it covers my nose and mouth. Paul Hollywood is in a different universe. My tea grows cold.

I'm at Mass. I'm five, maybe four. The congregation is standing, singing a hymn, and my mom holds me. The strands of her hair cover half my face, tickling my mouth. Her hair spray is strong and a bit sticky when I play with the hair against her back. Her perfume is a shield around me. I can even smell her blush, the sharp chalkiness of it, and feel the vibration of her voice as she sings and sways us to the song. She holds me tight because I'm tired, and when I'm tired, I'm extra needy for cuddles and hugs and physical affection.

Another deep breath of her.

I stop playing with her hair and tighten my little arms around her neck as I stare at the man in the pew behind us. He catches my eye for a split second, smiles, then raises his gaze to the front of the church and continues to hum along, peppering in a word every so often. And I just keep staring. He keeps noticing, then looking away. And I do not care an ounce about being rude and making this strange man uncomfortable. Because he can't do a damn thing about it. My mom is holding me. I am safe. I am home. I am Eileen's baby girl.

I wake from my daydream, my memory, with a long painful groan that startles me. Pull the blanket over my head entirely. Feel the darkness, the emptiness of it. How it creeps over me. The thing I dread every day.

I am not safe. This emptiness scares me.

I am not home. Home no longer exists.

I am nobody's baby girl. Because no one on this earth loves me the way Mom did.

CHAPTER FOUR

I don't know how much sleep I got last night. Sleep and sadness are the closest of friends. Mimicking each other, dancing together, playing tag and hide-and-seek. But two students commented on the bags under my eyes today, so I think I spent more time with sadness than sleep.

It's officially summer, the semester is over, and I leave for Europe in two weeks. I should probably cancel the trip and just take the financial hit. I'm dreading it now. Now that I'm used to being empty and alone, the idea of being with someone else—even if it's Florence—all day and all night for weeks at a time scares me to death. How can I collapse into my black hole when someone else is around?

My dad called to congratulate me on the culmination of my first year of teaching. I said thank you. We hung up after a few moments of awkward silence.

I haven't heard from Sean.

I haven't heard from Riley, save the email.

The ruined portrait of my mom leans against the wall in the upstairs hallway. I can't let it go.

And from what I can tell, people just keep on being, and the world just keeps on moving, no matter how devastatingly sad and lonely I am.

CHAPTER FIVE

@Gowithflo33: *I see how it is. Summer vacation starts, and I instantly lose my early morning buddy.*

I blink a few times until the glowing words become clear. My aching jaw strains as I grin. Though nothing feels quite as miserable as waking up on a couch with a crick in my neck and drool on my favorite pillow, I suppose I shouldn't be complaining because at least I got a few hours of sleep. I thought that after my mom died, I would see her in my dreams all the time. She was just here on this earth with me, shouldn't my brain be wanting to process her death and play me sweet memories and visions of her or something like that? I've even researched lucid dreaming to manifest her myself.

I'd do anything to see her one more time. Even if just in a dream.

"Coffee," I mutter to myself and carefully walk to the kitchen, keeping my neck steady. Nothing can happen without coffee. I rotate through phases of using a French press and my automatic brewer. But now that school's out and I have a little more time, I grind my beans and pour them into the press. It feels nice, not having to rush around in the morning. Especially knowing it's summer, and every morning will be this chill until late July.

"Yeah. It's nice," I repeat to myself, willing away the anxiety and depression.

While the coffee steeps, I write a text to Florence. She gave me her number, and we're about to embark on a huge trip together, so I want to move our communication off social media. She's my friend. We can text each other. Plus, I'd prefer to spend way less time on Instagram.

Would you settle for an anytime buddy?

I send it without a second thought, pour my first cup of coffee, and sit on my back deck to listen to the morning birds chirp. They're so loud here. It's always been one of my favorite things about spring and early summer in Atlanta. My phone vibrates with Flo's response.

I'm only mildly disappointed. Five a.m. is way less fun now.

My two a.m. slot is available if you're interested, I reply.

Having trouble sleeping?

Yeah. Got any tips for me?

Unfortunately, no. I usually put on a podcast or watch Great British Bake Off. The serenity knocks me right out.

I chuckle into my mug. *No way. I literally fell asleep to that show last night. It's kind of all I can watch right now.*

The sun warms my face as Florence types. It's so peaceful, talking to her over my morning coffee. She fills some hole in me. Not necessarily one that my mother's death left, but one that's always been there.

I've been there. The first time Riley and I split, it was Bake Off and a lot of horrible microwave mug cakes. Talk about soggy bottoms and clumps of flour. But that show is gentle on the soul. Especially with whatever soft filter they film it through.

I remember the first time she and Riley broke up. Though we didn't message or talk back then, I remember Riley coming over and grabbing a beer from my fridge. She was fidgety, as if nervous energy was escaping her body through her limbs. She drank half the beer in one chug before she wiped her mouth and said, "I think I fucked up."

She then proceeded to tell me about her latest trip and the woman who was working in the lobby of her hotel, a hotel she frequently stays at when she's in town on business. She told me they'd always had a flirty banter, but that it was completely harmless. This time, though, it wasn't just a business trip, it was the North American Medical Supplies convention, a convention that apparently is notorious for being a giant party. So Riley was quite intoxicated when the woman got off work at the hotel and invited Riley for a drink. Which led to another. Which led to said woman in Riley's bed.

Unforgiveable, sure. But the worst part was that Rye wasn't going to tell Florence. Florence was playing music over Rye's phone when a text from "Hot Marissa" popped up, describing how badly she wished Rye would come back to Miami and fuck her again.

Cue Riley and Florence's first breakup.

It makes me nauseous to even think about someone treating Florence that way. Riley is blood, but I could barely look at her when she told me what she'd done.

"It was just a mistake," she explained, shaking her head. "Mistakes happen. It's not like this is a full-blown affair. We aren't married or anything."

I know infidelity is often a symptom of something else not quite working in a relationship, but that didn't seem to be the case for them. It seemed like the only thing that wasn't "quite working" was Riley. Even from my limited time with Florence back then, I could tell that Riley had won the jackpot of life by receiving her love. She was steadfast, loyal, always trying to anticipate people's needs, talented and creative, and just simply stunning. And Riley spent her precious love like it was a week's allowance.

"Is this a one-time thing?" I asked Rye.

Her hand in her hair said *no*.

A week later, Florence showed up with her to my father's birthday party, and I caught her in the backyard by the cooler, sipping a cider. She blushed when she spotted me walking toward her. "It's good to see you," I said.

Her nostrils flared as she nodded, as if she was willing her emotions to settle. "It's not that I'm not mad at her, I just—"

I shook my head and gave her an awkward side hug. "It's none of my business. I'm just happy to see you around."

Maybe I should have let her tell me whatever she wanted to tell me, but I felt awkward that she felt awkward, and she didn't owe me any kind of explanation. That was five years ago, and since then, there have been multiple repeats of Riley's offense, multiple pardons from Florence, and ultimately, some kind of resolution where they're not officially in a relationship, but they're intimate. Now Florence lives with Riley's family—not with Riley—and Florence continues to have a deeper commitment to Riley than Riley does to her.

But for some reason, Florence can't let go. Whether it's the free rent while she scrapes together tuition for the graphic design program or the fear of being alone, something keeps her firmly in Riley's grasp. And maybe she really is just deeply in love with my cousin.

So now, when Flo mentions their first breakup, I don't poke or prod at the subject, even if I'm curious. Which I am. Because Florence is one of a kind. Though she must not know it, she can have anyone she wants.

Microwave mug cakes, huh? May have to make me one of those tonight, I message back, applauding myself for ignoring the topic of my cousin for the time being.

Oh, you should. Don't forget the secret ingredient.

I raise a brow as I type. *Which is?*

Tears. Really elevates the cake. Just cry right into that mug. Her text ends with a hysterical smiley.

I don't quite know how to respond. Instead, I lay my phone on the wrought iron side table and watch a sparrow splash in the birdbath. The birdbath which is just a flooded clay pot with a dead plant from last season. But the sparrow doesn't know that. My phone buzzes loudly against the metal. It's Florence again.

Sorry. That was probably too much.

My heart breaks a little for her. *Not too much. Flo, we're friends. You can talk to me.* I send it and start typing again. *Would you like to know something?*

Yes.

Okay. The sun makes my screen hard to see, but I don't mind. It's like a little layer of anonymity as I type my small confession. I want to give her something because she gave me something. She was vulnerable. *My mom's funeral was a disaster. On so many levels. And when Rye ruined your painting, it felt like the culmination of everything. Like, the end of everything good in my life. I know that's a selfish way to see it because it was all for my mother. But I had to get out of there, so I walked out back to the patio. I thought I'd be happy to never see a single soul again. Then you put your arm around me and somehow, in the darkest moment, made me smile. You were the only light that day.*

I send it, self-conscious and very aware that I just texted her a novel. But that doesn't stop me from adding one more bit, *I just wanted you to know I'm grateful for your friendship, and I'm here for you, too. Anytime.*

As I wait for her response, I gently remind myself that she wasn't there for me; she was there for Riley. Collateral kindness is what it was. Happenstance.

I wish I could have taken away all the pain of that day.

I do believe her, but a little part of me is annoyed. Riley ruined the painting and got in a literal fight with me at *my* mom's funeral. And there will still be zero consequences for her. At least, not from Florence. Again a good reminder, before we get coffee and travel together, that I am the third wheel. And though I've grown attached to her company in some way, she is not here because of our friendship; she is here because she is too in love with my unfaithful and sometimes unkind cousin to leave.

I should've just given Riley the wrong date. Her absence would've saved a lot of pain from that day.

I don't send it, though. I can't. Instead, I delete my truest words and write something more palatable because I'm not going to be the person who talks bad about my cousin to their partner. Ex-partner. Or whatever Florence is to her.

I appreciate it. I have to go run some errands. But it was nice chatting. I don't plan on leaving my house today. At all. But my mood is growing dark, and I don't want to put that on Florence.

Oh. Okay! Have a good day. Still on for coffee on Monday?

I thumbs-up the message and lay my phone back down. My mom would tell me to get outside and go for a walk. She knew I need fresh air when things get heavy. Vitamin D boosts serotonin, so it's less of an Eaden thing and more of a human thing. The sparrow and its friends fly off, flicking water on the black grill cover as they go. "Grill cover" is generous. Its sole purpose since I moved in has been a spider hotel. Never seen the point of grilling for just myself. The sun reflecting off the black plastic hurts my eyes, and I consider selling the damn thing.

No one wanted to share time and space with me before. Now my eyes look like month-old peaches, my cheek itches so badly I'm tempted to scrape off the remaining scab with a butterknife, and I'm so depressed, I don't know how to be Eaden anymore. I'm no one.

The wrought iron rattles with the vibration of my phone.

It's my dad. The last person I want to spend energy on. I ignore the call and walk inside to drown my day in *Bake Off*, a homemade mix of self-pity and self-loathing, and trying to find that one spot where the threads of my throw blanket still hold a bit of my mom's perfume.

CHAPTER SIX

If the one person who sees you disappears—dies—do you even exist anymore?

Do I even exist anymore?

My midnight musings from the funeral taunt me through Sunday. My throw blanket smells like stale coffee. Smells like I should shower. Feels like I should sleep in my bed. Can't feel much.

I fade in to Netflix asking if I'm still watching. I fade out to meaningless dreams of grocery shopping and checking my tire pressure. Not my mom. Nothing evocative or soothing. But anywhere other than alone on my couch in the darkness is more tolerable.

Faded.

I jolt upright when I hear my front door swing open and bang against the door stopper. I fling off the throw and swing to my feet, catching my knee on the corner of the coffee table and letting a low grumble of *fuck* roll from my throat. My adrenaline troughs when my dad's voice follows his steps up the stairs.

"Eaden?" he calls. My name tremors, threatens to crack on the sharp edges of his worried voice.

I'm in two-day-old underwear and a stained T-shirt, and my jeans are on the kitchen floor where I can't reach them. It's weird how I hardly remember last night, as if I blacked out from drinking, but I haven't had a drop of alcohol since beers with Hakim on Thursday.

A fuzzy image of me scrounging in my freezer for the mini chocolate chips I used to bake Mother's Day cookies last year flashes in my brain. Explains the little brown stain on the rib of my shirt.

"Eaden," my dad says again as he crests the stairs and steps into my living room. He swallows his obvious discomfort as his eyes take in his pants-less, depressed daughter, with a chocolate-stained shirt and a stale smell about her. He swallows again, harder this time, as his eyes flash back to the stain.

This is a new low.

"It's chocolate," I mutter.

"Okay." He nods and raises his hands as if to say *whatever you say.*

I sigh, his questioning glare, his palpable concern agitating my already frayed existence. "Just one second. Let me grab some clothes."

"Okay," he says in the same tone, like he's given up on reasoning with a hell-bent toddler.

"Why are you here, Dad?" I shout down the stairs as I walk up to my room. It's a rhetorical question, a manifestation of my annoyance. This is the closest I've ever been to a disrespectful teen, and I'm thirty-four. I only grow angrier that he's bringing this juvenile insolence out of me. As if I'm not dissociated enough from the woman I am. As if I'm not already the antithesis of the woman my mother hoped I would become.

I toss my dirty shirt in my already overflowing hamper and pull on clean underwear and sweats. It's nice, smelling the fresh cotton on my skin. I was planning on showering tomorrow before I met with Flo, but maybe I'll shower after my dad leaves, too. Try to become closer to a human on this earth. Hot water sounds heavenly.

My dad waits for me in the kitchen, his gargantuan ring of keys—house keys, shed keys, car keys, defunct keys from decades ago that he can't emotionally part with—is splayed over the center of the small kitchen table. He sits, twirling his thumbs, my dirty jeans folded neatly on the counter.

"Thanks for folding those," I say as I pour coffee into the grinder. "I was going to clean this afternoon. Just got—" I grind the beans, letting the loud crunch and whir overtake my voice and drown out the obvious lie that I got "Busy."

"Of course," he says. In that same maddening tone.

I toss the ground coffee into the press and whirl around. "Why are you white gloving me?"

He holds up his hands. "Eaden, I'm not—"

"It's fine, okay? *I'm fine.*" I pour hot water over the grounds, pull two mugs from the shelf, and snag the creamer from the fridge, aware that each movement is a little louder than necessary. Petulant.

"Okay, but"—he pushes his keys to the side and leans on his elbows—"you haven't answered my calls, and I got worried about you. Sean said he hasn't heard from you either, and Riley—"

"Dad." I grip the edge of the counter to anchor myself. "First of all, it's laughable that you think Sean has reached out to me. He cares about other people just as much as Riley does." I know he wants to protest, but to his credit, he sits silently, listening. It almost angers me more. Where was this concerned father months ago when he was having sex with someone who wasn't his wife? "And I answered your call on Friday."

"And you uttered all of five words to me." He furrows his brows. "That's not how we used to be."

He's right. It's not how we used to be. We used to love easily, trust easily, and have real capacity for one another. I'd go over to watch Sunday football with him, to help him in the shed with whatever little gift he was building for Mom, or just to kick back with a beer on the deck and catch up. He used to be my friend and a person I could depend on. So, no, it's not how we used to be.

We used to be free.

But when he decided to throw everything away to cheat on Mom, he threw away what our relationship used to be, too. I should be able to compartmentalize our relationship from their marriage, but I can't. A family is a cell, and if one part of the cell is malfunctioning, the others will, too.

In my dark moments, like last night, I wondered if it's a load off his shoulders. Mom dying.

I pour two cups of coffee and deliver his with a loud thud. "It's unfair for you to expect me to be normal and okay. Losing Mom"—I drop my head and let the steam of my coffee warm my face, unable to even look at him when I talk about her—"is enough of a reason to not want to talk. I'm processing. I'm mourning. But on top of that, I'm dealing with the pain you caused."

I place my coffee on the counter and lift my eyes to his, though I want to drop his gaze immediately. Because I see the pain it causes him, too. I don't want to hurt him, but hot achy rage cascades and avalanches over any sympathy that crops up in my heart. Maybe I do want to hurt him.

"And I have no one to talk about it with. I'm dealing with Mom's death like everyone else, but on top of that, I'm dealing with knowing that you had an affair, Dad. And it's"—my voice cracks, and he's by my side in a second, his arm over my shoulders gathering me to his chest—"so lonely."

"I know," he mutters against my hair. "I know, Eaden."

For a split second, I let him hold me. My body gives in to it. Gives in to someone who loves me. Until the avalanche comes roaring through again. I pull out of his grip and wipe my wet eyes.

He touches my shoulder, the delicate pressure hinting at his caution. His black hair is somehow grayer since the funeral. More salt than pepper now. Ashen skin bunches under his eyes like mine, and he seems to hunch just a bit more. He's still handsome, which presently annoys me, but he's aged through these few months.

"I have never asked you to hold this secret. The burden shouldn't fall on you."

"Should I just call up Sean and Aunt Susan to process with them, then? Just lay it all out there?" I slide out from under his hand and glare. "I can't do that, Dad."

He straightens and folds his arms. "Again, you can do whatever you want. Tell whomever you want. But I would suggest starting with a therapist."

My entire face elongates. Brows stretch, jaw drops. "You have the nerve to come over here and tell me to go get a therapist?" I point at him, the tip of my index finger an inch short of his chest. "This is your fault, and it sucks, but I'm dealing with it fine."

"Are you at least going to tell me what happened to your face?"

My fingers find the flaky raw skin. "I think I'll save that for my therapist, thanks."

"Right." He nods and takes a step back. "I get that you need space right now. But I want you to know that I'm here for you no matter what. I'd really love to see you before your trip, but if not, I get it."

I nod quietly as he grabs his keys.

"I know Riley isn't going anymore." He pauses between the kitchen and the living room. "But maybe that's for the best. Remember, call for anything." He starts down the steps. "Tell Florence hi for me. I love you," he calls.

I sigh when I hear the door shut. Hot coffee scalds my chest as I completely miss my mouth when I go for a sip. "Shit," I groan as I rip off my clean shirt.

My dad's concern pricks at me as I ascend the stairs to retrieve a fresh shirt. The mirror in the corner of my room displays a rough image of me with greasy hair, a scalded red chest, slumping shoulders, and clouded brown eyes. I've never been a beaming image of beauty, but this is a poor showing even for me. I normally at least look clean, kempt, and approachable. My hair used to have some shine in it. My eyes used to pop a little behind my green glasses. Now I can barely see through the fingerprint smudges on the lenses.

I ruffle my hair until it falls close to how it used to, at my shoulders with gentle waves. A glimmer of silver running down behind my ear catches my eye. Another gray hair popping up to torment me.

Instead of opting for another shirt, I strip, peeling off each layer until I stand naked in front of the mirror. It's a body I'm very familiar with. The acne scars are exactly where they should be. The faint birthmark next to my belly button is still there. It's my body. But something is muted now. My shoulders aren't as broad. I've lost a little weight I didn't mean to lose. My skin is papery and dry as I run my hands down my stomach.

I need to shower. And I need to eat a real meal.

My coffee will undoubtedly go cold.

❖

I consider texting Hakim to join me for a bite, but it's Sunday night. I'm sure he's enjoying the evening with his family, and he's too nice to say no to his grieving friend. It's not a position I want to put him in. My phone buzzes as I'm about to text Flo. But it's not from Flo or Hakim or my dad. It's from Riley.

Hey. You doing okay?

"What?" I mutter to myself as I lock my front door. Is today opposite day or something? A backward day where all the people who hurt me "check in" as if they care an ounce about me? If they cared, I wouldn't be emotionally scarred by my father cheating on my mother mere months before she died, and I wouldn't look like Harvey freaking Dent.

I start down the sidewalk to my favorite café in town that moonlights as a wine bar. They have the most delicious homemade lasagna that I'm hoping will solve all my problems and, if I'm lucky, fix my broken heart. It's probably for the best that I didn't text Florence. I need to just be on my own right now and not put my mess on anyone else. Especially not her. She already holds all of Riley's mess.

I open Rye's text again, unsure of what I'm going to say as I respond.

Hey. I'm okay. Meeting up for coffee tomorrow with Flo if you want to join.

It wouldn't be my dream, Rye joining us for coffee, but maybe it would alleviate one of the stresses in my life right now. To see Rye, to talk, to patch things up a little. It doesn't have to be perfect, but even just an ounce better would make a difference to me. Even though I firmly put all the blame on her—and my dad—I can't help but feel guilty for it.

No. Thanks. I'll let you guys connect and work out trip details. I still think it's for the best that I sit this one out. It's come to my attention that I may not be the best company right now, and I know this is your trip. I may have kind of taken it over.

Wow. Not what I was expecting. And now the guilt is tripled.

I appreciate you saying that. But seriously, I'd love for you to come if you change your mind. You and me, we're okay.

She messages back after I cross the street to the main road in my neighborhood.

Of course we're okay. We're family. I just need to hang back and work and figure some shit out.

I stop outside the door of Mina's and respond. *I get it. Maybe we can meet up just the two of us before the trip then.*

She thumbs-ups my message, and that is that. It's way more than I expected from her. Maybe I've been underestimating her. I open the door, and the breeze tickles my healing cheek. She is still the cousin who ruined my mom's funeral, and she is still the cousin who put that scab on my face, so maybe I'll be a little more lenient with myself and shelve the guilt for now.

I wave to Jamie, the bartender, and find my usual spot in the corner by the back window. This place is like my second home. I run through here in the mornings, snagging a coffee and croissant on my way to school on Fridays and picking up dinner to go when I'm desperate for a night in with my favorite show. And when I want to feel a part of society without feeling like I'm out at a busy bar, I come here, where I can say hi to the people I see multiple times a week, share some small talk, and be left alone to enjoy my meal, my coffee, my wine. Whatever it is.

They get me.

When my lasagna is placed in front of me, the smell of the roasted garlic and tomatoes and cheese makes me salivate. I know this food will cure me. I compile the perfect ratio of noodle, meat, cheese, and sauce onto my fork and take my first bite. It's bliss. I'm pretty sure I moan a little.

Is this what sex is like? I can't even remember because it's been so long.

I chuckle to myself. Who needs sex when I have this lasagna?

I'm going to be okay.

CHAPTER SEVEN

I wait for Flo at the coffee shop by Aunt Susan's house. It's just a short walk for her, and I felt like driving anyway. It's only been a few achy days since I saw her last at the funeral, but my nerves are prickling. My hands are wrapped tightly around my mug, and I will myself to not drink any more coffee until she arrives. I don't want her to feel like I've been waiting long. I have been, but only because I got here twenty minutes early. I should have just drunk the darn coffee and ordered a second in all that time.

Twenty minutes early.

I told myself it was because traffic around here can be unpredictable, and I loathe being late. But the truth is that I'm eager to see her. Eager for a hug from someone who hasn't hurt me. From the person who brings a little light to my days with her messages. She doesn't have to check in on me, but I can tell.

I'm the person who hasn't hurt her.

Maybe I light up her days with my messages.

My phone vibrates with a text from her. *I'm so sorry. Running about twenty minutes late. Stayed at Riley's last night. Got in a huge fight. Said she would drop me off this morning but bailed. On bus now.*

My lip burns under the clamp of my teeth. "Fucking Riley." Just because you've had an argument doesn't mean you have to let your girlfriend take the world's worst public transportation to get somewhere you promised you'd take her. I slug my coffee and order another at the counter, plus two almond croissants and a cortado. I didn't want to be weird and order for her before, but I think she'll be relieved to have a coffee in her hands as soon as she walks in.

Maybe their fight last night had something to do with Riley's softer messages. Maybe Flo talked to her about the funeral, the trip, how unacceptable her behavior has been. I reread her text. It brims with anxiety. It literally pains me to know how shitty Riley is to her. How she keeps her on the hook and takes everything she needs and wants from Florence while giving her nothing in return. Nothing as far as I can tell, at least.

It's all good, I type. *Just take your time and get here safely. Got an almond croissant and cortado with your name on it.*

We didn't message too much this weekend. She's not my person, so I think that would be a little inappropriate. But I know it's not just the caffeine that's tingling in my stomach. Florence is about to walk through those doors, and Riley will not be here to interrupt. It's just coffee. With a friend. But for the first time in a while, my energy is kinetic. For the first time in a while, I'm not saturated with the pain of mourning. My mind only sporadically pauses on my mom, on my dad, when it normally sticks as if caught in fly paper.

It's a feeling I'm aware of. Something to keep an eye on given our upcoming trip.

Florence crashes into the front doors, and half the coffee shop turns their attention to her. The barista mimics pulling the door.

"You pull it," one man shouts. As if she wasn't going to figure that out in one second.

She takes a visible breath and *pulls* open the door, giving an adorable half curtsey to her concerned, and adoring, audience. I don't blame the patrons. Florence is easy to be captivated by. Her flowing red waves cover her pale shoulders left exposed by a lilac sundress. A plaid button-down hangs over her cross-body leather purse, and a pink blush swells into her chest and cheeks. She spots me in the back and beelines toward our table.

I knock the table with my knee as I stand to hug her, and coffee sloshes over the edge of my mug. I ignore it. Florence ignores it. I notice her eyes are watering before she launches into my arms and hugs me. And I hug her. Tight. The kind of hug where you gather all of someone into you. Her hair smells like white flowers and vanilla, and her body is warm against my chest.

"It's okay," I murmur.

I feel her chest rise and fall with a deep breath before she nods against my shoulder and pulls away, quickly pulling off her purse and smoothing her hair.

"I should be the one saying that." She clears her throat and pulls out her chair. "Thank you for ordering for me. My favorites. I need them this morning."

She closes her watery, seafoam eyes as she takes her first sip of cortado. Her shoulders relax as she settles into her seat. Coffee really is healing.

"Do you want to talk about it?" I wipe the overboard coffee with a napkin, pretending not to watch as she tries to compose herself, smiling the kind of smile that serves as a dam for tears. I won't push it. She knows I'm here if she wants to share.

She blows out a breath and shakes her head. "No, no. It was just a silly disagreement. Par for the course with your cousin, really." She drums the table top with her white-painted nails before grabbing her coffee again. "You have enough on your plate without me burdening you with my problems, too."

"Flo." She pushes her clear plastic glasses up her nose, her quill wrist tattoo peeking at me as she sips. "You're not being a burden."

She chuckles into her mug. "Eaden, you're a scientist. You of all people should know one data point doesn't confirm a hypothesis." Her nails continue to drum. Softer now. "All I've ever been is a burden."

"Maybe," I start, and she stills her hand. She watches me as if she'll remember what comes out of my mouth next. At least for a week or two. I'm not even sure what I'm going to say. I stall with a sip of coffee. "Maybe it's other people's burdens you feel."

"Hmm"—she arches her brow—"maybe."

We both bite into our croissants, letting our previous words settle and fade. She brushes a crumb from her lip and gazes out the window.

"Hey," she says, bringing me back. "How has this weekend been? Are you okay?"

From the pained look on her face, I can only assume I'm donning the same kind of dam-for-tears smile she had on earlier. The sting in my eyes confirms it. She grabs my hand, her fingers cool against my warm skin. Aloe.

"I don't normally ask the world's most obvious questions," she says, her hand tightening over mine. "But I need to know. How's the storm, love?"

I squeeze her hand. A little anchor in my rough water.

"Raging," I whisper.

It's all I can say.

When I was fifteen, I tagged along with Riley to her friend's lake house in Arkansas. In February. She and Owen, her friend, were doing polar plunges into the lake off a huge boulder about fifteen feet above the water. I watched them carefully as they ran across the slick rock and leapt without a single care in the world. Without any hint of interest in self-preservation. It entranced me. Danger in so many different forms. I took solace in at least knowing the icy water would have a lower incidence of flesh-eating bacteria. Maybe.

It didn't take long for Riley and Owen to pressure me to the top of that rock. And it took even shorter for, at the first sign of my refusal, them to throw me off the edge into the lake. Phone in my pocket. Heart in my throat.

Surfaced. Gasped for oxygen until my lungs burned. Muffled shouting.

"Just get out of the fucking water!" Riley, more annoyed than concerned.

"Fuck, dude. I think she's drowning!" Owen, bang on.

Suffocating shock. Drowning. A nightmare full of silent shouts and sobs for help.

Florence squeezes my hand tighter, and the scent of coffee fills my lungs instead of the burning nothingness. Her brows are drawn tightly together in concern. "I can sit with you through it, you know?" She rubs the back of my hand with her thumb. "When it's raging."

I nod slowly as I track the movement of her thumb on my skin. She's so convincing, really. With her deep eyes and her cool fingers and the way she leans close to me over the table. Offering shelter. But I know how this works by now. I know that older brothers who used to tell you stories of Captain Blackjack and the unicorn pirates on sleepless nights grow up callous and distant. I know fathers falter, leaving emptiness and pain in their wake. Cousins watch as you literally drown before their eyes, until an Owen jumps in after you. Partners hold you tight until you feel that sweet sense of safety in their arms, then they pack their things while you're working overnight at the lab.

And mothers die when you need them most.

I don't know yet what a Florence Davis does.

Something tells me she could fill a person up. Fill up a whole life with art, love, slow living, and fast heartbeats.

Something tells me she could hollow a person out. Scarecrow a life with straw-brittle emptiness, excavate bones to leave sinew and strife, leave a crater in her wake.

"Okay. Thank you," I murmur.

The rings on her fingers pinch a bit of my flesh when she squeezes one more time as if for emphasis, and I delicately free myself from her grip. She piles her hands in her lap and forces a shallow smile.

"So," she starts. "About this trip."

"Yeah." I run my hand through my hair. Twice, out of paranoia that I left croissant crumbs from my first pass through. "Just two weeks away."

"I know the itinerary is down to the minute, but I just wanted to really check in with you." She casts a glance out the window, then turns back to me. "Are you sure you want to do this with me instead of alone?"

"I'm sure."

Christ. Apparently, I'm so terrified of being alone, I can't even take a single moment to verify within myself that this is the right decision for me. Cost-benefit analysis is out the window on this one.

Her eyes soften, and for the first time, I notice the shallow crow's feet that frame them. "You and me, then." She holds up her coffee in a toast.

I clink her smaller cup with mine. "You and me."

There's no more talk of storms, arguments, or shows of support. The rest of our time together at the café is filled with assuring each other we can explore at our leisure outside of Riley's itinerary and planning and where to meet when we first land in Barcelona. Riley booked Florence a direct flight that lands two hours after my non-direct, albeit much cheaper, flight.

I offer to drive her back to Aunt Susan's, but she politely declines.

I open my arms to hug her once we're outside. "I guess I'll see you in Spain, then."

"Yeah." She hugs me tight and fast before she pulls away and switches her eyeglasses for sunglasses. "Text me if you want."

I grin and unlock my car. "What would a day be like if I didn't?"

"Pure shit," she shouts as she crosses the parking lot toward Kline Street.

My car door closes with a thud, and I take a deep breath while I buckle my seat belt. "Pure shit," I whisper into the quiet. Then I drive home, thinking about if Florence could hurt me or abandon me just as everyone in my life seems to do. If at this point in time, I would care. Her relationship with Riley is tenuous at best, and if it crumbled completely, would I see her again? Are we friends without Riley?

I suppose this trip will tell.

CHAPTER EIGHT

Today is Florence's birthday. I know this because I received a flurry of texts from my aunt and Rye yesterday about trying to throw together a last-minute barbecue to celebrate, followed by another flurry of texts from Rye changing her mind and stating she's going to take her on a nice date instead. Just the two of them.

Florence plans out birthdays for Riley, for Aunt Susan and Uncle Bob, and for her mother with achingly thought-out detail and with more care and consideration than any of them are capable of. She is the most selfless person I know, surrounded by the most selfish people I know. It's hard to stomach, knowing when her birthday comes around, all she will receive is some haphazard, slapdash attempt at affection. An apathetic display that she receives with grace and appreciation.

Knowing that's all she has to look forward to today physically pains me. Almost as much as the idea of her spending the night with Riley.

Wonder if it crosses my aunt's mind that when Florence doesn't stay at her house, she's at Riley's midtown apartment, probably naked in her bed. My groan tickles my throat. Knuckles rub over my temples. Sit up against the headboard to keep the nausea from spilling up my esophagus. My coffee is cold, as always, and I'm pretty sure I'm sick. Truly ill, not just at the thought of Florence in Riley's bed after a lavish night of being wined and dined. Riley loves to throw money at people, especially if she's recently misbehaved.

"Not your business, Eaden," I mutter.

I open and close the message thread between me and Flo enough times to frustrate myself. We've exchanged a handful of messages every day since coffee. About nothing, about the trip, about the theories of infinite space. Normal stuff. So why am I being so juvenile about texting her happy birthday?

Even if she isn't spending it alone with Riley, it's not like I could've gone to the barbecue. I don't want to get anyone sick.

I take a swig of Gatorade and toss back a Tylenol, then I open our messages again and type a birthday note. Short and sweet: *Happy birthday, Flo. I'd say my days are fuller with you as my friend, so thank you for being in them. I hope you're showered with all the love today. You certainly deserve it.*

She doesn't respond. I turn off my lamp and slide back into the abyss of my bed, hoping to sleep off this cold and most of this day. For how much I was looking forward to my first summer as a teacher, it's been hard. The days are so long. Dinner is finished by six, the dishes are done by quarter past, and there's still four hours to kill before I can reasonably attempt sleep. The goal is to knock the days out quickly and as painlessly as possible until I can live again.

Living again, I suppose, is just on the other side of survival. Or grief, maybe.

I rub at the stubborn ache just above my brow.

Barcelona. I'm going to be living again when I land in Barcelona. At least, that's my goal for the trip.

Aww, thanks Eaden! A text from Flo comes through, followed by a second. *It's so weird though. There's no gift here from you.* She ends it with the skeptical smiley.

Despite the growing throb in my head, I grin. *I couldn't fit the string quartet in Riley's apartment.* I add a handful of violin emojis and a few musical notes.

She laugh reacts and starts typing. *What a shame. I'm at her aunt's for the night, and there's plenty of space for that gorgeous orchestra to perform in the backyard.*

I respond without thinking too much about it, though I know it's none of my business. *Oh, my bad. I thought you were staying over there after your birthday date with her. In that case, your next gift is an at-home spa day!* Again, I litter the text with emojis of nail polish, baths, and bubbles.

It takes a moment for her to respond, so I continue to hydrate and sink lower into bed, avoiding getting up to brush my teeth.

It wasn't a date, she sends. *I know everyone jokes about it, but we aren't together. Even if sometimes, that line is blurry for us. At least, she made the line pretty clear before you and I met up for coffee. Not together. Maybe she was trying to blur things again tonight, but I just can't right now. A spa day alone sounds perfect. Thank you.*

Riley treats her like garbage while they're officially together. Now she makes it clear to Florence that they're definitely not together. Then tries to take her on a romantic date for her birthday? I know Riley. I've seen how she walks through life so unaffected by the wake of her actions. Unaffected by the hearts she breaks. But it hits different when I know the woman on the end of her hook. My head threatens to explode.

Fingers twitch over the keys.

Would you choose something different? If you hadn't just moved into her family's basement? I mean, I know the graphic design program isn't cheap, and free rent makes that doable for you. But would you be open to a cleaner break from Riley and maybe dating other people? I bet you're just dying to get on the apps. I end it with a winky face to soften the question.

It takes a moment for her to respond. *That's a big question, Eaden. There are sides to Riley that you don't get to see. And even though she drives me crazy sometimes, I do love her. Or, I have love for her. I'm not looking to date anyone else, especially when her parents went out of their way to help me through SCAD. They're my home now, and I respect that.* She sends a quick follow-up. *For all her faults, Riley has been there for me in her own way, and she will grow up one day. Maybe once I finish the program and move into my own place again, we can reassess and reunite in a more meaningful way. Sorry, that was verbose.*

There it is. I lay my phone on my chest and digest what she said. She loves Riley. Loyal to Riley. Hopeful for Riley. She wants my flawed cousin still. Even after she watched her make a complete circus of my mother's funeral. If after that and the multiple infidelities, she can't let Riley go, she never will.

But I've become accustomed to her friendship. Her comradery. The banter and the bonding over early mornings and weird families, orange cat memes, and a mutual obsession with Emma Thompson. If Florence stayed with Riley forever, then I could enjoy her friendship forever.

It's scary to find solace in a person.

People are fleeting. Just a mass of living cells and stimulus responses. Little organisms that get sick, get lost, change their surroundings on a whim. They are, for all intents and purposes, momentary.

I open the message and respond.

I hear you. I'm glad you have them to see you through your program. And seriously, whatever you want to come from your relationship with Riley, I hope you get it. I think the world of you, and you deserve it all.

Then I add, *like a Parisian café full of birthday treats,* and a smattering of cake and croissant emojis.

It feels good to confirm what Florence wants. To confirm who I am to her and where I belong. To say I've been pining for her would be an overstatement. I'm more curious about our connection and how it relates to Riley and my family and if it correlates with potential chemistry beyond friendship. It does not.

I see my part more clearly now. My part in the darkness woven between me and Riley. She needs to dominate, to be the star, and that need has personified itself in taking from me people I've wanted in the past. Merely for sport. While I would never do that, especially not with someone I care for as deeply as Florence, I may have let my resentment of Riley's actions bleed into things. I let Riley's questionable behavior mask the seedling of my feelings for Florence in something resembling innocuousness. Something entirely moral because it was in response to the immoral.

So many sins have been branded by this fallacy.

I don't want to be that. I want to be loyal to my family even when they make it so damn difficult. I want to be at peace with who I am and what I have. And I have two very good friends in Hakim and Florence. That is my priority. I can't lose the bright parts of my life right now. Darkness consumes, and I'm just barely flickering as it is. What I need is to be more like Florence.

That means everything to me. Thank you for the support and the delicious pastries, she messages. A second one arrives quickly after. *And just so you know, you are also seeing me through. I quite honestly can't imagine not having you. I'd feel very alone without this connection of ours. It's special to me.*

I respond, *It's special to me, too. I don't want to lose our friendship.* Then *let's not. Let's protect it. You and me,* she replies.

You and me, I agree.

She sends a red heart, and I slide my phone on the nightstand, feeling a sense of calm and acceptance. I won't lose her.

The streetlamp casts just enough light through my window for me to see the faint outline of my mom in the photo on my dresser. An instant hollow ache fills my chest. I wonder if it will ever fade, that desperate, empty pain. Or if it becomes a part of one, like a scion on rootstock, forever altered for better or for worse.

❖

It's been over a week since Flo's birthday, and there are only three days left until my flight. Shampoo overflows my travel-sized squirt bottle as I catch myself in the bathroom mirror while I fill it. My cheek is completely healed, with just a whisper of dry pinkness across the bone. And my eyes are clearer, having lost some of that strange haze that had settled over the brown like fog in a decimated forest. I rinse the container and set the travel shampoo by its conditioner partner on my bag. It's a bit early to be packing, but it's how I manage my anxiety and excitement.

It also takes a lot of planning to pack for a three-week European adventure in a backpack. Well, a backpacking pack, but still. Sean let me borrow the Osprey pack he takes to the Burning Man festival in the desert of Nevada. I shudder to think what this pack has seen. It certainly has the physical scars; it took days to rid it of stray sand and air it out enough to lose the musty scent of stale wet cardboard. I picked it up from his place in Athens last week after I was sure I wouldn't spread whatever cold I had.

He handed it to me and wished me luck. Told me to be safe, as if he took ownership in my well-being. I thanked him and turned right back around for Atlanta.

It had never occurred to me that I could bring anything other than a giant suitcase to Europe. But Flo mentioned how much easier it is to hop trains and navigate new cities when you don't have to drag a swollen suitcase behind you on crowded platforms and side streets. We agreed that we wouldn't judge each other for wearing the same four outfits on repeat and vowed to find some laundry detergent leaflets for washing essentials in hotel sinks.

But as I fill the bottom half of the pack, it hits me just how little I'll have with me overseas. Maybe it's a metaphor. Shed the pain of last month and be free with my friend in new countries without the weight of my depression holding me down.

"Sure," I mutter, tucking the outlet adapter in the side pocket. "Or I'll just smell like sweat and faintly of Burning Man the entire time." I cringe as I sniff the faded nylon again, worried I've gone nose blind to the stench.

My phone lights up on the dresser.

How's packing going? Do you find that packing a year in advance is the superior method? It's from Flo.

I chuckle as I type, *Don't lie. I know you started making your packing list way before me.*

I have no idea what you're talking about. I'm not excited at all, she counters.

I let her message sit without a response for a few minutes. The letter my mom wrote her aunt is weighty on my open palm, as if each word has its own atomic weight. My mother's last thoughts, the thoughts she felt were most important to get down on paper, to send across the Atlantic, weren't for me. I sigh as I slide the letter carefully into the compartment meant to protect a laptop. The anger in me wants to look up Aunt Mary's address and just send the damn thing.

But I should meet this person. The only one from my mother's family still alive in Ireland, and she clearly meant something to my mom.

The Velcro secures the letter in its sleeve. Even if I left right now with what I have in this pack, I'd be fine. And that feels good.

I grab my phone to respond and find a new message from Riley: *Keep Florence safe for me. Have a good trip.*

There's zero chance that I will be responding to that. The mere fact that she could ever insinuate that she keeps Florence safe is wild to me. It makes zero sense. And it frankly insults me. I open Flo's message to respond instead.

Sure, sure. Tell that to your Duolingo.

Then, because I'm me and have the compulsive need to not rock the boat, I respond to Riley, *Have a good summer.* And that's that.

Finished for now, I move my packing supplies off the bed and review my schedule for the days before my flight. Drinks with Hakim tonight, lunch with my dad tomorrow, and fly out the day after that. Almost there. A nervous knot winds itself tight in my stomach. I'm not the best flyer, and I've never been on an international flight across an entire ocean. It freaks me out to do it alone, but I know it will be worth it. It will all be worth it.

CHAPTER NINE

"Flight attendants, please prepare the cabin for arrival," the captain announces over the choppy intercom.

Sitting up, I wipe my eyes and try to gain my bearings. I couldn't fall asleep on my first flight, which was an eight-and-a-half-hour red-eye into Frankfurt, but apparently, I finally closed my eyes on my short second flight into Barcelona. I wipe some crumbs off my lap and make sure I have my phone, passport, and wallet still on my being. And, wow, I feel disgusting. What is it about flying that completely wrecks a person? Unfortunately, a shower isn't available, so I'll need to wash my face and brush my teeth in the airport bathroom before Flo lands in a couple hours.

We messaged back and forth a few times when I was on my first flight, and we both had Wi-Fi. After we disembark, I connect to the airport network and wait for the messages to file in. Except I have zero messages. Hopefully, that means she's sleeping.

I walk to the gate she's supposed to arrive at and find a bathroom to freshen up in. Then I find a small bar in sight of her gate and buy a beer. Because why not? I'm in Spain, and I'm officially on vacation. Technically, I have been for the last few weeks, but now I'm forcing myself into relaxing, enjoying, and just taking things day by day. Starting with this Estrella. It's crisp and delicious and, after the twelve hours of traveling, goes straight to my head. I chug a pint of water and wait.

Florence and I haven't seen each other since our coffee date, and I've missed her. From her messages, I feel like she's missed me, too. Though she hasn't flat-out said it, I can feel it. That's the thing, I can always feel her. I can tell when she's trying to paint an illusion with her words, and I can tell when she's in pain. I can tell when she misses me. All the things she can't write in a message, I still see them woven in the words she chooses. It could be that I'm delusional. Or we're just connected like that. Either way, I'm dying to see her.

Passing the last half hour until her arrival, I check the news and message my dad that I've arrived safely. It pains me to do it, to allow him such paternal privilege, but I couldn't say no. At the end of the day, I am a rule follower, and I want to make the people I love happy. Even if they don't currently deserve it. He floated the idea of family therapy before I left.

"Oh? So you're gonna tell Sean about the affair?" I asked in response.

He shrugged as if it didn't matter to him. "If it's necessary for us all to heal from your mother's passing." I rolled my eyes at this. "Again, Eaden, I've never asked you to keep this a secret for me."

"No, you haven't," I scoffed. "You just enjoy knowing that I will."

Every prick of pain my words cause him has an equal and opposite effect on me. It's simply a law of physics, and nobody is winning. I know he's probably right about family therapy, but I'm just not there yet. He responds to my text with *Amazing. Have the best time, stay safe, and send Flo my love.*

I notice the plane arrive at Flo's gate and rush to pay before everyone disembarks. Slinging my pack on my shoulder, I take the last sip of beer and wash it down with the rest of my water. It will be another ten minutes at least until she gets off the plane, but I wait eagerly a few feet away from the service desk. I'm anxious to finally hug her again. Fingers thrum my thigh, and I check my phone over and over for a message from her until one finally comes through.

Welcome to Barcelona! I'm hereee!

My smile tugs hard against my cheeks as I slip my phone in my pocket and scan the passengers beginning to file into the gate. Chic strangers and kids rubbing their eyes stride past me. Then I spot her. Hair pulled into a messy bun, a nineties MTV hoodie draped lazily over her body, and a bright purple pack holding it all together. She spots me and delivers a megawatt smile that I'm pretty sure could jump-start my heart from a flatline.

She pushes a loose bang out of her face and drops her pack by her feet, nodding for me to do the same. My pack thuds against the carpet by my shoes as we stare at one another.

"Welcome to Barcelona," she says, looking up at me through a smile.

We crash into each other, her arms tight around my neck and my arms tight around her waist. My glasses go crooked against her hood as her fingers find the baby hairs at the back of my neck. It makes me twitch in her embrace. This is not the hug we shared at the coffee shop. This is not a hug we have shared ever. But there is something about being in a foreign country alone that casts a particularly powerful sense of anonymity over us. Yes, we were alone at the coffee shop, but now we're alone together in a place where no one knows who we are. Or who we are to each other. Or who we are to other people.

It's just Florence and me.

And the terrifying realization that we have almost three weeks of this anonymity, and her waist in my grip feels like my new addiction.

She gives the back of my neck a little squeeze, and we pull away from each other. Her cheeks are a bit flushed as she clears her throat and reaches for her bag. The sound of my heavy breath awakens my common sense, and I do the same, confident that the blood rushing into my face has betrayed my emotions. We let each other get away with it, though, and I follow her through customs, the two of us trying to maintain casual small talk but failing to fight the growing kernel of awkwardness between us.

The hug. It was too much.

In some indefinable way, it was too much.

"Did you sleep much on the plane?" she asks in the cab on the way to the hotel.

I'm mesmerized by the giant castle-looking building that looks like it was made from drip sand and gumdrops and the gentle mountains behind it. Never in my life have I seen a building so haunting and simultaneously playful. And imposing. Like a king with a sense of humor.

"That's Gaudí's Sagrada Família," she says, leaning over to look out my window with me. "It's amazing, right?"

I cannot respond.

I am so taken by this edifice.

Maybe it's because I've never been outside of the US, and the only imposing buildings I have seen are sleek, steel skyscrapers. The monuments in DC are gorgeous, but they are still severe and monotone. They command respect, surely. But this commands worship, adoration, obsession.

"Is this on the itinerary?" I finally ask as we drive beyond sight of it.

She narrows her eyes and grins, as if she just learned something curious about me. "Don't worry. We'll go see it tomorrow, itinerary be damned."

"It's not on there?" I ask, horrified.

We lean to the left as the driver makes a right.

She winces. "Riley thought it was too touristy. Wanted to stick to more local, underground stuff."

While I can appreciate the desire to experience a new city, a new country, authentically, I cannot imagine merely taking in the Sagrada Família in passing. The mere size of it, how it demands attention on the city's horizon, must at least speak to its cultural significance. I was ready to blindly trust Riley with this trip, but now, as the first detour from the itinerary is going to happen on the second day of the trip, I feel released from it.

A new sense of freedom and excitement settles in my chest as the cab slows in front of our hotel. This isn't Rye's trip.

Florence gives my knee a squeeze and says, "Think of it this way. We have all our travel and accommodations pre-booked. As for the rest, we can do whatever the hell we want. And if we need some suggestions, we can look at Rye's itinerary or ask the internet for all I care. But I kinda think the best way to experience a new city is to walk its streets and see what we find." She cracks open her door. "You ready?"

I nod and follow her into the hotel. It's our trip.

Flo takes care of check-in and leads us to a room on the second floor at the end of the hall. It's a small room—barely large enough for the two double beds—with tan walls studded by local art, and strangely tall ceilings. I toss my pack on the bed closest to the door, under the silly notion that I could defend us in case of an intruder. By no means am I weak, but I have also never won a fight with cousins nor brothers. They've kept me humble, to say the least. But as I watch Florence unzip her pack, so painfully organized and exact, as if the very apex of her existence is balanced on the neatness of her surroundings, I decide

I'd throw myself in front of anything if it meant an extra second of her safety.

Choosing this bed is less ego, more exaltation.

"I cheated," Flo says. She hangs her summer dresses in the small wardrobe, smoothing each one before adding the next. "I fit, like, three more outfits in my bag than we agreed on."

I chuckle as I pull out a fresh pair of shorts and a light button-down. "Trying to make me look bad, Flo?"

"No." She turns to me and delivers a potent little pout. "There's just not a ton of material to my sundresses, and I had a little extra space."

I ignore the little flame licking in my stomach at the mention of her dress's minimal material. And I pivot in an attempt to quell the little flame, to douse it in some reality. "Now you don't have any space to bring back gifts for Rye or Aunt Susan." I shake my head as if this is the gravest of mistakes. "They're gonna think you don't care about them." I don't realize the quiet of the room until after I drop my pack on the floor between the wall and my bed and turn to see Flo watching me. "I didn't actually mean—"

"First of all," she says, walking by me and grabbing my pack off the ground. "You and I are going to be sharing small spaces for a long time. Traveling is chaotic, and I really need our space to be organized, or I'll get, like, major anxiety. Is that okay?"

"Yea—yeah. Okay."

"And second of all, it's you and me on this trip together. Riley isn't here. Aunt Susan isn't here. And though Riley and her family permeate every minute of my life in Atlanta—which I'm not ungrateful for—it's just, I am across the world with *you*, my best friend. I'm not saying we can never talk about Rye or your aunt and uncle, but can we just embrace being away from it all?" She drops her head and sighs. "Honestly, between you and me, I need this break to just be me for a little while."

She picks the ridge of her nail bed, drawing my gaze to her fingers. They're painted a soft peach, the polish perfectly smooth and neat. But the skin around the nail is puffy and irritated, hinting at a longer history of picking them. Though it's none of my business, I can't ignore this physical evidence of her anxiety or pain or whatever it is that drives her toward relief. It kills me. It kills me that I'm not the person who will ever know what hurts her. I'm not the person who could ease that load for her. I'm not her person at all. Regardless, I hold this data close, tuck it away for another time.

"Hey," I say, grabbing her attention. She drops her hands and tucks them behind her back. "I hear you."

She scrunches her eyebrows, clearly wary of my response. "That's it? You hear me? No follow-ups, no objections. Just—"

"Just, I hear you." I nibble on a dry speck on my lip, trying to come up with more, but what she told me makes sense. Cut-and-dried. "And thank you for sharing it with me," I finally say, though it sounds like a question.

"Hmm." A grin splits the concern on her face, and her shoulders lose their tension. "Okay, then."

A deep breath fills my lungs, and I release it, along with my own tension. "Okay, then."

She chuckles and reaches for my bag again. "I can unpack for you if you want. So you don't have to fuss with it. I'm quite good at fitting things in small spaces." She whips around to face me, eyes wide. "Oh my God, I didn't mean it like—"

I storm over her words with delirious laughter. Eyes watering, doubled over, jet-lagged laughter. And she laughs, too. Hand on belly, gasping, beautiful laughter.

"It's the—" I cut myself off with more uncontrollable laughter. "It's the jet lag," I wheeze.

"Oh my God," she says, wiping the tears sliding down her cheeks. "That was so funny."

"Was it, though?" A few more chuckles pop from my chest before I straighten and wipe away my tears. "I blame it on how sleep-deprived I am."

"Okay." She plants a hand on her chest and takes a deep breath. "How about you shower while I unpack for you, and we can go grab an early dinner and come back and just chill? Watch a bad movie and get a good rest before we really get out there and explore tomorrow."

"What?" I shake my head, confused. "Florence, I'm an adult." When she only responds with a quizzical look, I elaborate. "I am perfectly capable of unpacking my own bag. I mean, thank you for the offer, but you really don't need to do that."

"Right." She shakes her head as if realizing it was a silly notion. "Obviously. You're right, I'm just used to..." She trails off.

"But the rest of it sounds perfect," I interject, saving her from an explanation. She said she wanted to embrace being away from it all, and I assume whatever she's *used to* falls under that umbrella. I couldn't understand more. The shadows of what I'm escaping on this trip flash before me. I ignore them. "Why don't you shower first while I finish unpacking, and we'll go from there?"

❖

I wake with a start. I wake with no idea where I am. I wake with the hollowest dread beating in place of my heart. With a damp tee stuck to my bare breasts, a cold shiver slipping down my back, and an ache thrumming in that familiar spot above my right brow. As awareness settles, I realize I'm completely stuck in an existence that's just as devastating as my nightmare.

Such that I find no reprieve in my sleep and none in my reality. No escape.

Florence stirs, and I remember where I am and who I'm with, not just what I've lost. But even knowing she's in the bed next to me can't rid me of the dread clinging to my chest like stubborn phlegm. I dreamt of my mom for the first time since she died. It wasn't beautiful, peaceful, or any iteration of what I hoped it would be.

It wasn't cathartic.

It was a haunting.

It poked at the very tender bit of me that holds the most sorrow. The bit that festered and flaked and fed on any good left in me. Mom's face haunted me, grayish and a sunken kind of swollen. As if she was found waterlogged then abandoned in the sun instead of ashen and dry on a gurney. She was so dry on that gurney. Like an autumn leaf, translucent between the veins. But not in this nightmare. In this nightmare, her eyes puffed red and doughy as tears flooded her cheeks, swelling her face into a distorted abstract of pain. Almost like the watercolor at her funeral. She sobbed that terrifying way. Wordless. Staring through me.

I saw her cry that way, though less grotesque and more of this world, a month or two before she died. She didn't know I was stopping by to check on her while my dad was at work. I let myself in the through the open garage and walked into the kitchen, noticing the sink full of dirty dishes, a sight I'd never seen in my mother's house. She was standing over the washing machine. I could tell it was mid-cycle by the way it reverberated through her planted hands and up her arms. Some news station was streaming through the wireless speaker we set up in there last Christmas. I stopped, careful not to make a noise.

I watched her sob in secret while my heart broke.

Then I went home.

CHAPTER TEN

My heart is only mildly broken when we learn that the Sagrada Família is closed for restoration. The excitement that overwhelmed me yesterday has been snuffed by the nightmare last night. It hangs all over me like Spanish moss. I can feel it, thick and itchy. A crawling thing. A parasite. I try to hide it, but it's so hard to pretend like I'm fully here in Barcelona with Florence when the horrendous image of my mom suffocates me.

"It's okay if you're not feeling good," Flo says, gently bumping my shoulder as we turn into an alley we haven't been down yet. "We can just go back to the hotel and chill."

It's hot. Like, really hot. And my stomach churns with anxiety and the omelet I accidentally ordered for breakfast. Eggs are not my friend, but apparently, a Spanish tortilla is not a tortilla at all. It's an omelet. I am the ignorant tourist who didn't know better, so I stuck with it. Ate just enough to not be rude and to not garner Flo's suspicion. But now I'm simultaneously starving and nauseated. And now I've worried Flo. I need to suck it up.

I adjust the secret travel pack I have strapped across my stomach to try to relieve some of my distress. Try to focus on something nice. Like this morning, when Florence made fun of me for my "grandpa getup" while she watched me store my passport and cash in the fanny pack, accusing me of wanting to flash my way through Barcelona every time I had to pay for something.

"Maybe, I'm not, like, the best at digesting eggs." I flash her a quick smile. "Sorry I haven't felt the best. Could we duck in somewhere, and I can get some water and a snack? Then I'll be good to go."

She quirks her brow as we hop onto the sidewalk to avoid a gaggle of children swarming through on their bikes. "Why did you order eggs? Especially on your first day in a foreign country?" I grimace, and she shoots me the most adorable smirk. "Eaden," she scolds.

I groan. "I know, I know."

"I told you to look it up if you didn't know what it meant," she says.

I hold out my arms in exasperation. "I didn't know that I didn't know what it meant. I thought a tortilla was a tortilla. Like a little breakfast burrito without eggs. Because it didn't say eggs. Seems very logical to me."

She rolls her eyes. "Well, not here. A Spanish tortilla is literally all eggs."

We stop and have a mini stare-down. Her chest is already beginning to freckle despite the 50 SPF sunscreen she lathered on this morning. Her green and blue floral dress is elegant and playful, and it suits her shy and cheeky personality perfectly. The messy bun atop her head is lopsided as she glares at me over her tortoiseshell sunglasses.

I grin and throw my hands up. "Well, now I know," I say in defeat.

She cracks into her usual gorgeous smile and sighs. "Come on." She tugs me down the alley as she opens Google Maps with the other hand. "One of the old-school bars I wanted to take you to is, like, a five-minute walk from here. They have some snacks, and we can rest and hydrate while simultaneously dehydrating with a drink. Deal?"

I skip by people to avoid knocking into passersby while hanging on to Flo's hand. I don't want to let it go, but she drops mine to zoom in on the map. "Yeah. That sounds good," I say. We take a left, then one more right and stop in front of a very old-looking bar with a new sign that reads *Pascal's*.

"Ready?" she asks.

"Let's do it."

The interior of the bar is a moment frozen in time. Empty bottles line the walls, serving almost as a timeline. The first bottles are wonky and esoteric, then the sequential bottles begin to resemble modern-day beer and wine bottles. But they are all equally covered in dust. Not just coated but dripping with soft gray clumps of it, which is a feat given the large, slow ceiling fans whirring above. The floor is a jigsaw of mismatched tiles that look meant for ballrooms or Spanish patios, not to be walked on by my worn-out Nikes.

Florence smiles as she takes it all in, then grabs my hand again, a habit that I hope sticks for the duration of our travels. "Come on," she says and guides me to the warped wooden bar. "This place is known for their house made vermouth and absinthe. They say Picasso and Hemingway used to drink here."

"Together?" I ask.

"I"—she stares at me, clearly taken aback—"have no idea."

I shrug. "Would've been quite the drinking buddies."

She chuckles and drops my hand. "They damn sure would have been. I bet we'll be good drinking buddies, too."

Emboldened and feeling infinitely better, I say, "Wanna find out?"

"Yes." She nods to the bar, and I follow.

The bartender is an older man with more gray than black in his trim beard and shaggier hair. A dark, brown-brimmed hat sits on the crown of his head, tipped back so we can see his gray blue eyes. "*Hola, hola, amigas,*" he greats us and slides a stained paper menu in front of us.

"*Hola, gracias,*" we respond in almost perfect unison.

"Okay," I say, glancing at the menu that is way easier to understand than the breakfast menu. "What about some patatas bravas, and we can split the Ibérico melt?"

She leans against me, and I can't help but enjoy the way her soft warm skin feels against mine. Her touch awakens me, and I stand a little straighter. "It's"—she checks her phone, ignoring a text from Riley—"half past three. I'm cool with starting with that and maybe another snack later. But, Eaden." She stares at me with the seriousness of Mrs. Aderton, the strictest teacher at my school. "You need to drink so much water. Please. I need you to be well."

Her eyes without glasses look almost naked. It's somehow intimate. Like maybe not a lot of people get to see her this way. Like last night when we got ready for bed, she came out of the bathroom clutching her dirty clothes to her chest, face pink and fresh from washing and no glasses. No armor. We had put on the TV to try to find a movie but quickly fell asleep. There was only slight awkwardness, but it faded as the exhaustion settled.

I run my hand through my hair. It's cut short for the summer—just about shoulder length—but the roots are still damp with sweat. Definitely need to hydrate.

"So much water," I promise.

She gives a concerned half-smile, then orders for us in pretty good Spanish, though her voice is soft and hesitant. She speaks with a shyness that I rarely experience with her anymore. It reminds me how careful she is with other people and in unfamiliar places. A duality exists in her of ferocity and power, fear and anxiety.

We have our pick of tables and choose one in the corner so we can enjoy a broad view of the faded teal room and all the mysterious peeling portraits that hang on its walls. I chug an entire pint of water in one go as Flo stares at me with the same curiosity that my eighth graders have with Bill Nye. I finish, only slightly gasping for breath, and wipe my wet lips on the back of my hand. What I'm learning about Europe is, water doesn't come unless ordered, it certainly doesn't come with ice, and the mountain of napkins you receive in America is distinctly absent. I enjoy the pattern of concentric circular stains on the face of the table, like years of little Venn diagrams from sweating drinks.

"Do you always drink your water like that?" Flo asks, brows still raised. She sips hers slowly as she waits for a response.

"Um." I fill my glass from the carafe. "I guess I do, yeah. But I was thirsty, so that probably added to the vigor." I grin as I raise the water to my mouth and take a small, measured sip. "Is that better?"

She shakes her head and chuckles. "You're weirder than I thought."

"Is that—"

"It's a good thing." She fingers the fat beads of condensation running down her glass. "It helps me feel like I can be all of me around you."

The bartender interrupts, sliding our *cervezas* and one glass of vermouth in front of us, followed by the food. It smells amazing. Salty and earthy from the potatoes to the truffle cheese on the ham sandwich. My stomach growls, and I want to dive in, but I can't let what Flo said pass me by. I want to know more. I hand her the vermouth and ask, "What do you mean?"

She smells the ruddy brown liquid but stops short of tasting it.

"Like, sometimes, I feel I have to be a certain version of me to satisfy people. For people to want to keep me. They seem to only want serious Florence in the tighter dresses, who makes sure everyone has what they need and doesn't ask for things she knows they don't want to give."

It feels like a very specific complaint about a very specific person, but it also feels like this is something that has always been building in her life.

"I'm silly, damn it," she adds.

I nod. "I know you are."

"I only want to wear tight dresses sometimes. But mostly, I want to wear my flowy ones with pockets." A grin begins to melt the pout clinging to her lips.

I nod again. "I know you do. So you can fill them with your treasures." I smile as she shoots me a sharp look. I always knew she was religious about journaling, but yesterday, I learned she likes to stash everything I'm about to throw away—coasters, receipts, tickets—in her pockets so she can paste them in her journal later. Now I call them her treasures.

"You're going to thank me one day." She shoves me softly. "Two years from now when you take your girlfriend to Barcelona to impress her, and you forget the name of that amazing little bar that makes their own vermouth, you're going to call me and beg me to look it up in my journal for you." Challenging me with a raised brow, she sips the vermouth. "Wow. That's delicious."

I taste it after. "It's a bittersweet whirlwind of herbal heaven," I say.

"Damn. That was poetic."

We go quiet as we fill our bellies with the hearty snacks and sip our beers to cut the grease. More patrons fill the bar, mostly older men but a few tourists as well. The breeze pours through the open windows and rustles through my hair. It's the most peaceful I've felt since before my mom died. It's so strange to have a "Before Christ" moment happen in my life. A moment that marks a permanent shift in my universe. The part of my life before my mom died and the part after.

Though I know it's not true—or I hope it's not true—it's difficult to imagine my best days are ahead. I have a dreadful feeling that I spent all the good in my life BD. Before Death.

I sip my beer and gaze at a couple at the table by the door. He rubs her thigh as they laugh over something she said. They are effervescent, chemically reacting to each other's cascading energy.

"I don't know," I say, breaking the comfortable quiet. "It's hard to imagine having a relationship strong enough to bring a girlfriend here one day. I can't really see that for myself. Or having a life partner at all." I shrug, taking the last sip of my beer, wondering if it's to blame for the admission.

"Hm," she says. The bartender brings the next round as Florence takes a moment to respond. Once he's departed with the empties and there are fresh bottles in front of us, she says, "Given you are kind, smart, marginally funny, and"—she tilts her head back and forth in appraisal—"we'll say quite attractive in a crushable teacher way, why on earth do you not see that for yourself? I mean, you've dated in the past, so I assume it's something you want, right?"

"I don't know." I pick at a hole in the leather of my chair top. Truth is, I've never known why I struggle so much to have successful relationships. "I mean, yes. I want that. I want a wife, I want kids, I want it all. I guess I've just never truly connected with someone in that soul way. And with the women I've dated, I was always willing to stay longer in the hope that it would grow into that. Actually, kind of makes me suspicious that it exists at all. Like maybe everyone's faking it."

"They aren't faking it," she counters.

I stare at her fingers gripping her beer. Pale and slender. "How do you know?" I ask, but I'm not entirely sure I want to know the answer.

"Maybe that kind of connection is something you can grow, but I don't really think so. I think you meet someone, and it happens then and there. Like, you brand each other's soul, and it's sharp and hot and sudden, like a wildfire in a drought. You may not know what it is when the first spark ignites to heat the iron, but you walk away feeling altered. Like you saw behind a curtain or something." She shrugs. "I think you can feel that spark the moment you meet someone meant for you."

While I'll never forget this description of meeting someone impactful, she didn't answer my question. And I'm a little tipsy, so I need to know the answer. "How many of those sparks have you felt before?"

She licks a speck of pepper from her finger, and I can't help but stare. Again, just a tad tipsy. "Two."

"Riley and…"

She clears her throat, wiping her hands in the napkin. "And Chloe. My first girlfriend. We dated for less than a year in high school."

I nod. "Gotcha."

"You'll find yours. Maybe multiple." She squeezes my knee.

Why on earth did I expect her to say three and add my name to the list? I don't know. Probably because I'm depressed and highly delusional about the way Florence cares about me. She's clearly just a good friend. To read into her eagerness to message me every morning or the way her fingers linger on me when we touch would be the inanest thing in the world for me to do. It doesn't matter that I felt a spark the first time I met her. That when her eyes met mine, it felt like she was branding me as hers. When she stopped me in my aunt's kitchen and took my hand to observe the scabs on my knuckles from falling on the sidewalk, I felt it in my marrow.

And at the end of the night, after talking all night, when we hugged good-bye, she slipped her hands inside my coat. It was strangely intimate.

"Maybe," I reply.

❖

After a few hours at the vermouth bar and a few rounds, we walk together to the bus stop. The sun is finally setting, casting the streets in a dusty orange glow. It's easy on the eyes, but somehow electric at the same time, how it paints the oddly familiar yet foreign buildings. It's finally cooled down a bit, and I feel just an ounce lighter. I try not to worry about tonight or if I'll have the same nightmare.

Focus on the sun spilling down the walls.

Florence answers her phone when it rings, and I can tell it's Riley. She sounds like she's talking to a parent she's been putting off calling. Chipper but short.

"We're fine. I promise. We're following the itinerary to a T, and it's been perfect. Thank you," she says.

I fall a couple steps behind to give her a bit of privacy.

"Yeah. No, of course. We're heading back toward the hotel now. Just going to walk around the neighborhood a bit, then call it a night. Exactly. Okay. You too. Wish you were here. Bye."

Wish you were here. That one hurts a bit. But it's okay because my threshold for pain is at an all-time high right now.

"How's she doing?" I ask.

Flo tucks her phone back in her purse. "I think she wishes she had come with us. But she's good. Just working."

We leave it at that and take the crowded bus back to our hotel. As we walk, a growing hum of music and shouting pulls us down the street adjacent to ours. When we round the corner, there is a crowd of people surrounding two flamenco dancers and a boom box on a wooden platform. Euros spill out of a hat on the ground next to a crate on a dolly.

"*Guapa!*" the dancing man shouts, clapping as his partner stomps, shaking the hem of her dress.

The onlookers cheer wildly and sway their hips with the dancers. When they stop to catch their breath, the people in the street start to dance. Some of them dance alone, an Estrella in hand. Some dance with a partner. From what I can tell, it's just an average weekend night in the neighborhood. But it feels so special.

"Come on, then," I say. I take her hand and lead us to the edge of the crowd. I haven't got much to lose at this point in my life, so why not dance with a beautiful woman? The whole neighborhood is dancing.

"You're serious?" she asks as we pull up to the dancing swarm.

I tug her by the purse strap crossing her chest, and she thuds into me with a small gasp. "As serious as a funeral at Endless Breadsticks."

"Eaden. You're terrible." And with that, she chuckles and wraps her arms around my shoulders. After a few moments of dancing together, she adds, "Thank you for this." And sinks into me just a little more.

I hold her against me and relish the closeness of her. How soft the fabric of her dress is, how tightly her waist curves into her hips, her perfume. Until the pace of the music ratchets up, and I spin her out of my arms. We dance until the performers take the small stage again and relinquish the floor to them. We cheer and watch, my arm over her shoulders and hers around the back of my waist. It's a nice fit, me being a couple inches taller.

"You ready to head back?" she says against my ear.

Her words warm the skin of my neck. "Let's do it."

We open the door to our room, and the scent of it makes my

stomach ache in an inconvenient way. An emotional way. It smells like Flo's perfume mixed with my shampoo. It smells like us. It's the first time I've ever encountered it, and I won't soon forget it. Another thing I will hold close from this trip, and it's only just begun.

Florence flops on her bed and groans. "I can't be bothered to shower tonight. I'm going to do it in morning, so it's all yours if you want it."

I notice her watching as I unclip my secret travel pouch from my sweaty stomach and toss it on the desk. She averts her eyes and pretends to look at something on her phone.

"I think I got a lot sweatier than you did," I say, running my hand through my matted hair. "I'm just going to rinse off real quick."

After I shower and brush my teeth, Florence changes in the bathroom and washes her face. She walks out in her adorable pajama set with tigers in plush emerald woods. "Hey," she says, tugging me away from folding my dirty clothes into a plastic laundry bag. "Thank you for today. I'm having a really amazing time with you, Eaden."

I drop the laundry and face her. "Of course. I don't think I would've had the courage to go on this trip by myself, so I should be thanking you."

She shakes her head and pulls me into a hug. It's intimate, like the hug in the airport. A saturated moment, threatening to flood. Because it feels too good. And I know it feels too good for her, too, since she doesn't let me go but pulls me tighter. We're not in Aunt Susan's house. Not at a funeral. Not in an airport. We are completely alone, so I pull her tighter too until her breath deepens.

"Wanna know a secret?" she whispers into my neck.

I nod against the top of her head without letting her go.

"No one's ever hugged me like this."

What I want to tell her is that no one has ever made me feel present like this. Rooted in a moment in my life because someone planted me there with them. I was lonely before my mom died and alone after she died. But I don't feel alone with Florence. I feel like me. And I feel like that could be an okay thing to be.

"Me neither," I admit.

After a moment, we release each other, the void of the hug like a black hole between us, pulling from us questions, tenderness, worry. I can see it all escaping Florence's features. Her brows coiled, her lips mouthing silent syllables, her eyes soft and watery. It's everything I feel, too, but I don't say it either. What I do say is pointless and insufficient.

"It's okay."

She nods, taking a casual step back. "Yeah, no. Totally okay."

"Do you want to put something on the TV?" I ask. Again, I have no idea what to say in this moment, but the music and crying of a Spanish soap sounds better to me than silence.

"We should get to bed," she says. She pulls back the covers and slips in. "I want to show you the Gaudí house tomorrow. It's no Sagrada Família, but it looks pretty awesome, from what I can tell."

"Sounds good to me." I switch off the lamp next to my bed and make sure my phone is charging. "And no Spanish tortillas for breakfast."

She chuckles. "Not for you, at least."

"Good night, Flo."

"Night, Eaden."

CHAPTER ELEVEN

I wake up to Florence turning on the shower and my heart thrumming hard in my chest, grateful for her impeccable timing. In my dream, I was just about to walk into my parents' house from the garage, and from the reaction in my body, I think I know what I would've found. A haunting just for me.

I have a text from Hakim and a missed call from my dad, who still doesn't understand how the time difference works, no matter how many times I explain it to him. Propping myself against the headboard, I text my dad even though he's asleep. *Dad, we're six hours ahead of you. It was one in the morning when you called.* And I wait to message Hakim until later. I know sleep is precious when you have a little one. I wipe my eyes and take a deep breath. Today is another day I get to spend with Florence in Spain. The last day. We take a train tomorrow to Paris.

Since this is my first time abroad, I have no idea what to expect from Paris, and it's hard to imagine anything could beat Barcelona. The mountains, the sea, the way the sun hits the buildings…it's stunning. And today, I get to see one of the Gaudí houses and am on a mission to eat my weight in paella.

"Oh, thought you'd still be sleeping. Sorry." Florence clutches a towel to her chest and shuffles through her bag for some clothes.

I get up and go to my own bag to busy my eyes with something other than her and how her red waves are heavy and golden when they're wet. Or how her freckles disappear into creamy pale skin at her chest. I tighten a fist in the linen shirt in my bag. This is Florence. *Riley's* Florence. I may hate my cousin right now, and they may not technically even be together, but it's a place I just can't go. I have honor, even if the rest of my family seems to lack it. Even if I didn't care about loyalty or respecting my cousin, I know Florence loves her. I know she stays because she wants it to be Riley in the end. She's basically told me as much. No matter what the hug felt like last night or how connected we may feel, the reality stands. And it stands between us.

Once we're ready, we head down to the lobby for a quick bite and some large coffees. We're going to need the caffeine for our last day in Spain. I avoid all the eggs and load up a piece of toast with avocado and Ibérico ham. Florence gives me a curious look.

"What? It's delicious," I explain.

"Okay." She grabs a yogurt parfait and a piece of toast. "Do you, Eaden."

"I will."

We eat quickly and mostly quietly, a combination of comfort and maybe a little shame from our hug last night. Which is silly, really. I mean, a hug is a hug. Right? I can tell I may be wrong from the energy between us this morning.

Few words but her knee presses against mine under the table. Always an anchor.

❖

The Gaudí house is magical even from the street. It looks like a rainbow-scaled ocean creature sandwiched between two laughably average homes. The front windows don masks as balconies, playfully drawing us in. Tripping over my own shoes as I walk to the entrance, I'm already hooked. All my attention hangs on every detail of the house. When I realize Florence isn't next to me, I turn to find her equally mesmerized on the opposite side of the street, capturing the house through her camera.

It's one of the things I love most about being her friend. How deeply she lives, wringing every drop of beauty she can from a moment. We all hold our own perception of beauty, our own filter through which we see the world. But knowing someone like Florence allows me to see things through her filters, too, and I count myself lucky to have access to her world.

"Don't forget," I shout at her from across the street.

"I know, I know." She caps her lens and looks for traffic before she jogs toward me. "I'll send you copies, I promise."

"Okay, good. 'Cause I'm just not great at taking photos on my phone, and I don't want to forget all this." I wave at the impressive building in front of us. "Plus, you're kind of amazing at photography."

"Don't worry. I've got you." She lifts her hand to my cheek and brushes her knuckles down to my jaw. "This has healed up nicely. I can barely even see it anymore."

I hesitate to respond. The warmth pooling in my chest from her touch burns into anger at the memory of Riley at my mom's funeral. Her entitled audacity. Her anger and aggression. Her complete selfishness. She robbed me of what could have been closure, and now I have recurring nightmares of my dead, decomposing, sobbing mother. And Riley acts as though I was the one who created the pain of that evening. There are zero consequences for her, as always, and it's hard not to be angry at Florence for letting her get away with it just to keep the peace.

I'm disappointed in her.

She must see it on me.

"Sorry," she mutters and steps back.

I clear my throat, wiping my cheek where her cool knuckles just were. "Yeah. Well, glad I don't have to remember that fucked-up night every time I look in the mirror anymore." I can feel the adrenaline, spurred by my anger, thrumming through me, but I can't take it out on Florence. It isn't her fault. Riley is her person. I'm not. What else was she supposed to do?

She lets the moment pass, directing her attention to the gentleman selling tickets and handing out headsets. I don't blame her. In fact, I'm grateful to table this. Though I have a feeling it's going to burst out of me one day. I just hope I don't direct it at her.

We get our headsets and are ushered inside the house. I think of nothing else except the way the walls seem to flow. How every single detail from banister to floor to windows seems to breathe with life. As we walk slowly through the masterpiece, listening to what it was like to live here, I watch Florence walk in front of me. Everyone here looks like a tourist, a visitor, but she's the only one magical enough to fit in, with the hem of her dress swirling like the ceilings with every step. Her countless earrings reflecting the light like the blue and green windows. The peaceful playfulness. The elegance.

We come to a sun-drenched hallway near the top of the house shaped like marine vertebrae. I try to capture the effect with my phone but quickly give up and try to soak in as much as I can in person. This house tickles something so satisfying in my scientific brain, to see all this biology and physics turned into art and architecture.

"I got a good one for you," Flo says, waving her camera as she walks past me.

I follow her to the stairs that lead to the roof. "Oh. Thank you."

The roof is somehow just as gorgeous as the rest of the house, except instead of sea creatures and shells, it was made to look like the iridescent back of a dragon. The rest of the tour group is lounging in the café section, enjoying cocktails and a few small bites. But I have a goal for today, and it isn't a café.

"You ready to go eat our faces off?" I ask.

"Let's do it. I'm starving."

We end up at a place that Flo found on Google Maps, which I'm beginning to realize is essential to international travel. The restaurant is a bustling two-story tapas house with a fan favorite paella on the menu that I have my eye on. The server brings us a bottle of still water and takes our orders.

"I'm sure it was no Sagrada Família, but damn, that was amazing," Flo says.

I pour us each a water. "Incredible. Like, how does someone's brain just come up with that? I swear, some people are pure magic."

"Well, next time we're here, we'll go see the Sagrada. Deal?" she asks.

I watch her sip her water, her hand curled around the small glass. The skin around her nails looks extra distressed today, and it sends a sharp pain through my chest. Is she stressed being here with just me? I'm almost too distracted to compute that she just referred to a future trip together.

"Yeah. That'd be perfect. Then Riley can see it, too."

"Mm-hmm." I don't mean it as a jab, but she sets her glass down with a clank. "Yeah. That'd be cool."

I finger the edge of the tablecloth, reeling for a pivot from this topic of Riley that I'm apparently obsessed with bringing up. "Would your mom ever go on a trip like this with you?" I finally ask.

"My mom?"

I shrug. "Yeah. Your mom."

"My mom's not big on wasting time or money. Thinks I should be focused on work instead of traveling. Saving money so I can be more financially secure. *Then* travel. So I don't know. Maybe when she's retired and I'm a full-time illustrator." She gives me a half-smile. "I don't know. I don't think I'm ever going to have that one solid job that she wants for me. I'm an artist. My work is going to be ever-changing and commissioned and not her idea of a traditional job."

I nod, enjoying learning more about her relationship with her mom. "But she trusts you, right? To handle your business and provide for yourself? Like, you're one of the most responsible people I know."

"And frugal as hell," she adds. "I mean, I'm literally living in my ex's parents' basement so I can afford tuition next fall. How fucking masochistic is that? Especially when said ex is a lesbian fuckboy, embarrassing me at literally every turn."

I stay quiet, watching her chest rise and fall with her deep breathing.

"Sorry," she says. "Just ignore that. Please."

"Um. Okay."

The server saves me from having to come up with another pivot, and thank God, because the first one didn't take us anywhere good. Only back to the conversation equivalent of a scab I'm dying to pick but know I shouldn't. Riley. I'm obsessed with wanting to talk about her. Not talk about her, talk *bad* about her. And it's just wrong. If I pick the scab, it will open a wound. And I'll be the kind of person I don't want to be.

"Wow," I say, taking in the golden treasure trove of rice and seafood before me. The briny, savory aroma wafting over me. My mouth literally waters.

"That looks incredible," Flo says. "I think you're about to be a very happy camper."

"Great food, great company. What more could a girl want?" I ask.

She chuckles and pulls her plate of steamed mussels in front of her. As is becoming tradition, we embrace a few minutes of quiet as we both indulge in our meals, taking in the food as we did the Gaudí house, exploring, getting to know it. We both emit contented groans and eventually trade bites.

"Wanna say screw it all and move here?" I suggest.

She dips a crusty piece of bread in the broth of her mussels and nods. "That's the best idea I've ever heard."

"I think you're amazing, by the way," I say. Out of nowhere, apparently, because Flo shoots me a confused look.

"Amazing?" She leans back in her chair and shakes her head. "Thet's funny. I don't feel very amazing."

"You are." I lean forward on my elbows. "Flo, you are one of the most creative, talented, loving, funny, and gorgeous people I know."

She shoots me a sharp look. "Gorgeous, huh?"

"Of course that's all you retained from that list." I roll my eyes. "But yes. You can't be surprised. It's empirically valid."

"That may be the nicest thing anyone has ever said to me." A soft blush overtakes her cheeks as she smiles. She eats a mussel and sips her drink. "You know, I think you're pretty amazing, too."

I smack the table lightly and laugh. "Okay. Now I know the drink has gone straight to your head because that is absolutely—"

"Empirical truth," she says through a grin. "You are wildly smart. Your students adore you, which I know for a fact from the birthday card they made you. You carry the responsibility of your family with grace, even when it's hard. You're funny. And you're so damn cute in your little button-ups and khakis and glasses."

I point at her with my fork. "You wear glasses, too."

She shrugs. "We're both cute."

The compliments fill me with an air of vitality. Feels like I'm warm-blooded for the first time in years, and the more Flo smiles at me, the more I believe what she just told me. Maybe someone, somewhere could love me after all. I fork my paella, pushing a few pieces of sausage to the corner of my plate. It's so hard not to fall into Florence when she's literally the only person in my life who makes me feel seen. It's like a lasso around my ankles pulling me in, and the effortless way she shines keeps me bound. It's helpless.

I finally take a bite and fully indulge in the beauty of Barcelona while we're still here. "You ready to conquer a new city together tomorrow?" I ask.

She nods as she wipes her mouth in a napkin. "So ready. We can conquer anything together. Florence and Eaden. *Floden.*"

"We sound like a malevolent Norse god." My shoulders shake with laughter at the celebrity couple name she just gave us. "Wait. I got it, I got it. What about *Eadence?*"

She drops her fork and leans back, shaking her head while she laughs. "Oh my God, that's terrible. It sounds like something you catch. Like you have a case of *Eadence* so you can't go out today. *Floden* is clearly superior."

"I think you should stick with Riley for this celebrity name. *Flowy* is not only fun and easygoing, but it's actually a word," I say, grinning like I just solved a *Times* crossword.

She sets down her fork and stares at her plate. "You're an idiot, Eaden."

"What?" I can't tell if she's joking until she shakes her head and looks dead at me, her eyes hard and icy.

"I get it, okay?" She says, leaning back in her chair in apparent exhaustion. "I get it. Riley hurt you. Riley hurt me. And given the funeral, given what happened, and the fact that I live in her family home, it's really hard not to bring her up. But I want to be here with you, and I don't want to be referred to as being in a relationship with her. Because I'm not. And I don't want to be right now."

"Come on, Flo." I push my glasses up my nose and lick my lips. "That's kind of bullshit, if you ask—"

"Excuse me?" The rage is apparent in every inch of her. From how she's glued to the back of her chair as if she can't get far enough away from me. To her fist clenching her glass. Her shoulders an inch higher than usual.

But it *is* bullshit. And I'm tired of dancing around her and Riley when the truth is right there, and Florence just wants to pretend that it isn't.

"First off, you literally just started this evening by complaining about her. So it's pretty hypocritical for you to get pissed about my mentioning her when you do it just as much. And you can't just bow the knee to her and take zero responsibility for the way she makes you feel and the way she makes me feel." I jab my chest with my pointer finger as she crosses her arms while she listens. It's a weird place to be, opposing her. We've only ever been teammates. Clandestine friends who sit with each other through the storms. We've never been each other's storm.

She nods for me to continue.

"You don't want to be referred to as her girlfriend, yet you call her every day to check in, tell her it's going 'fine' but would be so much better if she was here. You let her fuck whomever she wants, whenever she wants, while simultaneously allowing her to control your dating life by making sure it's nonexistent. And I know you don't owe me anything. But you also did nothing, said nothing, when she literally ruined my mother's funeral and smashed my face in the ground." I swallow hard and grip the edges of my chair. "I don't expect you to choose our friendship over her, but you can't come at me for observing the facts."

"And what are the facts, Eaden?" she asks, words slipping through her set jaw.

I sit up straight. "That you let Riley control every facet of your life while she gives you nothing."

"That's ridiculous."

"No. It's true." I lean on my elbows, closing some of the distance she's trying to create. "You don't think your girl was over at our place constantly complaining about how you should live with her family and scheming up ways to pitch it to you to make it make sense? Because she knew you wanted to live in that house off Candler with the two roommates who just started nursing at Emory. Four hundred dollars a month, right? A *steal*. But let you have your own life? Your own space? Live with friends who could influence you to be you?" I gasp like I'm trying to make sure the back row heard me. "No way. She wanted you where you'd be isolated and dependent on her."

She stares at me. I feel a few strangers staring, too. I don't think I was *that* loud, but my tone may have caught their attention. The smell of the seafood makes me nauseated. Every second Florence doesn't speak makes me regret every word. Makes me want to vomit. Makes me think this was all one big exercise in how to lose it all. How to push away the one person left who matters to me.

"Eaden." She clears her throat. "You have no idea what the fuck you're talking about."

I feel her slipping away from me. Like everyone else. Like Mom, Dad, Sean. I feel our mornings together disappearing, and the space of respite we built together—the cabin in the woods away from it all—crumbling.

"Florence, I—"

"I want to go back to the hotel."

My mom haunts me in my dreams. Again. Every night. Only this night is accompanied with another little delight. A little *accoutrement* of terror. I want to tell her something. A desperate little something that sticks in my throat and festers and swells. Swells so big I choke. Can't cough it up, so I reach down the back of my throat and pull clumps of wet hair and chewed gum. Pulling and pulling and never really clearing it.

I launch upright, gasping for air and clawing at my throat. From my desperate breaths, it's clear I hadn't been breathing. *Fuck.* Slow steady breaths and my firm palm on my chest bring me down enough to realize the sound of our thick door shutting is what woke me. Florence is gone. I fling the sheets off me and grab my phone and a room key. A slithering of panic mingles with the fear from my nightmare. A potent combination that has my heart beating double time.

She's okay. I know she's going to be okay, or I would have heard something more than our door shutting. A commotion. There would have been a commotion if there was anything happening beyond Florence just leaving to go…*where?*

Home?

I run a shaky hand through my sleep-matted hair. Maybe I'd know if she had *left* left if I'd taken one second to see if her bag was still in the room. I shake out my arms and hands and try to master some calm, easy breaths.

I spot her when I round the corner into the darkened lobby. She's sitting in an armchair in the far corner with her knees drawn to her chest and red tendrils of hair spilling from her hood. I stutter-step, unsure of what to do next. She hasn't noticed me. I could just turn around and go back to the room. She's clearly not trying to run off to the airport in the middle of the night. But it's also kind of strange to be huddled alone in a hotel lobby at… I have no idea what time it is. Only that besides the front desk agent, we're the only ones here.

She's my friend. I decide to check on her.

When I'm a few paces away, she looks up at me and sighs. I realize she's on the phone and stop walking.

"Hang on, Rye. Can I call you back?" Her voice is low and raspy. "No. Eaden just walked up. It'll just take a minute. Love you, too." She plops her phone in her lap and glares. "What do you need, Eaden?"

"Sorry, I…" I fumble for something to say, dying in my discomfort at being an intruder. "Just saw you weren't in the room and wanted to make sure you were okay."

"I'm fine." She holds her arms out as if to display her *fine* self. "I'm perfectly capable of taking care of myself. I just missed Riley and wanted to call before she went to sleep. Just a touch homesick tonight. Is that okay with you?"

It's as if she chose every word just to hurt me. "Of course. I'm sorry. Just care about you."

She continues to stare at me, every second making me feel more and more like a burden. A nuisance that she's tasked with babysitting. "Well, I'm okay. So?"

"Right," I say and walk away.

I crawl back into bed and stare at the ceiling. It's a cruel night.

CHAPTER TWELVE

Cruel nights make for cruel mornings.

We wake to Flo's alarm at a quarter past five. My head aches at my temple, a hangover from only a few hours of nightmarish sleep, coupled with a heavy dose of self-loathing. Maybe a sprinkle of discontent with her. She slides out of bed wordlessly and disappears into the bathroom. A second later, I hear the echo of the shower spraying the tile floor. I am too damn exhausted to shower. Instead, I change into jeans and a hoodie and triple-check I have everything packed and ready to go for the world's most uncomfortable train ride from Barcelona to Paris.

I've never been good at being in a fight with someone. *Are we in a fight?* We're in something, and I hate it. Ten minutes into any argument and I'm ready to roll over and expose all my vital organs to the person. Like, go ahead. Gut me.

But I don't feel that way with Flo. What I feel is frustration. I'm so frustrated that she allows herself to be kept in Riley's prison, even when the key is in Flo's pocket. She could be free at any moment. But she grovels to my cousin as if Riley is the best thing to ever happen to her. And yeah, it makes me sick. I know Riley doesn't care about her beyond knowing that Flo is there, on the end of her hook whenever she wants her.

It frustrates me that at the end of the day, no matter how close Florence and I are, and no matter what shitty thing Riley does, Florence will always choose her over me. Over our friendship.

I know this. I've *known* this. And yes, that's Florence's right, her prerogative. But I don't have to pretend along with her that Riley doesn't exist and that she's her own free, independent person. I don't have to pretend that my relationship with Riley is good and that she didn't break my already thrashed heart mere weeks ago. I will not just roll over on this because to give in to Florence's delusion is to give in to Riley's power. And honestly, fuck that.

Maybe I've had a change of heart. Maybe it's okay to be angry. To express my anger for once and take up space.

The train station buzzes with travelers and commuters bouncing from ticket booths to coffee shops to platforms. We wait in uncomfortable silence, coffees in hand, in front of the big central screen listing departures until our platform appears. It almost feels like we've been in competition all morning.

Who knows which way to turn first?

Who can produce the train tickets first?

Who can rattle off which platform appears next to our train first?

"Platform seven," she huffs.

Damn it.

I scan every sign above us in a pathetic attempt to win something. "This way," I grumble and proudly stomp off.

We drop our bags on the small belt of the security scanner and walk through to the other side. Her bag comes out first, and mine follows with a stray apple bobbing along behind it and an OJ threatening to fall off the ledge. They're the snacks I got with my morning coffee. She catches the juice before it hits the ground in an impressive show of athleticism that I honestly didn't know she possessed.

"Thanks," I mutter as she passes it to me.

We walk down the platform almost the entire length of the train until we find our carriage and board. I don't know why I had such a romanticized idea of what a European train to Paris would be like. But I was wrong. The only thing separating the train aesthetic from a tired old Spirit Airlines plane is the space. We pile our bags on the closest baggage carrier and find our seats. I offer Florence the window seat, which appears to have slightly fewer stains on the purple and gray fabric than my seat. I swipe some torn bits of paper that were left on the table in front of us and toss them in the little trash receptacle on the side of my seat.

She puts her purse on the table and pulls her headphones from the side pocket, signaling that there will be no conversation between us. At least for now. Which I guess is fine by me, given I don't have much to say. I already said my piece at the restaurant. Maybe we just take a step back from here.

I double-check I have my phone and wallet, then settle into my seat. My limbs are achy from the nonstop walking, and my head is fuzzy with exhaustion. The warmth of the train pushes me closer to sleep, and when I hear the conductor announce Paris as our destination and the train starts moving, I close my eyes and let it take me.

Even in my sleep, I'm becoming used to the nightmare. And this time, I walk into my parents' house through the garage with a mission. I'm not choking on gummed up hair this time, and I'm growing familiar with the grotesque version of my mother's face that's waiting for me. I'm not so scared when I walk into the kitchen and see the sink full of dirty dishes and hear the speaker echoing in the laundry room. Maybe it's the bit of anger in me that Florence stoked. That Riley stoked. That Sean and Dad stoked. Maybe it's not a bit of anger. Maybe it's a lot of anger.

I'm angry at her, too. Mom. For only being here for me in this space. For haunting me instead of appearing to me as something nice, like a butterfly or a cardinal or something. Like a dream.

There is something new in my nightmare. I hear my mom singing, singing and humming. I grin. She always sang every word of songs she knew until the words she didn't know. Then she'd hum. I drag my fingers along the cool, smooth surface of the island and peek into the laundry room where I normally find her. But the small space is empty.

The living room is empty.

I walk up the stairs, no longer feeling the bravery of anger. No longer feeling like this is in any way familiar to me. The steps whine underfoot, and the banister feels brittle under my hand. Maybe I die in this version of the nightmare. Surely, the house is about to collapse on me and snap my neck. It would probably be better than seeing my mom's swollen, dead face, but I'm on a mission this time. A mission to say something to her.

So why is my brain making it so hard on me?

I walk down the hallway of our childhood home. The carpet sinks strange inches under my feet, and I can hear voices that sound like young versions of me and Sean bickering in his room. I hear the TV from my parents' room streaming some loud sports show with commentators arguing over this year's NFL draft picks. She could be in there, folding laundry with my dad. That'd be okay. I want him to hear what I have to say, too.

The handle is strangely warm in my hand as I push open the door. It's not my mom. I stare as a lithe, smooth-skinned girl with perfect brown waves cascading down her bare back rides my dad, fucking him as he moans. His hairy white legs kick and tense as she picks up speed. I barely register my feet sinking farther into the carpet as the girl— or woman, I guess—lets out a long deep moan before she says, "Yes, daddy. Yes," and picks up the pace again.

I need to leave.

I can't move.

My feet are stuck in the carpet. I'm sinking.

I'm dying.

A strong hand grips my shoulder and yanks me out of the room. "Eaden," my mother's voice screams in my ear.

"Eaden," Florence says. Her hand on my other shoulder.

A train crew member watches me, wide-eyed as I heave for air. Fucking tired of waking up this way, barely alive, scared to death, gasping. Why can't I breathe?

"I'm sorry. Sorry," the man says. "Ticket. Ticket."

"It's okay," Florence tells him. She pulls a piece of paper from her purse. "She was just having a nightmare." She hands him the tickets to check, and he takes them carefully, keeping his eyes on me.

"It's okay," she says again. Softer. To me.

I nod, avoiding the gazes of other passengers attempting to see what the commotion was all about. I wonder if I screamed or just gasped or how big a fool I've made of myself. The man hands her back the tickets and apologizes again before moving to the next seats.

Once I've caught my breath enough, I turn to Florence. "I'm so sorry. I don't know what—"

"You're okay. You're okay. I promise." She rubs my shoulder, her eyes soft with concern. "He startled you awake by grabbing your arm instead of just letting me handle it. Completely inappropriate. I wanted to let you sleep because I know you've been struggling with it lately."

"Yeah." I lean back in my seat and nod. "Yeah, I've been having this recurring nightmare. Every night." My jaw aches with my last words, and I give it a rub with my knuckle. Florence zips her headphones back inside her purse pocket. "Well, every time I sleep, I guess."

"I noticed something was up, but I didn't want to intrude," she says.

"Intrude?"

She angles herself toward me and tucks a leg under herself. "Yeah. I don't know what you want to talk about or if you want some space. I know it's a lot."

"Flo, you're my best…" I can't finish what I want to say because it feels impossible that she sees me the same way, especially after the very public fight we had, thanks to me. Someone as amazing and likeable and fun as Flo would have countless people she would deem her best friend over me. Also, we're in our thirties. Something about declaring a best friend feels of the Tamagotchi and JT Squared era. If not, just a little desperate.

"I thought Hakim was your best friend." She gives me a pointed look. The feigned jealousy is a relief, a step away from our fight. A step back to us.

"I mean, yeah. He's my best work friend." Especially after a fight, it's weird showing all my cards here. It's not normally the moment I would choose to be vulnerable. But it's Florence, and I trust her in some indescribable, innate way. "But, Flo, the mornings when we're awake so early before anyone else—especially when my mom was dying— they mean a lot to me. And I think, somewhere along the way, you became a really big rock in my life. So thank you."

Her hand finds my knee under the table, and she squeezes it. "I know the feeling. I wake up and hope you're online. You mean a lot to me, Eaden."

I nod, trying desperately to not move my leg, needing her hand to stay exactly where it is. Because I swear, her touch may be healing.

A soft blush curls up her neck as she drops her gaze to her lap. "It's the first thing I do in the morning, look for you."

She rubs the denim of my jeans with her pointer finger, and I feel her touch consume every atom of me. It's like fire. And her words are the oxygen feeding it. The desperation I feel to hold her hand is a wild want thrumming in my limbs, in my chest. But there's so much hate in me. It paralyzes. I blame Florence for being helpless for Riley, beholden to Riley. And yet I sit here immobile because of Riley, beholden to Riley.

The thing is, I can't fucking breathe these days.

Everywhere I look, I can't stand what I see. My family. My empty apartment. My mom's funeral notice on my kitchen table. The letter to her aunt. The goddamn mirror. I could swear I'm hollowing out. Mummifying somehow. And the only thing I see that feels anything like life is her.

Florence.

"The nightmare"—I squeeze my eyes shut and push the back of my skull firmly into my seat—"it's been the same every night, except for just now. It was so much worse just now."

"Okay. It's okay if you don't want to talk about—"

I cover her hand gently with mine. Squeeze my eyes shut even harder. Because *wow*, was it always supposed to feel this way? I wonder if she feels it, too. If that's the reason she lost her words. Because she's combusting next to me. Our fingers mingle and stroke and squeeze. Our fingers are flint and striker.

Frenetic. Kinetic.

We slow, our hands curling into one another like cats settling for a nap. I open my eyes to find her staring at me. Her pupils wide and stunned, her lips parted.

"You okay?" I mouth, as if not speaking of it aloud could keep it ours. Could keep this connection, this precious tender thing between us safe.

Her chest rises with a deep breath, and she nods after she releases it. I nod back.

"So in these dreams, I see my mom," I continue.

"Oh, that must be nice, right?"

I shake my head. "I wish. I wanted so badly to see her. After the funeral, I thought I would dream about her all the time. But nothing. Until the first nightmare, and now when I see her in my dreams, she's like, really dead. Like, decomposing and swollen and sad."

She squeezes my hand a little tighter. "Oh my God, Eaden. That's horrible."

I can't help but chuckle. "Yeah. It really is. And I don't know how to stop them. I feel like maybe it's guilt because of how much of a disaster her funeral was. Or the guilt of not being able to forgive my brother or my dad."

"Your dad? What happened with your dad?"

I stop talking. Look at her. "I didn't mean to say that."

"It's just you and me here. It's just us. You can trust me with anything. But you also don't have to share anything you don't want to."

I take a deep breath. "A couple months before my mom's surgery, she found out my dad was having an affair."

"No," she gasps.

"Oh, it gets so much worse."

"How could it?" She presses her fingers to her lips in anticipation.

The image of the brunette riding my dad flashes in my brain, and I bite my lip hard to try to focus on the physical pain instead of the agonizing scene. "He was fucking his personal trainer. Who is the same age as me."

"I—" She cuts herself off with another disgusted sounding gasp. "And your mom knew?"

"Yeah." I wipe my eyes under my glasses. "The last months of her life were basically filled with heartbreak and torture. And I can't"—I choke on a sob that shocks me. I haven't cried this entire trip, and it just erupts from me like vomit.

She pulls me into her chest and strokes my hair, her fingers occasionally getting caught in the tangled waves. "I've got you," she whispers. "I've got you."

"It's like I'm reliving the nightmare that was her life. Every night," I mutter against her sweatshirt. The fresh floral smell of her makes me ache in a way that isn't so miserable. "I just miss her so much already. I don't know how I'm supposed to do this life without her. She was my safety. She was the person who saw me. And now she's just *gone*."

"She's not gone." She kisses the top of my hair, and it feels amazing to be held and cared for, but it's not enough to keep me from drowning in this emptiness.

"She's gone, Flo. Dead. Decomposing. Literally nothing. Soon, every atom will be recycled into the ecosystem, and it will be like she never existed. And when she knew something was seriously wrong, when she knew she was probably dying, she wrote a letter. She wrote a letter with her thoughts and feelings and words that would exist after she was gone, and she didn't write it to me. And now I have to go deliver it to my great-aunt, when in reality, I'm fucking brokenhearted that she didn't write it to me. So please, don't lie to me. Don't say something trite like she'll always be in my heart. We don't lie to each other."

"Yeah," she says. Her limbs tense, and the energy shifts. I sit upright and wait for her to confess the words rushing through her mind.

"What is it?"

She shakes her head, briefly playing at keeping her thoughts from me.

"Flo."

"Riley got a letter from your mom. I'm so sorry. There must have been some misunderstanding. Maybe she meant to write—"

"Stop. Please. Just stop." I stare at the dirty table top, unblinking. Enjoying the sting in my eyes. I pile my hands into overlapping fists and crunch my knuckles until they pop. A pop for each emotion rushing through me.

Jealousy. *Pop.* Anger. *Pop.* Betrayal. *Pop. Pop. Pop.*

"It's wild, isn't it?" I mutter, avoiding her eyes.

"What?"

"How Riley spends every ounce of love she's so lucky to receive like a fucking gambling addict."

She inhales deeply, as if she took that one in the chest. "Hey, I don't think—"

"Like a fucking black hole. A vacuum. Sucking up every goddamn thing that's in front of her with zero thought of consequence. Zero thought of the pain she causes others. Zero concept of what it means to be in a symbiotic relationship with people." I look her in the eye, borrowing a page from Riley's book, not caring how it makes her feel. "A parasite. And you're telling me that my dying mother, with the last bits of strength she had left, wrote a letter to that narcissist instead of me?"

Florence watches me through watering eyes, but she doesn't cry. She's probably used to an outburst. She's probably used to catching the shrapnel of someone's blowup. Sharp words and angry glares probably ricochet off her battle-weary chest like dulled arrows.

"How could you love someone like that?" I bite my lip until I think I may pierce it. "You let her keep you small so you don't threaten her ego. I don't get it."

She nods slowly. No tears. Hands curled into her lap. I'm too resentful to regret.

"My father left when I was six," she starts. "My mom had just gotten fired for hiding a bottle of vodka in her classroom desk. This was before she got sober, before she went back to school and became a nurse. And we moved around a lot back then. Sometimes she'd get a hotel room, sometimes we couch surfed, sometimes we had an apartment for a month or two." Her stare hardens. Her eyes dry and focused. "Do you know what that kind of instability feels like? Not knowing where you'll be sleeping the next week or if you'll get in trouble for poor attendance at school because your mother doesn't 'believe in the system' anymore?"

I shake my head.

"That's exactly right. You don't know what that feels like." She closes her eyes for a moment as she takes a deep breath. Then, she licks her lips and continues. "You don't know how it feels to never be on steady ground. How it feels to have a bald patch at the base of your skull because that soft pale spot of skin on your head is the only thing you can control in your life."

"Florence—"

She holds up a hand to stop me. "I'm sorry you lost your mother, I really am. I'm sorry you have issues with your cousin. I get it. I am here for you as your friend, as someone who cares deeply about you. I love you, Eaden. But if I'm not mistaken, I haven't wronged you. I haven't lied to you. I haven't meddled between you and Riley. So if you'd like to continue this friendship with me, let me be very clear about my needs and expectations. Unless my actions directly harm you, don't you dare judge me for keeping Riley and her family in my life. It is my choice, my prerogative, to carry on whatever relationship with her I see fit. And until I ask for your opinion or advice, keep your judgments and displeasure to yourself, because I didn't tell your mom who to write those letters to. And your relationship with Riley has nothing to do with me."

I nod, tuck my phone in my pocket, and stand. "I'm going to give you some space until we get there."

"Wow. Okay." She nods in a dismal appraisal of me. "Suddenly not feeling so confrontational, huh? You really just aren't going to respond?"

"Doesn't feel productive right now," I say.

"To your agenda. Don't paint it as something else. You just don't want to hear what I feel or what I have to say. You know, I'm starting to see the family resemblance between you and Rye."

Her words impale me. Quick and deft and deep. I am completely wounded. A searing burn quickly numbing. Alone again. A kind of peace settles over me. Maybe I was always waiting for the other shoe to drop with Florence. Always waiting to lose her. Now I know exactly where I stand and exactly where she stands. Apart.

"That's where you're wrong. I'm nothing like her." I bow a little closer to her. "Were you mine, I'd make sure you felt it. Make damn sure you knew I'm just as much yours."

Her mouth splits open in silence, and I walk to the next carriage in search of an empty space. I find it two carriages down and collapse into the window seat, exhausted and wired and empty. I can't sleep. Can't eat. Can't do much of anything besides sit in this murky lake of anger and disgust.

I heard her. I always hear her. When Florence speaks, I tuck each of her words safely into my chest. Every little tendril of knowledge I learn of her, I curl into my trellis with care, curious what will grow of it. So when she told me about growing up and feeling unstable, out of control, I listened. I ached. I learned. But that doesn't change the base of my frustration. If I'd been honest, I would've told Florence I'm angry because I want what Riley has, what she takes. I want to be chosen. I want Ashley West in my shotgun seat, smiling at me that way she did in high school at the little park along the Chattahoochee. And when Riley called her, I wish she hadn't answered.

I wish she'd chosen me.

I want Justine, the doctor I dated, in my bed, whispering how she wishes she could stay even five more minutes. But that she's excited to see me tonight for dinner. When her schedule got tight, I wish she'd found a place for me. Tucked me in and kept me.

I want a letter from my mom. I wish when I desperately looked for her, I'd find her. Any bit of her. Any last connection to her.

It's warm on the train, and I peel off my hoodie to use as a pillow against the window. I close my eyes and think of all the times I wasn't chosen. Surely, it means I'm weak, needy, to crave so much validation from others when I should just accept what I am to the world: no one. There's an alternate answer to the question, "If a tree falls in a forest and no one is there to hear it, does it make a noise?" Sure. But one of the definitions of sound requires receival of sound waves to be defined as noise. Therefore, if no one is there to receive the sound waves, no noise.

I could crash into the hard forest floor from a hundred feet up, my old, hard oak slamming into the earth, splintering with a ferocious crack. And not a goddamn person would care.

Florence cares. But she'll never care enough to choose our friendship over her need for Riley's pseudo stability. And no, I can't begrudge her that. She's her own human, with her own desires. But it stings, especially in tandem with learning my mom wrote her a letter. These fucking letters.

They're a cruel exercise in starving.

But I'm nothing if not dutiful, especially to my mom. I unlock my phone, ignore the unread text from my dad, and open the email from my great-aunt Mary. I type out a quick response, confirming our arrival date and that I'm excited to meet her. Maybe she'll have Mom's mannerisms. Maybe I'll feel closer to her there.

CHAPTER THIRTEEN

I wake to the sound of Flo's voice. I'd been in and out of sleep the entire train ride with zero dreams, just peaceful nothingness, waking when we slowed for stops. It felt like being back on my couch, sleeping and waking and sleeping, reality almost indiscernible from dreams.

"We're almost to our stop," she says. She doesn't seem outwardly angry, and somehow, that's worse. Instead, she seems like she bottled me up and put me far away from her. Like she's unaffected by me. She drops my bag in the seat next to me.

"Okay," I say, wiping my hands down my face. I tuck my hoodie through the arm of my bag so I don't have to carry it. Pat my pockets. Look under my seat.

"What is it?" she asks.

"Can't find my phone."

We search together for a few minutes before the realization settles on me. "Exactly what I need," I mutter.

"Where was it the last time you had it?"

I gesture to where I was sitting. "In my lap."

She rolls her eyes. "You left your phone in your lap, just out there for anyone to walk by and take? This is Europe, Eaden. You can't even hold your phone too far from your face without it getting stolen." She sighs. "We'll find you a store after we get to the rental. It's fine."

"I can handle it."

"You can handle it? Without a phone, without a laptop, you're just going to magically find an Apple store and sort this out?"

The train begins to slow, and I hike the pack up my back, grateful that it wasn't stolen instead. As annoyed as I am about it all, I need to deliver this letter. I can replace a phone, but I can't replace that.

"I don't want to burden you." I sway to the left as the train's momentum slows. "Plus, it will give us some more space to—"

"Eaden." She grabs my arm to steady herself. "I don't want space from you. I never asked for space from you."

"But you're upset," I say, confused.

"And you're upset. So what? We can be upset next to each other."

In that moment, with her holding on to me, it hits me for the first time that Riley isn't her only stability. "Okay," I say.

"Okay."

She turns away but stays pressed against the length of me, her hair tickling my nose. I stay close. It feels like I'm always meant to be close to her. She leans into me even more, as if our argument has helped shed some of the aloofness of mere friendship. It's hard to pretend I don't feel cosmically bound to Florence. With the soft weight of her settling against me, I know she feels the same. I curl my fingers around her hip and hold her to me. The feeling of her curves and bones and flesh just under the thin fabric of her dress makes me dizzy. I whisper into her ear, "I'm sorry, Flo."

With zero hesitation, she takes my hand from her hip and pulls it tighter around her waist. "It's okay."

"I know I'm a mess." I drop my head against her shoulder blade as the train comes to a complete stop, and all the passengers fill the aisle around us. "It was wrong of me to spill all over you like that, especially since you're the only thing keeping me sane. And to walk away after you shared so much of yourself with me. I'm just really sorry."

She spins in my arms, careful not to whack anyone with her pack. Her eyes meet mine, and I feel something I've never felt in my life. It's unique and strange and nascent. And somehow familiar. Like déjà vu.

She grabs the straps of my bag and gives them a tug. "I've got you, Eaden. I promise. You and me."

"You and me," I repeat. "We've got each other."

"Always have," she says.

I grin. "Always will."

A stranger taps me on the shoulder and points for us to disembark. Flo and I stay close, shoulders brushing and backpacks knocking, as we find signage directing us to an exit. It takes a few minutes for us to navigate out of the train station and onto a bus to the rental. And it takes even less time for us to take one look at the place, an admittedly cute apartment in a vibrant little Parisian neighborhood, and see that Riley booked this for her and Florence with zero regard for me.

Unsurprising. She loves to torment me.

We drop our bags in the small kitchen and take a look around. There's one bedroom that accounts for half the apartment. It has a well-appointed queen bed with beautiful linens and an armchair in the corner. What I assume is Parisian art hangs on the walls, and fresh flowers adorn the side tables.

"Well, the bedroom is nice," I say.

"Sure, but where's the other bed?"

I can't help but laugh. "You didn't see it when we walked in?" Her brows rise in apparent surprise. One thing I'm learning about me and Florence is that no matter the argument or the misunderstanding, we always come back. There's something that feels so safe about us.

"No," she says.

I laugh and lead her into the living room. "There it is." I pull the sad cushion off the tiny, worn couch and find the crossbar of the pullout beneath. It whines with effort as I stretch it open. The mattress is about an inch thick.

"That cannot be considered a place to sleep." She shakes her head with a horrified smile. "I mean, that is barely a cot. No way is that a pullout bed."

"I mean, I'm not too picky." I sit on the edge of the contraption to prove my point, my expression purposefully blank so I don't give away the pain shooting up my ass from sitting directly on the thick crossbar. "I promise, I won't hold it against Rye, but I may just sleep on it as a couch." I chuckle, not wanting to make Flo feel bad about it. There's no way I'm letting her sleep on this piece of shit.

"We're staying here for five days," she says, arms crossed and a stray bang falling across her forehead. "She booked this place for five days, knowing it was going to be wildly uncomfortable for you. For what?" She throws her hands in the air. "So we could sleep in a nice room with fresh flowers?"

I stand and fold the couch back into itself, the tired creaking only emphasizing its shittiness. I wait for Flo to keep talking, but she doesn't. She stares at the floor, picking her pointer finger.

"I don't know what to say. Kind of feels like a trap," I admit.

"Say what you're thinking."

"You sure?"

She nods, turning her attention to her thumb.

"This doesn't surprise me at all. This is the most Riley move in the history of Riley." She abandons her nails to run her hands through her hair. A speck of blood soaks into her dress where her hands just were. I walk to her and tug the bit of fabric, flattening it so she can see. "You bled a little here."

"Oh, it's fine. It happens." She brushes the dress free of my hands and sighs. "It'll come out, no problem."

She smooths the familiar floral fabric over her stomach, and I take her hands in mine. I'm slow, gentle, just in case it's too much for her to let me really see her fingers. I look into her eyes, searching for consent before I look at her hands. Her lip slips between her teeth as she nods. I feel her stare as I observe her fingers. Some of her nail beds are smooth and pale like the rest of her, but some are puffy and angry, red and raw from constant picking and peeling and biting.

"I know," she says. "It's gross."

"It's absolutely not gross." I meet her concerned gaze. "Is this kind of like the bald spot?"

She nods. "I've gotten better at managing those feelings as an adult. No more plucking hair. But sometimes, when things feel too scattered or unstable, I pick my nails." She rolls her eyes like she's disappointed in herself. "I'm working on it. I promise."

"Does Rye know about it? Is there anything she does to calm you that I could be doing?"

She breaks into a startling laughter. A laughter more sardonic than any I've ever heard before. "To calm me? She's the one who said it was gross. When I tried to talk to her about it, she just got uncomfortable and told me to get a therapist."

It's simply the most enraging thing I've ever heard about my cousin. Somehow more enraging than her infidelity is her apathy. Her apathy to the pain and anxiety of the most beautiful human on this planet. She made Florence feel judged, alone, like she had too much darkness in her to be seen by someone else.

"I know what it's like to feel so dark. So ocean blue." I lift her fingers to my mouth, acting on pure instinct. I can't stop. "I can sit with you in the dark. We can weather the storm together." Her eyes water as I brush my lips so gently over her fingers, pausing over each nail to kiss it softly. To kiss her scars. To taste her pain. To show her it doesn't scare me. Her lips pluck apart as she watches me. I don't stop. "The night of my mom's funeral, I was ocean blue. Midnight dark," I whisper over her knuckles. "But you had me. And I remember thinking you were the moonlight in my midnight. You're the moon to me, Florence."

"Eaden." Her gaze flits to my mouth, her fingers against my lips, then back to me. "We can't do this."

I softly kiss her knuckle and drop her hand. "I'm not asking for anything from you except to be close to you. I don't care if you date Riley or someone else entirely. I can't lose you. Whatever goes on in the world outside, I just need to know that we can rest in our friendship. That's it."

Her brows arch together with a soft stitch. "But what if..." She shakes her head as if to shake away the thought.

"What if?" I ask.

"What if I have a small crush on my friend?"

My fingers twitch at my sides. Heart leaps. "Oh. Well. I'm sure that's completely normal." I shrug. "Mundane, even." She shoots me a skeptical glare that makes me chuckle. "So what friend are we talking about?"

"You're the worst." She scoffs, but a blatant smile slips through her facade. "But really. I can't lose you either. And I can't betray my history with Riley." She looks away as if to shield me from the obvious pain that losing Riley would cause her, even if it may not be a romantic loss at this point.

It stings, like always, but is a small price for admission to this strange and intimate friendship I just can't replace. I meant what I said, I need Florence in my life. She doesn't need to be *mine*. The moon reflects light on everyone. Besides, I know our connection is deeper than her connection with Riley. It's wrong of me, but I cherish knowing that.

"I meant what I said." I squeeze her hand in the most friendly and unromantic way I possibly can, which mostly amounts to a quick tug of her fingers. "Your friendship is the most important thing to me, and

I won't jeopardize that. If things feel a little too *Florence is about to accidentally kiss me*, then we can cool off before we derail. Get our cart back on the track."

She swats my shoulder. "Why am I the one to derail us? That's absolute bullshit. You were literally just kissing my fingers."

"I don't know." I grin like I have an ace up my sleeve. "Gotta be careful with that big old crush of yours. Could derail things pretty fast." I laugh. It feels good to laugh.

"I knew I should've never told you that. But honestly, how could I not? You're so nerdy and adorable." She rolls her eyes and swats me again. "Go on. Say something nice about me before we get this friendship cart back on track."

The majority of "nice things" that pepper my thoughts are too much for this moment. This is a moment for light flirting, an easily digestible compliment. Not telling her that she's my only anchor to a world that feels like a paper cut between my fingers. Even then, that isn't a compliment. It's self-centered to only appreciate the utility someone provides me, even if that utility is based in their incredibly warm personality.

She winces. "Really leaving me in the wind here, pal. Surely, after this talk, it can't be too hard to find something nice to—"

"You're, like, completely devastating."

Her mouth freezes in the formation of a word. "What?" she finally asks.

"It's my nice thing to say before we cart this conversation. I think you are completely devastating. And when you walk into a room, you're all I see. No other woman, no other person, can even come close to the kind of energy you radiate."

"My energy, huh?" She traps her lip between her teeth before she breaks into a grin. "Sounds a lot like you're talking about my aura, Ms. Bilbo."

"Christ." I run my hand through my messy hair and chuckle. "No need to cart this, you just doused it in ice water, my friend."

"Oh?" Her grin deepens, freckles disappearing into her dimples. "Was it the aura talk or calling you by your sexy last name?"

"I mean, you really missed an opportunity here. Why not go all the way and call me Dildo? You definitely wouldn't be at any flirting risk then. And I'd probably vow sweet revenge and strike up an evil plan to slowly drive you mad by making Aunt Susan let me in your basement apartment and moving all your furniture by an inch every day. Until one day, you wake up and think you're in a different dimension. And trust me, no one wants that." I raise a stern finger to emphasize the pure evil I'm willing embrace in the case of being dildo-ed.

"The horror," she whispers as she grabs my finger and pushes my hand down.

A smile breaks my character before I regain composure and deliver my final threat. "You have no idea, Ms. Davis."

"Cart," she says, taking a step away from me. "Cart, cart, cart. You can't call me that." She takes a deep breath, a patchy red blush blooming above her neckline. This is why friendship is enough. I could live on the thrill of making Florence blush for decades.

"The cart is back on track. But just saying, the fact that your last name is off-limits and mine is just a joke"—I wince, shoulders skimming my earlobes—"kinda hurts my feelings."

"Besides the fact that I know you're full of shit right now, you're the only one making a joke of it. I wasn't joking when I said it like that." She pats my shoulder. "Now. Let's go sort out your phone."

"Deal."

❖

Finding an Apple store and replacing my phone with Florence is strangely nice. The way that grocery shopping with a partner is nice. While we wait to be helped, we play with all the display gadgets, musing about why anyone would ever want a smartwatch and deciding what the ideal tablet for Florence is for her illustrative needs. It could've just been another day in Atlanta. Except I walk out eight hundred dollars lighter.

After we take the bus back to our neighborhood, we find a cute little café to grab lunch at. Well, we don't find it, we pick it randomly from the thousands of options presented to us. But it seems like a good choice, with Parisians studding the tables instead of tourists. I lay my phone facedown on the table, unable to get it up and running until we get back to the apartment and connect to Wi-Fi. I don't mind, though.

It feels kind of nice being disconnected from the world, not knowing who has tried to text me, email me, call me. But I can't lie, the monetary hit hurts, especially after paying for this trip and being on a teacher's salary.

"Hey." Florence smacks the table lightly to get my attention. "Where's your brand-new phone?"

I lay down the menu that I most definitely will need help translating and instantly panic. My phone is gone. My brand-new, eight hundred dollar iPhone has vanished. "Oh my God. Shit. Oh my God." I stand and almost knock over the small round table.

Florence pulls my new phone from her lap, and I sit back down, panting still. "You seriously need to learn your lesson." She smirks and hands me the phone. "I swear, I don't know what you'd do without me."

I take my phone and zip it away in my hidden travel pack under my shirt, not caring that I'm exposing myself as a silly American. A silly tourist. My heart is hammering. "Thanks," I manage to say.

"Hey, are you okay?" she asks, curling her fingers around my wrist. "I'm sorry. I shouldn't have hidden your phone. It was just a joke. I promise, I won't touch it again."

Her voice is soft and placating, but I'm not angry with her. It's not that she played a trick on me, it's that I truly could've lost my new phone. *Again.* I'm not quite sure why the thought of it, truly believing I lost it, makes me feel out of control. I had just gotten a new phone before my mom died. Made the switch to iPhone after the endless bullying from my family, annoyed about the "green bubbles" and the missing texts and pixelated photos in our group chat. Sure, that phone was free, but I value the things I have.

"Are you okay?" she asks in the same soft tone.

I nod, able to partially snap out of my trance. "Yeah. Yeah, sorry. I'm not mad you." I squeeze her hand to prove my words. "It's silly, but thinking I had lost my phone again made me feel a little out of control. Like I'm spiraling. Made me feel kind of panicky." I wince. "And it's not like I don't have money, but I'm a teacher who just paid for an expensive European trip *and* an iPhone. A second phone would have been hard."

"I get it. Two iPhones would have sunk me, and you're dealing with a lot right now. I'm sorry I scared you."

"It's okay." I smile. "Now, what the heck is all this stuff?" I wave the menu, and she snatches it out of my hand.

As she translates the menu items, she says each French word and works out the English equivalent, rubbing her fingers together in the air as if she's physically untangling the languages. I watch and listen, completely mesmerized by Florence speaking French. My heart rate stabilizes, and I'm back in this safe world with her. Apart from Riley and my dad and Sean. Apart from my mother's death. I can find happiness here, and temporary relief, with Florence in Paris.

She catches me watching and smiles. A knowing smile. Sure, it's mildly terrifying that this little "crush" is reciprocated and out in the open now. It's mildly terrifying that we can't help but have some form of physical connection always; the edge of the sole of her sandal is currently pressed tightly to the edge of my sneaker.

And it's mildly terrifying that she will most likely insist that we just share the real bed tonight. Because why not? We're two mature adults with very compelling reasons to not act on these mutual feelings.

But mildly terrifying things are just that. Mild.

CHAPTER FOURTEEN

We end up spending most of the afternoon wandering around the neighborhood, admiring the café culture and how the community seems to gather every night: adults drinking wine, chatting, and smoking, and children playing in the streets as the sun sets. It's a gorgeous way of life, and I'm beginning to see why people fall fast and hard for Paris. The romance in this city is palpable.

Though it is tempting to spend the entire night café hopping and basking in a sweet Parisian haze of wine and charcuterie and pastries, we're exhausted and opt for an early first night.

We walk home, letting the quiet of the evening hold us tight. There are broken bottles of wine and cigarette butts scattered along the edges of the streets, remnants of a Saturday we were not here for but that hint at an energetic city. A city that isn't afraid to be authentic and free.

The Eiffel Tower is slightly visible when we turn onto our street. I absently wonder if Riley knew we'd be able to see it from this spot. It hits me that we'll be able to see it from the balcony of the bedroom, too, and her booking the apartment with the shitty pullout makes a lot more sense. She wanted to spend Paris with Flo, gazing at the Eiffel Tower from their room. While I slept—or struggled to sleep—on the world's sorriest excuse for a pullout.

Florence's knuckles skim mine as we approach our building, and I can't help but smile. Maybe it was always meant to be just us on this trip. No matter in what capacity.

We pause at the doorway, both taking in the view of the glowing tower. It's way bigger than I thought it was.

"I really want to touch it," I murmur, entranced by the hazy orange glow of the landmark. I turn to Florence. "Is that weird?"

She gives me a warm grin, her dimples making a quick appearance before she says, "Well, you're weird. So yes and no, really."

"You're weird, too," I fire back.

"Oh, I know." She chuckles, making the yellow rays from the porchlight dance through her hair. "It's why we're two peas in a pod. You and me." She pokes me softly in the shoulder as if adding a little period to the statement. It slays me. Lights me up and devastates me in all the beautiful and painful ways. The way I have her and will never have her. Can't have her. She must register the duality of pain and healing she causes me because her finger rises to my cheek, and she caresses me. "Can I say something? Something I don't want to have a conversation about. I say it, then we get our cart back on track, no questions?"

I nod against her knuckle. Terrified. Thrilled.

"I know you have resentment toward me from that night. From the funeral." She pauses as if waiting for me to confirm. As if confirmation is ever needed.

I nod again because there's no point in lying. She knows me. And I've explicitly told her how I feel about it all. In the most callous way possible, yes. But I was honest.

"Just know, seeing you get hurt—and I don't mean Riley wrestling you—shattered my heart. But what I abhorred the most that night was not being able to fix it. To be there for you completely. Because I had to be there completely for someone else. And I know hearing that may only hurt you more because we're stuck in this paralyzing space of family and stability and loyalty. But I can't do this, I can't be on this trip with you, without you knowing that I hold a little bit of you in me. Always."

Her dusky brown lashes clump under the weight of her gathering tears, and my stomach coils around the terrifying fact that we may spin out of control. That we've hit some critical mass of feelings for one another that cannot be undone. A juggernaut of sorts with no direction that would guarantee us—Florence, me, Riley—a way out unscathed.

Unscathed.

Is anyone unscathed? Maybe I was Before Death, but I was also just a different shade of miserable. What is it worth, being good and unhurt if the only thing we're putting on a puppet show for is the borderline emotionally abusive hold my cousin has over Flo and Flo's tenuous stability under Aunt Susan's roof? That she doesn't even need in the first place.

We nod at an older couple walking by, and I swear I can smell Mom's perfume in the woman's wake. And that ache, oh, that *ache*. I am not the person to trash things that I don't understand and that don't belong to me. I am not my father. And I will not let this love between me and Florence pull me under. If I have only myself, I need to at least be able to stomach the person I am.

"I know," she whispers, watching my face carefully.

Only she couldn't know the agonizing roller coaster I just took myself on.

"I promise you, Eaden, we can do this together. As friends. Please don't leave." Her hand slips down my arm, and she squeezes my wrist in a soft desperation. "Please don't leave. I won't say anything else like that. We can focus on this trip and your aunt, and we can be okay. I promise. Just, please, don't leave."

"Leave?" The wounded look in her eyes crushes me, and I flash back to Barcelona when I thought Florence had abandoned me in the night. "I'm not leaving."

"Oh, thank God." She collapses into me, her head on my chest, and her arms wrapped tightly around me. "I thought I went and fucked everything up between us. And I meant what I said, I need your friendship. Please don't take you from me."

"I'm not taking me from you," I whisper into her hair.

"I mean"—she pulls back with a jolt—"of course you can leave. I'm sorry, jet lag has got me so emotional. Just promise you won't disappear without letting me know you're going. I just want to know you're safe."

"I'm not leaving. I promise." I pull her back into a hug with an attempt at a friendly chuckle. "Did we just have our first emotional breakdown on an international trip together?"

She nods against my chest before she pulls away and enters the building code on the keypad. "Yes. We definitely did. Well, maybe second. Welcome to the joys of world travel."

We laugh as she pushes open the door, and we walk up the stairs to the apartment.

"I kind of like it," I say as we drop our things on the counter.

"Me too." She pulls the bottle of wine from the welcome basket and waggles it. "Nightcap?"

I nod and fetch the glasses from the cabinet. They're suspiciously cloudy, so I wash them quickly before presenting them to Flo. I feel better somehow. As if we finally reached this understanding of what our priorities are. Being good people and loving one another as friends.

"So I was thinking," she says and pulls the cork from the bottle with a wet *pop*. She fills both glasses and hands me one. "And I don't want to argue with you, Eaden, so just say yes."

"I don't even know what—"

"The sleeping arrangements. I think, given tonight and how we're both feeling, it's probably best to have our own space and not share the bed. At least, that's what I'm most comfortable with."

I nod. "Of course. I agree completely."

"I propose we alternate nights. I get the bed tonight, and you get the bed tomorrow. Back and forth. Any more than one night on that couch for either of us, and I don't think we'll have a functioning neck." She shrugs and takes a sip. "You know, being post-thirty and all."

"I tweaked my neck sneezing last month." I chuckle over the rim of my glass. "It's too real, isn't it?"

"Too real," she agrees.

I flip open the welcome packet to find the Wi-Fi info and connect my phone. A few texts begin to roll in along with two missed calls from my dad. I open the messages from Riley that read: *I haven't heard from Flo in a couple hours. Tell her to check in.* And the second: *I'm not playing. I told her to check in every two hours. Make her call me.*

I glance at Florence. She's gazing out the kitchen window, looking so free and unburdened. I don't want to bring her down with these controlling messages, and honestly, I don't want to be involved with whatever agreement or relationship they have for this trip.

"My new phone is officially functional," I say.

She flashes me a quick smile. "Oh, good. I'm so glad."

"Is yours working okay? No trouble connecting to the Wi-Fi?" I ask.

"I haven't connected to the Wi-Fi, but Rye made sure I had an international plan set up, so I've been receiving texts and calls regardless. It's how we've been using Google Maps everywhere."

"Right. Good," I say. She directs her gaze to the view again, and I type a response to Riley.

Hey, Rye. Everyone is safe and sound. Things are going great over here, but we definitely miss you.

She messages back immediately. *Tell her to text me back, Eaden. Now.*

I get a little paranoid that there may be some emergency back home, and maybe that's why Riley is desperate to get in contact with Flo. "Hey, I got a few texts from Riley. She was concerned you haven't responded to her. Not sure if you have received her messages. Just a heads up."

She scoffs. "Her ten texts and seven calls? Yeah, I received them. But I'm going to respond on my own time."

That's a good enough response for me. If it is an emergency, Rye should say so. *Sorry, Rye. It's none of my business. She said she'll reply when she can.* It feels extremely good to send that message. And though I refuse to cross more lines with Flo out of loyalty to her, I'm still allowed to feel all my complicated Riley feelings.

Fuck you too.

Her response doesn't surprise me. Even though she was "kind" leading up to the trip, with Riley, it's always one step forward, five steps back. The kindness is just manipulation or a means to get what she wants. Truly, she just kind of sucks. I shrug it off and slide my phone in my pocket. Ignoring my dad for one more day won't hurt anyone.

I take the last swig of my wine. "All right. I'm going to brush my teeth and get ready for bed. Night, Flo."

She gives me a quick hug. "Good luck on the couch. Try to sleep well, we have an adventure-filled day tomorrow."

"Can't wait."

❖

The non-pulled out pullout is rough. Not rough enough to complain or sleep together in a bed with Florence, but I'm foggy through breakfast the next morning. And through the bus ride to the Centre Pompidou, a museum with an outer escalator that gives an iconic view of the city

THE MOON TO ME

and another view of the Eiffel Tower, Florence has asked me multiple times if I'm okay. Finally, I joke, "I promise, I'm fine. Plus, it's your turn tonight, so good luck."

"Oh dear God," she says. "Good thing I brought a pharmacy's worth of ibuprofen."

I squeeze her shoulder. "You're going to need it."

She smacks me away, and we both fall into a comfortable quiet for the rest of the rainy bus ride. Paris looks good in any weather. The dark skies match the brooding, artsy vibe of its residents. I, too, welcome the rain. It's soft and easy on the senses. The perfect day to spend in an amazing gallery with Florence. Though I really want to get to a natural history museum with her, the Pompidou looks incredible, from what I can tell online.

We hop out of the bus and jog across the wet asphalt street to the industrial-looking building. I wouldn't have guessed it was a museum, except for the iconic escalator that gives it away. We walk inside the atrium and shake off the rain, our hair a little wild and wet.

I spot a café on the next floor up. "I'm going to grab a quick cappuccino before we start. Do you want anything?"

"No, thanks. But damn, that pullout really sucks, huh?"

"It's fine. Honestly. I'll be right back."

I take the stairs up to the café and order my drink. They have a few spinning stacks of postcards, journals, and little trinkets from the museum. I spin through them while I wait, particularly enjoying the postcard with the view from the top of the escalator. An excitement bubbles within me, and I consider buying it, but my decision-making is interrupted by my phone ringing in my pocket.

It's my dad. It's six in the morning for him, but I guess he finally figured out the time zone enough to not call me while I'm asleep, even if he did overcorrect.

"Dad, why are you calling so early?"

"Good morning to you, too."

I roll my eyes and try to physically harness the annoyance I feel, as if I am literally sixteen again. "Look, we're at a museum, and it isn't the best time to chat."

"I just wanted to check in. You haven't been returning my calls, and I worry about you, Eaden. Even if you don't want me to. I worry."

They call my name for the cappuccino, and I grab it, mouthing a *merci* to the barista. I hate being on the phone while I'm being waited on or I'm buying something. It's beyond rude, and I'm even more agitated that my dad called and made me be that person. I try to take a calming sip, but it's piping hot.

"I'm sorry you're worried. I really am. But, Dad, I only receive your calls and texts when I have Wi-Fi, and as you can imagine, we're pretty busy exploring out here."

"And I'm so happy you're having a great time. All I ask is for the occasional check-in. Please."

"No." I scoff, taking a sip and not caring if it burns my throat. "Dad, I'm thirty-four. In no world do I need to check in with you. I am living my life, and right now, I need some space from you to figure out my own shit. And to maybe figure out what our relationship looks like from now on."

"But, Eaden—"

"No, Dad. I'm literally in Paris at the coolest gallery I've ever been to, making Florence wait on me because I'm on the phone with you. We aren't doing this. I need space, and I need you to respect that." I huff into my phone.

"Okay," he finally says, seeming defeated. "Okay, I hear you. Just know, I love you so much. And I'm here for you whenever you need me."

I've never been one to think much about money, but for the first time since she died, I wonder if Mom was planning on divorcing him. And I wonder if he feels lucky that she didn't get the chance to because now all her money and retirement and assets are his. He is completely off the hook for everything.

Fuck him. I hang up without saying good-bye.

Immature, sure. But I could not care less at this point. How does he not understand that not only am I struggling through losing Mom, but every time I hear his voice or see his face, I'm absolutely gutted all over again. Drowning in my mother's heartbreak. And it's so much more painful than drowning in her death.

Fuck him. I wish it was him instead of her. I really do.

Florence looks concerned as I descend the steps to her, her brows stitched tightly above her eyes. "What's wrong?" she asks.

I wrap myself around her, holding out my cappuccino in case I drip on her cardigan. "I just need a hug."

"I got you," she says, pulling me tight and softly stroking my hair. "I got you. It's okay."

I untangle myself from her before I lose control of these emotions and let the tears start falling. And there's nothing I want less than to be the gaudy, dramatic American crying in the atrium of one of the most iconic galleries in Paris. Cappuccino in hand.

"I'm sorry," I say, fixing my hair and wiping a hand down my face. "My dad called, and I felt like I had to answer, which was a mistake because every time I talk to him, it makes me miserable." I shake my head and pick a point on the second floor to stare at as I hold back the tears. The image of him fucking that girl from my dream strangles me to within an inch of collapse. I don't know how to be his daughter anymore. I don't know how to receive his love. To love him.

"You don't have to talk to him. That's the beauty of being an adult." She rubs my bicep as I gather myself. "Take your space. Especially on this trip. Take all the space you need from him. Then you can begin to understand what kind of relationship you want with him if any. It's okay."

"Yeah," I mutter, still staring at my point on the second floor. "You're right. I'm an adult, and I don't have to abide people in my life who hurt me." I look at her. It's clear she heard every meaning behind my statement by the sad, slow way she nods. But she doesn't argue. My dad, Riley, and Sean—I'm in control of how much access they have to me, and that knowledge gives me reprieve.

"That's right. You don't," she says. "But, Eaden—this is coming from a friend who loves you—you should really find a good therapist when you get back home. Just to help you untangle all your feelings and find the best solutions for them. You've been through it this summer." I stay quiet for a moment, digesting her suggestion. Then she adds, "I honestly don't know where I'd be without mine. And, no, I'm clearly not perfect, but I'm on a trajectory of growth and have built a relationship with my mother that feels good to me. And I'm not saying you have to build that with your dad. I'm just saying, get someone good in your corner to help you through it all. Lord knows life doesn't quit throwing punches."

I nod, knowing she's right. It's only because I trust her so much that I'm able to receive her words without getting defensive. No one in my family has ever seen a therapist. But maybe we would have all been better to each other if we had.

I take a deep breath to release my anger from the phone call with my dad and attempt a smile. "You're not going to bill me for that, are you?"

She cracks into a grin and shoves me. "Shut up."

"Because I'm going to be pissed if I come home to a giant therapy bill from you, Flo."

"Come on, loser. You're my worst patient." She pulls me toward the first exhibit on the second floor.

It's all very modern cubism, with bright primary colors and concentric patterns. I abhor it. But Florence seems at least mildly interested, so I follow her around quietly and wait for her to comment on what she sees. Maybe there's some hidden message of why it's so alarming and loud looking. Some meaning that would make it beautiful. But we don't speak, and I continue to follow her like a ghost until we finish the exhibit and walk back into the atrium area. My eyes water with relief at the soft light replacing the barrage of modernism we just saw.

"What'd you think?" I ask hesitantly.

She looks up and taps her mouth with her pointer finger, the soft lilac of her nail popping against the strawberry red of her lips. "Well, I think the choice of the colors and shapes in tandem with the use of layering is an interesting commentary on the juxtaposition of society and the—"

"Shut *up*." I laugh as she scoffs at me. "I know you're full of shit."

"What?" she gasps. "You don't know that. I could have loved it."

"Even if you did love it, which I know you didn't, you wouldn't use all your fancy art talk to describe why. Not to me. You would have been real with me and used vocabulary I could follow. You're not one to show off. Plus, if you actually liked it, you wouldn't have been able to stay silent the entire time. You'd have been overflowing, wanting to show me every little thing that makes it gorgeous."

She stares at me for a moment, apparently sizing up my words. "Fuck. You really know me, don't you?"

I shrug. "I mean, I'm basically your best friend. So, yeah. I'd say I really know you."

She grabs my hand and tugs me to the next exhibit. "All right, then. Now you're really in for it."

The next exhibit has a warning for explicit content. We shoot one another an intrigued look. It must be quite explicit if they have to give a warning for it in Paris. The gentleman scans our tickets, and we walk in, wondering what's so explicit about some cool, grainy-looking images on the wall. They're large and made of steel blues and melty greens, what I assume a computer chip would look like if it was liquified somehow. Then we notice people looking through binocular type things that are mounted a few feet away from the images. We wait a beat before one becomes available.

Florence offers it to me first. I lower my eyes to the lens, and a new image immediately comes into focus. It's an older woman sitting on a toilet. Her legs are spread wide so I can see the curls of her pubic hair. She's smoking a cigarette and looking at her phone, her elbows planted on her white thighs, and her shoulders hunched. It's not disgusting. It's jolting. Too real. Like I opened the door of a dollhouse and found the most mundane version of the innermost part of someone's day. A place I was not invited to and should not be. Or was I invited? I'm instantly uncomfortable.

"Fuck," I mutter and pull away from the lens.

Florence raises her brows in surprise. "Well, it made you feel something, apparently. Any idea what?"

I lift my arms in a weak shrug. "It made me feel kind of perverse for looking. But the whole point is to look. I have no fucking idea what it means." I touch both my temples with my fingers.

"Stop being so adorable. Let me look, and we'll brainstorm together." She bows to the lens. "Oh," I hear her murmur. But she stays longer than I did. Finally, she pulls back up. "Okay. I see what you mean now."

"Right?" I say in exasperation. "It's so confusing. Like, is it sexual? Or maybe, I don't know. *Not* sexual?"

"No. I don't think it's supposed to be sexual at all. On the surface, these images are grainy and fuzzy and obscured. They're hidden to the naked eye, dressed up as something they're not. Not truly. But when we're invited to uncover the mask, we see the raw realness of the subjects. Not posing in a coy nightdress, not lounging with an expertly picked book, but pissing on the toilet and checking their phone like we all do." She pats me on the chest. "And somehow, that made both of us feel a metric fuckton."

"And that's art," I say.

She smiles. "And that's art." She bows into the next lens and instantly bursts into giggles. "I'm sorry. It's not funny. It's just that, you're really going to love this one," she says when she pulls up.

"Oh God." I hesitantly press my forehead to the viewer and look through the lens. I see a middle-aged man, probably in his sixties, laid back in an old, ripped army green recliner. He has his hard, veiny penis gripped firmly in his hand. Clearly masturbating. It would be funny—I can see why it felt like a joke to Flo—but it's not funny at all to me. I am staring at an image of a man masturbating in a Paris gallery, and all I see is my father.

I pull up sharply, knocking my face on the outer shell of the eyepiece. Florence squints at me, so I come up with something on the fly. Something that's very far from my dad having sex with his personal trainer.

"I didn't know they got so veiny." I run my hand through my hair. "But, uh, it makes sense. Given that erections are powered by blood flow, and well, veins enlarge when mass amounts of blood are traveling through them." I widen my hands for effect. "The veins. They engorge."

"Oh my God, I broke you." Florence yanks me away from the exhibit and back to the atrium. "Maybe we'll skip the 'explicit' exhibitions until you're older," she jokes.

"Ugh. I totally lost my cool, didn't I?"

We walk to the outer shell of the building and step onto the escalator. I can already tell the view is going to take my breath away just as much as peeing lady did.

"It's cute when you're flustered. Don't worry about it. I know the penis was a lot," she says as she steps on with me. "How about we go straight to the top, enjoy the view, then work our way back down through the exhibits?"

"Sounds good to me."

We grow quiet as the escalator lifts us into the Paris skyline floor by floor. It's breathtaking to me. Calm. All those roofs and balconies and potted plants. I can see people reading through their windows until we lift even higher, and my focus becomes the Eiffel Tower. It's hard to imagine beating this view of the city, and I get to experience it with her.

We get off at the top and join the crowd of people snapping photos and taking videos. It seems like a lot of people just come to ride to the top of the escalator because most of them are still wet from the rain, dripping everywhere with their sopping black umbrellas and sleek raincoats. I dodge a few children to catch up with Florence, who has found a peaceful corner amongst the chaos.

"What do you think?" she asks.

"I think it's stunning."

She leans into my shoulder. Completely harmless, but it feels so good to feel her pressed against the side of me. We stand quietly together, indulging in the open-air view and this new calm between us. Maybe it won't last forever, this sweet spot of friendship we've settled in, but that is not a problem for today. Today, I'm with my favorite person, at this weirdly cool museum in Paris, enjoying the view from the top. And I feel happy.

Life could be good.

"Ready?" she asks, nodding to the door across the crowded walkway.

"Yeah. Let's see what the next one is all about."

We bid a silent farewell to the view for now and weave through the wet throng of people. For how artsy and chill Parisians seem to be, they also always seem to be in a hurry, just like Americans. Men push by us, undeterred in their journey to get to the escalator or doorway or wherever they're going, and I stay close to Flo. My anchor.

My phone buzzes, and I pull it from my pocket to check. I have a message from Riley that I cannot be bothered to read. I sidestep a running child and reach behind me to slip my phone back into my pocket. A man I didn't see when I was avoiding the child checks me hard in the shoulder, and I slip on the wet metal utility cap underfoot. It's that strange moment where I realize I'm going down. All the fail-safes of the human body have failed, and now, I'm about to completely eat it.

And I do eat it. I eat complete shit. My leg flies out from under me, and I fly backward, trying to catch myself with the hand that is already behind me. And my brand-new phone.

One crack. Two cracks.

And a firestorm of pain.

CHAPTER FIFTEEN

"Oh fuck," I hear Florence say.

I scramble to my knees, running on adrenaline and sheer embarrassment. The man didn't even stop to see if I was okay, but from the acid burning in my wrist, I know I'm not okay. From the tunnel vision I'm experiencing, I know I'm not okay. But I can't bring myself to look at the damage yet. Instead, I brace my wrist by cradling it just under my elbow and holding it to my stomach. *Oh.* My stomach doesn't feel so good.

"Eaden. Fuck. Can you stand? Don't rush it if you can't."

I nod and let her assist me to my feet. Nobody around us seems to realize I have seriously injured myself, which simultaneously relieves and enrages me. I may pass out. I may—

I vomit.

It splashes into the puddle beneath our feet and sprays Flo's ankles. Also covered in my vomit is my phone. My phone, with its freshly shattered screen, lies in the puddle of rain and puke. Serves me right for being too cheap to buy the device protection plan.

I am drunk on the pain. Maybe I can save the phone.

I need to save the phone.

Oh my God, I don't have a travel health insurance plan.

That's it. I'm sunk.

I'm ruined.

I grab my phone and try to swish it in the puddle to get most of the vomit off it and hold it up to Florence.

"Oh my God. Okay." She takes the hem of her dress and cradles my phone in it, trying to dry it. "It's okay. I have your phone, and it's going to be completely fine." She tucks my phone in her purse, then guides me to the edge of the crowd. "Can I see your wrist? Please?"

Another wave of nausea hits. "I don't wanna look," I mumble.

"You don't have to," she says as she gently guides my arm away from my stomach. Her face contorts into disgust and concern. "Oh, Eaden. We have to go to the doctor, okay?"

"No. We can't. I don't have insurance here," I plead.

She shakes her head. "We don't have a choice. You clearly broke your wrist."

I muster the confidence to look at it. Florence holds it like a broken bird. It almost feels disconnected from my body as I observe the strange appendage of mine. Crooked and wrong, fat and swollen.

"I'm so fucked." Tears stream down my cheeks. "I'm so fucked," I repeat. It's the only thing going through my brain. How fucked I truly am. I'll be broke after this. I know someone who got appendicitis in the small time frame that they didn't have health insurance. They had to file for bankruptcy.

I'm so fucking weak.

Why would anyone want to love this? How could anyone love this?

"Let's go." Florence's tone doesn't leave room for discussion. And though I don't know what the fuck I'm doing or what the fuck I need to be doing, I follow her. Down the escalator, the pretty view faded in my fuzzy vision. "Come on." She ushers me through the small crowd of people as if she's my bodyguard until we get to the edge of the street, and she flags down a taxi.

We climb in, and Florence has a short, urgent conversation with the driver before we set off down the road. She is busy on her phone the entire drive as I focus on cradling my arm tight and not throwing up every time we hit a small bump in the road. Lucky for me, we aren't in the taxi long until it pulls up to the entrance of a small building that looks like an emergency room.

"Flo, I can't afford—"

"You can't afford to not go to the doctor. We're going. End of discussion." Florence pays the man and beckons me out of the cab. I follow her to the doors and am immersed in the small chaos of a French emergency room. I am so glad she speaks French.

She sits me in an open chair and directs me to stay put.

I do as I'm commanded, admitting to myself that I'm not in control. I don't want to be in control. My wrist is half-numb and half erupting volcano. It's confusing. There's no question it's broken. A five-year-old could look at it and diagnose it. The question is, how I'm going to afford it. What do I do? How do I come back from this? From the phone?

The garbled French of the people waiting with me makes me feel isolated in the world of pain and fear and confusion. I close my eyes and do my best to dissociate. Try to find my mom but I can't. I can never find her. I faintly register Florence sitting in the chair next to me, but I keep my eyes closed. I'm so tired. But her hand on my knee is nice. I'm not sure how much time passes before we're ushered through the door to an exam room. Thankfully, I have a doctor who speaks English, though it's hard for me to understand her through her thick accent. Florence still has to translate a few words for me.

"Quite the fall," the doctor says. She reaches for my arm. "May I?"

I let her examine my wrist. It feels embarrassing, breaking a bone just by slipping in a puddle. Florence is busy on her phone again. Can't really look her in the eye right now anyway. I'm basically a child. No wonder I'm unlovable. No wonder every woman on earth would choose Riley over me. She has money. She has confidence. She doesn't have a broken fucking wrist.

"Okay. We need to take an X-ray image of the wrist. Then we set it, give it about five days for the swelling to subside, put you in a cast, and you'll be nice and secure until you get back to America."

I don't remember telling her we were traveling.

"Sound good?" she asks.

I just nod.

"Can we get her something for the pain? Please?" Florence asks.

"Of course. I'm going to get you something strong for while you're here. And write you a prescription for a high dose ibuprofen for when you're discharged. Is that okay?"

Again, I nod.

The whole experience takes about two hours.

I broke my wrist in two places. But the pain meds are doing some heavy lifting, and some relief begins to cool me down. Once I'm splinted and Flo is given instructions, we're discharged with orders to come back in five days. Which does not fit into our travel schedule. But I can't think about that right now. My brain can't take any more stress. No more room at the inn. We're at capacity here.

I'm caught between a painkiller haze and sleep in the cab ride back to the apartment. Open my eyes to Florence's gentle command to follow her out of the car onto our street. We walk up the stairs slowly, and she opens the door for me, giving me a list of commands as she does.

"Drink this water. Sit. Let me help you with your shoes."

I drink the water. Sit. Let her help me with my shoes.

"Follow me."

I follow her.

"I'm going to get you set up in bed." She moves some pillows out of the way and pulls down the quilt. "Okay. Can I help you with your pants, please?"

"Uh, yeah." My voice is hoarse. Mouth full of cotton.

Flo unbuttons my pants and pulls down my zipper, then nods for me to shimmy out of them. Being in my underwear in front of Flo feels normal. I guess. I crawl into bed and lean my head against the headboard. "I'm so tired," I mumble.

"I know. I know. It's been a long day. Just close your eyes." She scoots onto the bed next to me and smiles a worried little smile. A one-dimple smile. "I'm going to be right here, reading next to you."

"No. You have to go out and enjoy Paris. I'm fine. I promise, I'm fine." What more trouble could I possibly get into?

"I'm staying. And I'm not arguing with you, Eaden. Close your eyes. You need to rest."

"I can take care of myself," I say. Petulant and probably untrue.

She sighs. "No offense, but you're high on painkillers and no longer have a functioning phone because it drowned in your puke. I'm not leaving you."

I crack a grin. "You're, like, obsessed with me."

A healing chuckle escapes her lips. "Says the girl who broke her wrist to get my attention."

"It worked, though." I think I'm entering the loopy part of painkillers.

She closes her book. "You know, you're, like, especially bad in an emergency."

"Yeah, but you're amazing in an emergency, so we're good." I point at her with my good hand. *Uh-oh. My good hand is my left hand, and I'm definitely right-handed.*

She laughs with her entire chest, shaking the bed frame enough to make my wrist hurt. But the sound is worth it. "I just watched you realize that you broke the wrist of your dominant hand." She wipes the tears of laughter from the corner of her eyes. "Oh man, it's going to be a fun couple weeks."

"Oh no. I'm fucked, Flo."

"Nah." She pats my knee. "You're not fucked. I've got you, Bilbo."

"Hey," I scold, but I'm already half asleep.

The sleep isn't peaceful. The sleep is never peaceful.

But this sleep is different, fueled by stress and painkillers, a fantastically disturbing combination that has melted my standard nightmare into a warped, dark portrayal of my parents' house. There is nothing happy, not even poignant, waiting for me inside that decrepit door, but it creaks open for me, welcoming me home. I know I should run, force myself to wake up, anything but walk inside. But this recurring nightmare isn't over for a reason, and I need to figure out why. I need to make it to the end.

It feels powerful walking through the front door instead of the garage, though it throws off the normal sequence of seeing my mom crying in the laundry room. The living room is empty except for the mold colonizing the damp cloth of the sofa. Even the drapes are heavy with it. Maybe that's why it's so damn hard to breathe in these dreams. I'm choking on spores.

I grip the rotting banister and consider walking upstairs, but I don't think I'm ready to see my dad with that woman. That *girl*. Definitely not. I let go, wiping soft wood particles from my hands, and follow the faint sound of music I just noticed. *The office.* I walk through the living room, and turn left down the hall. The door to my parents' office is cracked, and the music pours through it. It's Janis Joplin—my mom's favorite—singing about someone breaking another little piece of her heart.

"Mom?" I knock as I push open the door.

It takes my breath away, seeing her grading papers and belting along with the song. She can't hit the notes, but that never stopped her from singing. She looks up and captures me with her bright blue eyes framed by healthy, glowing skin. Her hair is combed and neat around her shoulders. She wears her favorite cardigan.

"Oh hi, babygirl. I didn't expect you." She stands and walks around the desk to me. Seeing her, feeling her embrace me, it's all so overwhelming. My face is wet with tears. I've waited so long for this, and I finally found her. I squeeze her tight until she pulls back and asks, "Is everything okay? That's a tight hold you've got on me."

Nothing is okay. How can she sit here singing when her husband is upstairs having an affair right under her nose? She's being made a fool of, and I can't abide it. "Mom, I need to show you something."

Her brows rise in question. "Okay, honey."

I take her hand and lead her through the rotting living room that doesn't seem to clock as unusual to her. We stop at the stairs, and I look at her one more time, trying to memorize everything about her. Her wrinkles, her confused smile, the warmth of her hand, in case I wake up and never find her again. I need to hold this image of her in my heart forever.

"Ready?" I ask.

She shrugs with a smile. "Sure."

"Just be careful," I say, nodding to the carpeted steps. "They're a little sinky."

"Oh, I've been asking your dad to fix that for months, but don't worry, he'll get to it soon. Mother's Day is coming up, so I can guilt him into it before everyone comes over for brunch."

Tears sting my eyes. "Yeah. Perfect."

She follows me quietly up the soft steps. The sense of impending doom grows with each one until we reach the top, and I turn to her, though her fresh face has already begun to swell and morph into the decomposing one I've grown so familiar with. Maybe I should have left her downstairs, happy in her office, singing her favorite song.

But I can't leave her in the dark. My dad needs to be caught. There need to be consequences for what he's doing.

I walk her to the door of her bedroom.

"Eaden, I don't want to." Her voice is garbled, as if it were coming through a drowned speaker.

"I know, Mom. But we have to."

"We don't," she says.

But I don't listen. We do. There is right and wrong, and wrong must be exposed and dealt with. No matter if it hurts.

I open the door to the same scene I remember from last time. Pale legs, moaning, the way the strange girl moves atop my dad. It hits me in the chest like a lightning bolt. The pain and disgust sears itself in my brain like a scar on top of the one image I actually wanted to keep, the image of my mom healthy and happy. But I ruined that. I can't stop looking at the grotesque thing happening in my parents' bed.

I watch his hairy toes curl until my mom snaps me back by the arm, breaking my bone and tearing tendons, muscle, skin. She shakes my flopping hand in my face. Every recognizable part of her is gone. She is gone.

She yanks me close so I can smell the decay on her words. "I was fine. Until you did this."

"Eaden, wake up!"

I wake with the usual gasp and raw throat but also with a searing pain in my wrist. "What? What'd I do?"

Florence is next to me, fumbling with my sling. "You started thrashing around in your sleep and decided to fling your arm out of the sling. *Shit*. Just lean back and let me get your arm back in, please."

I grip my eyes shut and let her wrangle my broken wrist back into the safety of its sling, though the painkillers are wearing off, and I feel each centimeter of movement with the ache of a hundred exposed nerves.

She tucks my arm back in and runs her fingers down my shoulder. "All done."

I nod, painfully aware of the incessant stream of tears down my face.

"Call me crazy, but I have a feeling these tears aren't about your wrist," she says.

I stay quiet because she's right. I keep my eyes shut because she's right. She brushes her knuckles down each of my cheeks. There's no drying them, but the tenderness of it pushes me closer to the edge of losing it. When I open my eyes, and I see her, I know I'm going to break.

"Eaden. I'm right here." She strokes her thumb over my brow. The move that breaks me open, cracks what little control I have left over my fear, my emotions, my tiny grasp on normal life.

I lean forward, trying not to choke on my heavy sobs. They fill my throat like vomit and flood from me in tears and snot and spit. This is the hardest I've ever cried. At least in my memory. Florence wraps her arms around me, careful to avoid my wrist, and pulls my head to her shoulder. My sore eyes hit soft cotton that I saturate in seconds. I fish my good arm around her and hold on for dear life as the barrage of waves crash on top of me.

She anchors me.

"I've got you," she whispers, rubbing my back. "It's okay, honey. I've got you."

My breaths stutter through my teeth. Each time I think I can calm down enough to speak, a new barrage of sobs drowns my words, and I collapse against her chest again. It's not just the sorrow or the pain of missing my mom. It's not just the anger I feel for my cheating father.

I take a deep, salty breath, rubbing my sore eyes on her collar bone. "I was the one who told her," I finally say.

Florence takes a moment to respond, never breaking from rubbing my back. "What are you talking about?"

I burrow into the crook of her neck, my safety and anonymity. "My mom found out about my dad's affair from me. I told her. I'm the reason she was heartbroken before she died."

"Oh, Eaden." She pulls back, gripping my shoulders gently to take a good look at me. It was easy to say it, taking shelter under her chin. It was easy to cry into her sweatshirt. But sitting in front of her now as this crying mess of a human, I feel exposed and naked. Like the lowest expression of myself. "You have to know it's not your fault."

I shake my head. "It is, though. I know that deep down, but I couldn't admit it to myself until I started having these goddamn nightmares. And my mom"—I drop my chin to my chest and take a blubbering breath—"she just begged me not to show her in my dream, but I dragged her to my parents' room and made her watch my dad in the act. And then she rotted into nothing before my eyes with that same look of anguish on her face from every other dream. From when I told her in real life." I wipe my nose with the back of my hand. "She was happy, singing Janis Joplin, before I came and ruined it all."

"*Shh.*" She rubs my shoulders as if to keep me warm. "You didn't ruin it all. Your dad made a huge mistake."

"I feel like I lost my mom and my dad. Like I'm mourning both of them. And then, to top it off, I feel this crushing guilt. I know it's my dad's fault for having an affair, but it was not my place and none of my damn business to tell my mom." I sniffle and wipe my eyes. "If you'd seen how heartbroken she was, Flo, you'd have regretted telling her, too."

"Of course you feel that way now because her life was cut short. Hindsight is always twenty-twenty. But, Eaden, anyone would have told her. You were giving her the truth. Affairs don't just randomly happen. You were giving her the opportunity to fix something broken or move on." She leans in to kiss my temple. Her lips glisten with my tears as she pulls away. "And the sum of a life is more than a person's last couple of months. So much more. She may not have gotten to make it through processing your dad's infidelity, but that doesn't mean she didn't have joy in her life."

I shake my head, unsure if I believe her.

She gnaws her lip, tears growing in her own eyes. The sadness is apparently contagious. "That wasn't your mom in your dream. You know it wasn't. She wouldn't appear to you that way."

"You don't think so?" I mumble.

"No. Those nightmares were about you expressing the guilt you feel. Do you really think if your mom were here right now, she'd be angry at you? Do you really think she'd feel anything but bursting joy to be with you again, even just for a minute?"

"I guess you're right."

"I know I'm right."

A small chuckle puffs from my chest, and I grin. "It would have been really scary to be alone on this trip, having these nightmares by myself in foreign cities. No one to call." She drops her hands in her lap, and I squeeze her wrist. "Thank you for coming with me and for being here for me. Especially today."

"Even if for some reason I wasn't on this trip with you, I'd be your person to call. You know that."

I nod, abandoning her wrist to wipe my eyes. "I don't know how to forgive my dad. Like, I need him. But I can't let him off the hook. I'm so damn angry."

She nods, rubbing my knee. "You know, you're not the only one to have a parent be unfaithful. They're just average, painfully real people who do things that average, painfully real people do. They cheat and lie and fail. But it doesn't mean they don't strive and hope and love. Doesn't mean they don't love us." She sighs. "Welcome to, like, fifty percent of the population."

"What's fifty percent of the population?"

"Children of cheating parents," she says.

I adjust myself against the headboard to stop slouching. "That can't be right."

"It's the sentiment," she says, shrugging as if she doesn't care if I agree.

"But your dad doesn't—"

"What? Love me?"

"I didn't say that." My cheeks warm at the realization that I did, in fact, insinuate just that.

"Don't lie to me, Eaden. You and me, we don't do that to each other," she says.

I pause for a beat, sure of Florence's capacity to handle a truth she's known for decades but unsure if I want to say it out loud to her. If I want those words in my mouth at all. Because the fact that someone who was supposed to give every breath to love and protect her so easily abandoned her is simply enraging to me.

"Your dad doesn't love you," I say. It tastes even more acrid than I thought it would. A painful truth that has been dulled by the ever-gentle lapping of other love in her life but one that will be forever a part of her landscape. Maybe if he had been there through the hard times with her mother, she wouldn't have felt so much fear and insecurity. Maybe she could have trusted the ground beneath her feet. And maybe he could have held her hand when she felt the urge to pluck her hair or pick her fingers.

But he wasn't there.

She nods. "But your dad loves you."

My gut reaction is to argue, to throw a fit and hold up all the evidence against him, all the pain he caused me, the disregard for how his actions would affect me. I know, deep in my heart, he loves me, but love is so muddled by human mediocrity and failure, it's hard to accept the shabby broken thing that it truly is. My expectation of love is a broad-shouldered singularity of will and strength, not the barely holding on bruised knuckles of a complex being with multiple priorities, needs, and scars. The latter makes accepting that love not so simple.

To accept my father's love would be to accept all of him.

"You don't have to," Florence says.

"What?"

"You can allow him to be there for you, to love you. And figure out how to forgive him over time. You guys will figure it out."

"Tomorrow," I say.

"What about tomorrow?"

"I'll let him love me tomorrow." I scooch down in bed and pull the covers up to my chest. "But I'm so damn tired from today, so I'm going to close my eyes again."

She leans in and kisses my temple again in the same place. It makes me melt. "Okay. I'll leave you to it."

"Please don't leave me." I grab her arm and give it a little tug. "Just sleep here tonight. It's not like anything untoward can happen with this between us." I nod to my sling.

She smiles and walks to the bathroom. "Okay. I'll stay."

After she brushes her teeth, she slides into bed. I can tell she's being careful not to wake me or rock the mattress too much in case of my arm. But I'm not asleep yet. I'm still thinking of her. Of what it must have been like for her growing up with just her unstable mom. Considering her scars, it isn't so difficult to imagine why it's so hard for her to let go of Riley and her parents.

But Florence is meant for so much more. So much more love.

"Flo," I mutter.

She turns to me slowly. "You should be sleeping."

She says it in such a doting way. Sweet and doting.

"I wish you'd had more love than you'd know what to do with when you were little. But I know you're going to receive it back a hundredfold one day." I sigh, sleep and pain making my tongue heavy. "And I'll always be jealous of the woman who gets to love you like that. But I'll be so happy, too." I smile at the thought of her bathed in love. "I'd even dance at your wedding."

"I'm feeling very loved these days." She bends down and kisses my cheek before turning off the lamp.

CHAPTER SIXTEEN

Sleeping next to Florence isn't erotic or sexy, especially not with my broken wrist between us. But it is something more startling than erotic. It's extremely peaceful. Even though I am up half the night, shifting positions and trying to figure out the best way to sleep with my broken wrist, I'm not anxious. I'm not having nightmares all night. It's like finally being safe at home, when I haven't felt that way in months. Not since my mom got sick.

It's extraordinary, really. Sleeping next to someone I trust.

Just her breathing deeply next to me is enough to steady me.

"Good morning," she says through a sleepy yawn.

We've slept in the same room for a while now, but I've never really noticed her in the morning. Her hair is adorably messy and falling all over the pillow and her shoulders. She runs her hand through it, but it only makes it messier. Her eyes are soft and satiated, and she turns on her side to look at me. It feels so intimate. Miles away from where we were yesterday.

"I hope I didn't keep you up with all my tossing and turning," I say.

She scoots a few inches closer, careful to avoid my arm. "No. I slept great."

"Good." I shift closer to her, too. "We need to change our travel plans, don't we? I can't leave Paris until I get my cast."

She plays with the hem of my sleeve. "I took care of all that yesterday while we were at the doctor."

"You did?"

"Yeah. Riley messaged the owner of this place and got us a few more days. I figured we should skip Scotland and slow things down a little. Let you recover. Flights to Ireland from here are cheaper than a round of drinks, anyway. Is that okay?"

"I mean, you owe me a trip to Scotland now, but yes. Thank you for handling that."

She rolls onto her back with a desperate sigh. "Oh no. A trip to Scotland? With *you*? How did I earn such a cursed fate?"

"Shut up." I throw my pillow on her and swing my legs over the edge of the bed.

"Easy, killer. You need a hand?"

"No, thank you." I lift myself to my feet and give her a little bow. She claps for me. "Well done."

I search through my suitcase with one hand. A shower sounds too hard at this point, but a fresh pair of clothes is a necessity. I pull out my last clean shirt. "We should find a laundromat today," I say.

"Definitely. Coffee first, though."

"Always coffee first." I look at my sling and the shirt on the bed. "Okay. So maybe I do need some help."

"I've got you." She climbs out of bed, smoothing her hair and adjusting her pajamas. The cutoff shirt hits just above her hip bones, and the waistband of her sleep shorts sits a couple inches below it. It's hard not to stare. She's stunning.

"I guess the sling has to come off, huh?" I say.

"Yeah." She fingers the strap over my shoulder, and her breath tickles my cheek. "But at least you're splinted, too. Ready?"

"Yeah."

She lifts the strap, and I duck out from underneath it, the sling going slack and releasing my arm. I cradle it to my stomach, feeling naked and unprotected. "Step one," I say.

"Done." She grips the bottom of my T-shirt. "We're going to go nice and slow. You ready?"

I'm not so much worried about my wrist as I am about the cascade of chemicals avalanching though my body at the feeling of her knuckles against my stomach. I was so chill sleeping next to her, but now, with my shirt in her grip, I am the opposite of chill. "Ready."

She lifts, pulling the shirt up and away from my body as I try to delicately fish my arm through without snagging the splint. I pull the shirt over my head once my arms are free. Then I'm standing in front of Florence without a shirt. Sure, I have a bra on, but it doesn't change the fact that we're only inches apart, and her knuckles skim my bare stomach again. I tense at her touch. Not because it's unwelcome but because I feel it everywhere.

"Is this okay?" she whispers.

I nod, closing the distance between us, pressing my face into her neck as if it is my home. I'm convinced it may be my home. Her skin is so warm and soft, and she smells like fresh-baked cookies. We hold each other like that for what feels like hours. Me and her in our own world. Safe and sound.

"I love you," I mutter against her skin.

She lifts my chin so she can look in my eyes. Hers are mesmerizing up close, her gaze hopping from left to right. Like she's trying to confirm something before she responds.

"I've loved you for a while," she finally says.

I don't mean to sway closer, not consciously, at least. But I do. I wrap my arm around her waist and pull her into me, holding my broken wrist to the side as if I am leading prayers. Then I feel her breath on my lips. I can taste its heat.

"Eaden, we shouldn't." Her words are soft and quiet, and I don't believe them. But I have to respect them.

Before I have the chance to clarify, she holds my cheek in her palm and pulls my mouth down to hers. Her lips are devastatingly soft and still warm from sleep. She's the only thing I feel. Her mouth on mine. The small whimper against my teeth, like she wants to climb up my body to get even closer to me. Like the big bang, chain reactions cascading so quickly, igniting and exploding. Entire galaxies being birthed.

I didn't know first kisses could still feel this way at our age. I didn't know first kisses could feel this way at all. Because what I'm experiencing is something foreign to me. This satiated happiness paired with ravenous hunger. It makes my head spin. As her lips meet mine again, I grip her waist tighter, needing her to anchor me as she always does.

I brush her bottom lip with my tongue and hear myself moan with the pleasure of tasting her. She opens her mouth to me, and we slowly explore one another, our hips grinding into each other, searching for something a little more.

She pulls away with a gasp, and I watch her, worried we went too far. Worried she'll never come back. But she leans in to give me a quick kiss on the cheek as if reading my mind, then tugs off her shirt so she's matching me in only a bra and shorts. She opens her arms for me, and we hold each other in an embrace that's growing more familiar to me. Only this embrace means slightly more. We've just crossed a very big line in our friendship, and there lies a vast sea of unknown ahead of us. But we hold each other at the crest of it all, skin on skin, breath against neck.

It has always felt like there was an *us* when it comes to Florence. And now I know there is.

"Okay," I say, my voice shaking.

We pull away, watching each other carefully, probably scared to see something like regret on the other. But I don't see regret in Florence. Her eyes take me in as if I've always belonged to her. Unabashedly and thoroughly. It feels more like she's coming to terms with a new reality. Not one she regrets or wants to change but maybe one she thought she couldn't have.

"Yeah," she says, reaching for my clean shirt. "Okay, then."

Not that I would be brave enough, but I really wish my damn wrist wasn't shattered so I could take Florence, push her against the wall, show her what she doesn't know about me. About who I could be with her.

Instead, I let her gently work my shirt over me and situate my arm back in the sling. She brushes her knuckles down my cheek again, smiling and shaking her head. "You're too cute for your own good, you know that?"

I can't help but laugh. I catch her hand and bring it to my mouth, kissing her fingers as she grins. "Only to you."

A flash of heat crosses her features. "Good."

"Have you always felt that way?" I feel my own cheeks go warm. "Um, about me?"

"I'm going to shower." She squeezes my arm as she walks to the bathroom. "Then let's get coffee, and we can spill all our secrets. Deal?"

I nod.

"Good." She closes the bathroom door, and I wait with my heart in my throat.

I kissed Flo. Or we kissed each other.

Really, she kissed me. It feels like I'm driving too fast. Like I've busted through all the stop signs, and now I can't turn around. The line has been crossed, and whatever the consequences are, they will come. Riley will actually murder me. She almost maimed me just for hosting my mom's funeral at Olive Garden.

But she and Flo are legitimately not together. And I'm pretty sure Florence doesn't even want to be with her like that.

I take a deep breath and sit on the foot of the bed while Florence finishes her shower. Whatever Riley may think and whatever consequences there are, they are not happening right now. Right now, the only thing that is happening is coffee with Florence. And even if things get crazy with Riley, I know that Florence and I will protect each other. There's just this knowing in my chest that I can't explain.

Once she's dressed and ready, we walk to the café on the corner of our street that's known for its espresso and hot chocolate. I do not understand what hot chocolate truly is, however, until I see it presented to the table next to us in all its thick, flowing glory. It even has a little candle under the cup to keep the chocolate warm.

"I'm definitely getting a hot chocolate," I say as we sit.

She slaps my good hand gently with the menu. "I told you you'd be obsessed with the hot chocolate here."

I can't help but stare. She looks different sitting across from me now. More at ease or something, which is funny because her life just got way more complicated. Just like mine.

We order a hot chocolate to share, two espressos, and two croissants. Once they arrive and we take the ceremonial time to enjoy our food and drink, we lean back in our chairs and look at one another.

"That is ridiculously delicious," I say, awkwardly trying to tidy my area with one hand.

She smiles and folds her hands over her stomach. "It really is. You ready to eat your weight in cheese later, too?"

I laugh. "I mean, sure. If you want to, you know I'm down."

We let the silence linger for a beat.

"So we kissed," she says, twiddling her thumbs as if trying to figure the sum of a simple equation.

"Well, one could argue that you kissed me." I grin with pride.

She rolls her eyes and leans forward on her elbows. "You kissed me back like you've been dreaming of kissing me for years."

"Maybe I have."

"Have you?"

I shrug. "Maybe." I lean forward the best I can to match her posture. "Look, I know that we've always had a connection, like, as friends. But, Florence, I'm really vulnerable right now, and you happen to be my best friend." I look away for a second before I can face her again. "Well, way more than my best friend. And I need to know how you feel about me. Because if that was just a fun kiss between friends, I need to step back. I can't let myself get hurt on top of everything with my parents. And most of all, I can't lose you."

"I hear you." She takes a deep breath and nods. "I may not have every answer for you. I didn't meticulously plan out kissing you. I didn't mean to fall for you."

"Fall for me?" I straighten in my chair.

"Well." She scoffs. "I'm trying to figure it all out, but yeah. I love you, Eaden. I meant it when I said that. Did you?"

"Yes. Of course."

She nods, her shoulders relaxing a bit. "Good. Because I'm nervous, too. I can't lose you."

I grab her hand over the table and squeeze. "You're never going to lose me."

"You sure? Because a lot of people love me for a moment, then disappear the next day. And just like you, I can't take any more of that."

"I'm sure."

"No. This is messy." She shakes her head. "It's easy to say you won't abandon me, but we have no idea what will come of this." She bounces a pointer finger between us. "What if it's not us romantically? Would you still be my friend?"

It hits me that there's a strong possibility we won't work out romantically. And it hits me even harder that it's because she may still choose Riley over me. I don't know if Florence would still pursue a romantic relationship with her, but she could. If Riley apologized for everything and begged for her back, who knows what Florence would do? I sit with that. Consider if I could truly still be friends with her if she chooses Riley, knowing now that she loves me and wants me in this way. That kiss…

"I think I could," I say, scratching my neck. "But I'd need things to be different. I'd truly need it to be just a normal friendship. No flirting.

No looks, no touches, no promises that feel like poems. I couldn't handle that if you were with someone else. But I'd never hold that against you. And I'd do my very best to keep you in my life."

I watch her process my answer. It's the most honest words to pair with how I feel. Except I left one part out.

"But, Florence, I want you. I've never..." I look around the café for the right words. True words. Words that aren't too much. "Remember when I said you were the moon to me?" She nods. "I have a suspicion that I'm your tide. I can dance to your gravity and still be steady and consistent for you."

Her gaze falls to her lap, and I think I may have blown it. Maybe we just hit the line that she can't cross. Or won't cross. But she whispers, "I want you, too. So badly."

I look around the café to make sure I'm still in reality and not in some dream world. Not that my mind has been treating me to such lovely dreams lately. "So what does it mean? We want each other. We love each other. But?"

The delicate laughter lines deepen at the corner of her eyes. Only, they look like worry lines now. "Is it okay if I don't know what it means yet? Things are complicated, and I hope you can understand that. I'm in a tricky position. The program is starting next month, and I can't really blow up my living situation right now. And I know we're not together, but I have to consider Riley."

I never know when the jealousy will flare in me. I know Riley exists. I know she's important to Florence. But is Florence still waiting for her? I should be feeling guilty about kissing my cousin's ex, but I just don't have the capacity right now.

"Do you still love her?" I ask.

"Of course I have love for Riley." She plucks at the napkin on her plate. "We've been through a lot together over the years."

"I mean"—I shake my head, completely unsatisfied—"do you want her? Like, if you woke up tomorrow and she was suddenly the perfect partner, would you want her?"

She smooths the napkin. "I don't know the answer to that."

I nod. "Florence, I can't lie. I don't really see a scenario here where I don't get hurt in this."

"Do you want to stop?" she asks so quickly, it takes me off guard. Makes me think she believes the same thing.

It's so very frustrating to me that she doesn't have a clear priority of feelings, and it's even more frustrating that I need that from her after one kiss. Only, I know it's not just a kiss between us. It's an entire deep world of connection and trust and love and support. The kind of things that we don't get from anyone else. I know she's scared to lose what she perceives as stability in her life, but I also know—or I hope—that if it came to it, she wouldn't be able to let go of what we have.

And I choose to trust in that scary unknown. Even if she can't see it yet, I choose to trust that it's us. I may fall hard on my face, but it's no stranger to the concrete. So screw it.

"I don't want to stop," I say.

Her eyes widen slightly. "You're sure?"

"Yes. Just"—I scratch my arm where the edge of the sling rubs against it—"be honest with me about what you feel and when you feel it. If you know it's not me, don't lead me on. I'm not interested in being strung along."

"I promise, I will be honest with you. And at the same time, I'm trusting you to be able to handle the murky in-between. And if you change your mind, I need you to tell me."

"Okay." I nod. "I can do that."

Her shoulders relax. "Good. Because it hurts to imagine never kissing you again."

"Same." Terror and excitement gather in my gut at the thought of kissing her again. "I guess we carry on for the rest of the trip and reconvene about how everyone's feeling stateside?"

She winces. "I think it will help me to see things more clearly, being home, but what if I can't promise anything by then?"

I shrug. "Then I'll have my own decision to make, too."

"I can't lose you, Eaden," she whispers.

And I feel the truth in it. I feel all the sincerity and need. I can't lose her, either, but it's going to take both of us to avoid it.

"Then don't," I say.

She nods slowly, and I swear, I can see all the possible outcomes of us racing through her mind.

"Can we go?" she asks.

"Sure."

We don't go home and make out like teenagers. Flo asks me to lie on her side of the bed so my sling is facing outward, then she finds some French movie on television and lies next to me, her hand resting on my stomach. We lie like that for about an hour. She cuddles in a bit closer, and I lift my arm for her to rest her head on my chest. She nuzzles into me, and we enjoy the quiet.

I can only assume she is processing the same way I am. We said we'd come back to the conversation when we got back to America, but we still have all this new unknown taking up space in our brains. It can't be good for either of us, sitting here ruminating, no matter how amazing it feels to hold her this way for the first time.

I kiss her hair and say, "Do you want to get back out there and explore? Maybe that bookstore you were talking about? Or Notre Dame?"

She sighs deeply, and I feel the warmth of her breath through my shirt. "But it's so cozy in your arms."

"Come on." I gently lift my arm again and ease away from her. She makes it extremely difficult with her pouting protest. "I know you didn't come to Paris to waste the days in an apartment. Let's go see some stuff."

She sits on the edge of the bed as I look for my shoes. "You're sure you're up for it with your arm?"

"Yeah. I mean, I probably can't dance the night away with you tonight, but I can walk around and enjoy the city." She levels me with a skeptical look, so I add, "I promise, I'll let you know when I need to come back. It's the heat more than anything that gets me."

She stands and takes my cheek in her hand, a move I'm falling more in love with by the second. I hold my breath as she presses her lips to my brow. "Call your dad," she whispers.

"Right now?" I complain.

"Yes." She rubs my collarbone. "And it's none of my business, but you mentioned being worried about paying the medical bill for your wrist. Not to mention your phone. I'm not saying you need to call to forgive, but maybe you should ask for help."

"Okay." I groan. It's the last thing I want to do right now, especially with my head and heart scrambled over Flo. "Can I borrow your phone?"

She hands it to me without a hint of anxiety. I notice this because my partners in the past were obsessed with not letting their phones out of their sight, which in hindsight, probably wasn't a positive marker for our relationship. And it probably meant they were up to things they didn't want me to see. Not that I would ever look, but it feels good to be trusted.

"This won't screw up your phone plan or anything?" I ask.

She chuckles. "You're not getting out of this, Eaden. And, no, it won't screw up my phone plan. I'll be in the living room."

I stare at her screensaver as she walks away. It's an artist's palette with globs of colorful paint and a messy paintbrush.

"It's Riley's birthday," she shouts from the living room.

Of course, it is. I type *0815* and unlock the phone. I type my father's cell phone number with the same begrudging taps. Nothing left to do now except call. The phone rings three times before my dad picks up.

CHAPTER SEVENTEEN

F lorence? Is everything okay?" He sounds slightly out of breath and worried. I tell myself he's out of breath from running across the house to grab his phone. Not for any other reason. Though the thought that my dad may date other women openly at any point he wants now hits me hard in the chest. Any high I've been riding from kissing Flo is now over. I'm back in the lows.

"It's Eaden."

"What's wrong?" His breathing is starting to even out.

I shake my head, unable to just let it be. "Are you with a woman right now or something? Why are you so out of breath?"

He pauses for a moment, surely taken off guard by my accusation. "No. No, I was getting out of the bath. I was going to let it go to voice mail, but I thought it could be you, and you could need me."

Something about him running to the phone, hectic and trying not to slip, just to make sure I'm okay, softens something in me. "Dad." My voice cracks on his name. I'm so tired of being angry at him. I'm so tired of avoiding him and not listening when he speaks. I'm so tired of being in pain.

"Why did you do it?" I finally ask. It's the thing I need to know. The thing I wouldn't let him tell me. I can't forgive him until we talk about it.

"Hold on." I hear him scurry around, probably to put on some clothes so he doesn't have to answer this vulnerable question naked. "You there?" he asks.

"Yeah," I say and sit on the edge of the bed.

"This isn't an excuse, Eaden. What I did was simply wrong, and I'd give anything to go back and do things differently."

"I know, Dad. Just tell me."

"I loved your mother with all my heart." He's quiet for a beat before he sighs. "Still love her." His voice cracks before he quiets for another moment. "Marriage is complex. On the one hand, I am so in love with her, but on the other, she just lost all interest in being intimate with me."

I inhale sharply at the level of detail he is sharing.

"Do you want me to stop?" he asks.

"No. I'm fine." Nothing can be worse than the nightmares I torture myself with.

He takes a deep breath. "I wanted to go to marriage counseling, but she wasn't convinced we needed it. She said it's what happens when people age, they transition out of sexual relationships. Eaden, we were sixty-three. Then her back got worse, and it was an easy excuse to pin the lack of intimacy on. It just felt like my life force was extinguished in some deep way. Like the knowledge that I'd never be touched again festered in me."

I shudder, holding the phone away from my ear for some distance from this.

"She just didn't need that to feel fulfilled in our marriage, but I did. Then I had to choose what to do, and I chose dead wrong."

"If you could go back," I say, my throat dry and tight, "what would you choose?"

"Well, given your mom was as stubborn as they come"—we both let a small chuckle of relief fill the phone—"and knowing I couldn't lose this part of my life, I wouldn't have let her tell me no to counseling. I would have told her to get in the car and driven her. The affair was unspeakable, but not putting my foot down there was what led to everything. The resentment. The loneliness. It was the crack in me that let someone else in."

"Was it just your trainer?"

"Yes."

"Are you still seeing her?"

"No." He sounds disgusted. "Not because of her but because she reminds me of the worst of myself."

I nod against the phone, gathering the words for what I want to say next. "I'm sorry I told Mom. If I hadn't, she wouldn't have died so sad." Tears well in my eyes.

"Hey," he says, and I almost feel his big hand gripping my shoulder. "The pain my affair caused her is on me. Only on me. And, sweetheart?"

"Yeah?"

"You actually gave us a gift by telling her."

"What do you mean?" My words sound more wet by the second.

He chuckles. "Well, we finally made it to a marriage counselor. And sure, we had only been going for a month, and we had a very long road ahead, but we hadn't truly seen each other in so long, and we finally had the opportunity to get past all the layers of stagnation and resignation. We had the chance to be vulnerable with each other again. We laughed. We cried a lot. It was a gift, you telling her." His voice trembles with emotion. "I'm not saying she had forgiven me. And I'm not saying she wasn't sad. I'm just saying there was a new joy, too."

I feel such strange emotions building in my chest. The deepest urge to sob mixes with relief and pain.

"But, Eaden, I'm just so very sorry I ever put you in that position. And I'm so very sorry that I hurt you."

My dream is not how I found out about my father's affair. I don't think he would have *ever* brought someone to the house like that. It's the same way Flo found out about Riley the first time. My dad is too sincere and bad at technology to get away with an affair. His phone was on the counter, and yeah, he had a passcode, but he also had text previews on the home screen. So, when his trainer texted, "Can you swing by mine after for that extra workout?" followed by a winky face, I was suspicious. But she cleared it right up when she followed it with "I'm a little sweaty, and I want you to lick it off me."

Those two messages are how I found out.

I've been holding so much anger. But maybe it's not mine to hold. For better or worse, my parents were figuring it out. The anger was my mom's to carry. It was hers to choose to let go of or not. It was their relationship, and she wasn't faultless in it.

The tears burst from me. Everything I've been holding on to so tightly slips from my grasp.

"I miss her so much," I sob.

"I know. I know, sweetheart. I miss her, too." His tone is soft and steady.

"And I missed you so much." I wipe my nose in my fresh shirt. "I got my phone stolen and had to buy a new one, then I broke my wrist and my brand-new phone, and I don't know if I can afford a second phone, much less the medical bill I'm going to have because I was an idiot and didn't purchase a travel health insurance plan. I'm scared to dip into my savings." I take a deep, stuttering breath. "And Florence and I kissed, and I don't know what that makes me. If it makes me a bad person because I'm betraying Riley."

"Okay. Slow down, slow down. First of all, are you physically okay? Your wrist, I mean."

"Yeah. It's in a splint for a few more days, and then they're putting me in a cast." I pause to catch my breath. "We canceled Scotland and are going to Ireland straight from here."

"Good. Good call. I'm so glad you're okay. Second, Eaden, you're covered for emergency medical care during international travel under your regular health insurance plan. Trust me, I checked before you left. A broken bone will definitely be covered."

"Seriously?"

He chuckles. "Yes. So can we cross that off your worry list?"

"Yes, please." My breathing starts to even out, and I pull the phone away from my ear to wipe my tears with the back of my hand. Turns out, even as a grown-ass woman, I need my dad sometimes. It's lucky I still have him.

"It sucks that you broke your new phone right after you got it, but without having to worry about the medical bills, you should be okay to take that loss, right?"

"Yeah, I can manage that."

"Okay, good. We'll chalk it up to an adventure tax. Just go back and get yourself a new one again." He pauses for a moment and clears his throat. "Now, about Florence."

I groan, hoping she can't hear this conversation. Even if she could, she'd put in her headphones to give me privacy. I know this about her. Love it about her.

"Dad, it's not just a crush."

"I know it's not. I've always thought maybe there was something deeper between you guys. So did your mom."

"Seriously? But Riley…"

"She's your cousin. And though she hasn't always treated you well, I know you will always do your best to treat her with respect. And I trust that, together, you and Florence will decide what that means."

I shake my head. "She could pick Riley. She lives with Aunt Susan and Uncle Bob. Riley is in every facet of her life."

"Then she wasn't meant for you, Eaden. You can't force these things. If your connection is what you think it is, and if she's who you think she is, she will be strong enough to step away from Riley. And if not, it wasn't meant for you." I can feel him smile through the phone. It's soft somehow. "Just enjoy yourself and try your best to mitigate the mess. I know they're not together, but that still won't make it easy for Riley to swallow."

"No shit," I say through my laughter.

"I missed that sound," he says softly.

I smile against the phone. "Me swearing?"

"No, smartass." He takes a beat. "Your laughter."

"I missed you, Dad." I take a breath and let this moment fill me. Charge me. "I'm still angry at you. In a way."

"I know. It's okay."

"But I love you, and I need you. I need us to be okay because without you, especially if Florence and I crash and burn, I don't have anyone. Sean is off doing whatever it is he does these days, and Riley has never been there for me. And Mom—"

"Will always be with us. And I will always be here for you."

I tell him I love him one more time before I hang up and return the phone to Florence. She lounges on the shabby couch with a French architecture magazine and a cup of orange juice.

"How'd it go?" she asks, making room on the couch for me.

"It was really great, actually. Like I think you knew it would be. But is it okay if I take a minute? There's just a lot going on in my head that I want to process before we go out again."

She tucks her phone in her pocket and stands. "Of course. Take all the time you need. I've been avoiding checking in with Rye, so I'm going to go on a little walk and give her a call. You can have some space then. Okay?"

Something about talking to my dad makes her calling Rye hurt less. I smile. "Deal."

After she leaves, I pour myself a glass of the fresh-squeezed orange juice we got from the local market and sit in the small wicker chair that looks out the bedroom window. It's a sunny day, with soft clouds that take the edge off the brightness. People walk along the streets, dodging cars and bikes, smoking and talking, and the cafés are filled for the lunch rush. And I watch.

I didn't realize I'd become so accustomed to waiting. Waiting to act until someone else acts first. Waiting for reactions before I react. Waiting to see if Riley or Sean want something before I want it. Holding my dad's guilt that he never asked me to hold. It would seem that in an attempt to keep the boat steady, I forgot that I matter. And what I want matters.

I'm free to want.

I'm free.

No one and nothing holds me back. I have responsibilities to my family, yes. I needed to plan my mother's funeral, and Sean was never going to be helpful. But that's his choice, and I don't have to hold the guilt for it being anything less than gorgeous. And, damn, was it less.

I'm letting that go.

No one else will hold it over me. Especially not Riley.

It's inconvenient and messy that Florence is her ex, and they are still so connected. But they are not in a committed relationship and are both free to date as they please. And though it's probably against "cousin code," that never seemed to matter to Rye before, like when she dated Ashley West.

I shake my head.

That's irrelevant to me and doesn't mean what I'm doing with Florence is going to be easy on anyone. The three of us are normal messy people living our normal messy lives with our normal messy relationships. And we're all doing the best we can. That's what's happening.

I take a deep breath, feeling renewed and lighter. But I have zero idea what to expect in the next few weeks.

I hear the apartment door open, and a mixture of excitement and nerves swarms in my stomach. I guess I'll find out.

CHAPTER EIGHTEEN

Florence fills a glass with water at the kitchen sink, her cheeks a soft pink from the heat and her hair tousled over her shoulders. She holds up a finger as she takes a long drink, water dripping down her chin and neck, disappearing beneath her dress. My fingers crave to touch her flushed skin, but I wait patiently as she dries her face on the hand towel and pulls her hair into a quick bun. She leans against the kitchen counter and crosses her arms.

"I told Riley about us," she says, looking at her sandals.

"What?" I step in front of her so she looks at me. "What do you mean you told her? Like, you told her we kissed? You told her we have feelings for each other?"

She piles her hands in front of her dress, her fingers finding any little cuticle to pick. "I told her everything."

"Florence. What?" I stand in front of her with my palm up, confused and exasperated. "I thought we were waiting until we got back to tell her in person. I don't even have a phone for her to contact me on."

She looks to the ceiling and shakes her head. "I know, but I was talking to her, telling her about your accident, and out of nowhere, she asked, 'What aren't you telling me?' And I just couldn't straight-up lie to her. She may lie to me, but that's not who I am, Eaden. I can't."

I tuck my hand in my pocket and take a moment to understand why she told Riley. It's not too far from me telling myself I wouldn't be vindictive like Riley. I groan. "Look, I get it. I never wanted you to lie, and I guess that's what you would have been doing if you didn't tell her. I just wasn't expecting that until we got back home, and I thought we were on the same page. The same team."

"We are always on the same team," she says.

"Yeah, but I feel frustrated because now I'm caught off guard and haven't considered what I'm going to say to my *cousin* about us."

She pushes off the counter and slips her hand around my waist, careful not to jostle my sling. "I hear you, and I'm sorry. In the moment, I didn't even consider that." She presses her forehead softly to mine and looks up at me with her deep blue eyes. "I'm sorry, Eaden. No matter what, we've got each other through this. I promise."

Her thumb rubs the small of my back as I fall deeper into her eyes. The remnants of heat from the sun still cling to her dress and her skin, a bath I want to sink in. It's hard to stay frustrated with her in my arms. I close my eyes and nod slowly, pulling her hips flush against mine. To call it a gasp would be an overstatement, but I don't miss the small breath that escapes her throat when our bodies meet. Her mouth is still half-open from its escape.

"I can never be close enough to you," I whisper.

"I feel exactly the same way. I look for you in every room."

"We've got this," I say.

I move my hand up the back of her neck and kiss her soft and deep until her hips start to grind into me. I don't even think she's consciously doing it, and it makes me wild for her. I walk her back a step until we butt up to the kitchen counter.

"Careful," she whispers between kisses. "Your arm."

"I'm done being careful."

She opens her mouth to me, and I drink her up, never experiencing such freedom before. Such safety. She responds to every nip of her lip, every brush of my tongue, with little gasps and sighs and grinds, and I can't take it. I'm about to rip this damn sling off me. It's hot and in the way and scratchy against my neck. "Fucking sling," I murmur.

Her fingers tangle in the back of my hair, and she pulls me deeper into her. "Fuck the sling. Just keep kissing me. Don't you dare stop."

I don't.

We make out in a desperate, needy way that I've never experienced before, until the warmth of the sun on her clothes is replaced by the warmth of us. Heartbeats and oxytocin and respiration. The heat building and building.

Flo knocks over her water glass with her hip, and it startles us out of our haze.

"Shit." She wipes the drips rolling down the front of the cabinet with the hand towel as she chuckles. She folds the towel neatly and places it next to the sink.

"At least it didn't break," I say, smiling as I step away to catch my breath.

"Fuck." She turns and leans against the counter again, touching her fingers to her swollen bottom lip. "I don't think I've ever been kissed like that."

I run my hand through my hair, trying to get some of it back into place. "Good. I think I'd be jealous if you had."

"Have you?"

I can't help but laugh. "No. No, whatever was in that kiss…" I shake my head, still amazed at the chemistry I feel with her. "I've never had."

She flashes me a coy grin. "Not even with the superhot doctor?"

"I think if we'd had it, she wouldn't have left."

"Mm-hmm. Yeah. Makes sense. Can't lie, I was a little jealous when you were dating," she says, looking away to the living room.

I close the distance between us and kiss her on the cheek, earning a smile in return. "Well, that's fair. I've always been a little jealous of Rye, so we're even." I kiss her softly on the lips and pull away again. "Did you guys have it? You and Rye?"

I regret my question the moment it leaves my mouth. How could she not have it with Rye? My cousin is objectively hot. Obviously not in a way I can appreciate, but I'm very aware of her effect on women. It's incredible. And it's not hard for me to imagine Florence champing at the bit to get her hands on Rye. *Ugh.*

"We have something. But not like this." She brushes my cheek with her thumb. "This connection between us…I don't know. It really snuck up on me."

"Same." She brushes her thumb over my lips, and I kiss it. "So is she pissed?"

"So pissed." She rolls her eyes. "It's a huge mess."

"I'm sorry." I grin. "I guess it's kind of nice not having a phone right now. Maybe I'll even go another day or two without one."

"I'm not sorry. I could never regret this. And honestly, if Riley wanted to be with me and cared enough about me, then we'd be together, full stop. And this would have never happened. But as it stands, she didn't want me like that, and we're no longer together. We're both single, and though it's an awkward situation we need to navigate, it's not like we're cheating or something."

"Yeah." I step back again. Not because I'm freaking out, just to get a breath and to talk more. It's hard not to kiss her when I'm so close. "So where does that leave things with you and Riley?"

She shrugs. "We honestly didn't talk much about it."

"Seriously?"

"Yeah. I mean, I told her that we had kissed and that I have feelings for you, and she didn't take it well. She said she thought I had to be joking. And when she finally believed I wasn't, she hung up on me." She winces. "Communication has never been her strong point."

I wipe my hand down my face. "Shit."

"Yeah. I guess I don't know where that leaves us. Is that still okay with you? I just need some time to figure it all out when we get back."

I nod. "Yeah. I don't expect you to marry me tomorrow." Her brows rise at the hint of marriage. "Or ever," I add, just in case.

"We can slow it down a little, then?" she asks.

"Of course."

❖

I walk out of the doctor's office with a fresh cast and a new sense of freedom. Though it's not healed yet, not having the sling makes me feel like a new woman. With new mobility. And I can think of a few reasons to be excited for that. The top reason is definitely the woman standing next to me right now.

I picked green for my short cast because green is the best color in the world, and it matches the shirt I'm wearing. I take a deep breath of fresh air. I've got a new phone in a very expensive, protective case in my pocket, a solid cast, and I don't have to worry about paying this medical bill.

Florence stands next to me and carefully takes my cast in her hands. "Does it hurt?"

"Not really. It's nice to be able to move around more freely now."

She runs her finger over the dried plaster. "The green suits you."

The last couple of days with her have been relaxed and nice, if a little distant. We are still undeniably attracted and connected to one another, but since Riley hung up on her, we've both been a little more careful. She asked to take it slow, and I just want to give her what she needs. The space and time have been peppered with kisses on the cheek and the occasional flirty comment. But the sling and splint has given us the needed space at night in bed. I sleep with it between us, and it's the barrier we need.

She directs me to a bench while we wait for our ride. I sit next to her as she looks for something in her purse.

"I got you something from the market last time we went. Had a sneaking suspicion you'd pick something like green for your cast." She pulls out a silver Sharpie and smiles. "May I sign your cast?"

I can't help but laugh. "You know, I've never had a cast before, but I was always jealous of all the kids growing up who got to get their casts signed."

She shoots me a devious grin. "Well, here's your chance."

I lay my cast in her lap and let her pick the perfect spot for her signature. She flips it over to take the inside of my wrist. "Why there?" I ask.

"Two reasons. I want it to be close to you. And it's where you broke it. A tender spot for tender words."

I try to watch as she writes, but she blocks my view with her arm. Instead, I watch an older man across the street crumble the end of his baguette at his feet for the birds to enjoy. His shoulders shake as he chuckles, clearly delighted by the scurrying joy of the birds.

"Done."

I take my arm back into my lap.

No matter the storm,
Always your Moon.
Flo

Under the words is a simple yet gorgeous depiction of a crescent moon and ocean wave. I swallow, unable to find the words to match the warmth in my chest. How those words fill me. I point to the wave. "What's this?"

"That's you." She leans closer to my ear. "My tide."

I can't help it. My lips are on hers. The kiss only lasts for a quick hot moment, but it lingers on my lips after I pull away. "Sorry," I mutter.

"Don't be," she says, grinning. "I deserved that."

"It's true." I pat her knee, and she holds my hand there, not allowing me to pull away. "You can't write something like that and not expect me to kiss you."

"See? I knew you were smart." We sit in quiet for a few moments, watching the man feed the birds. "Would you be up for going out tonight? You haven't taken pain medication in the last couple days. Fancy a beer?"

I shrug. "Sure. Sounds great."

"I have a pretty fun idea for a bar game. Trust me?"

"Oh God."

CHAPTER NINETEEN

Even more so than Barcelona, Paris is a party on the weekend. The streets brim with people dancing and partying and jumping around. As an American, it's a shock to see such casual celebration and comradery in the streets without tickets being sold or police coming to break up the crowds to allow for road access again. Cars are king, of course. But this is not America. And though I want to be immersed in this casual joy, I feel so blatantly American in my khaki shorts and linen button-down. A boring shirt to hide a boring travel pack underneath.

"Come on." Florence leads me through the crowds, guarding my new cast from anyone bumping into it. "Let's get a couple drinks before we dance."

She pulls me into a dimly lit bar with soft neon lights whispering across a stone interior. It's less chaotic than the street but is still brimming with chattering people and music. She stops short, and I bump into her back.

She shoots me a scandalized grin over her shoulder, her eyes narrowed. "Was that your cast or are you just happy to see me?"

I hide my cast behind my back and squeeze her hip with my other hand. "I'm just happy to see you."

"Good." She continues to lead us to the bar and shoulders us into a tight spot at the end. "I'm buying you a drink, and you're not allowed to argue."

"But—"

"What did I just say?" she scolds.

"Thank you." I roll my eyes and offer her the only free barstool.

She gives me a skeptical look, but I gesture for her to sit. "Please. I feel like standing, and you're not allowed to argue."

She slides onto the stool and smiles. "Thank you."

"No problem."

As we browse the small cocktail menu, she lets her hand drop to her side and brushes her knuckles against my thigh. Her touch makes it hard to focus on the cocktails, the letters becoming hazy like me. A few people begin to dance to a song I've never heard before in the open space between the banquet-style tables, and I sway to the beat until she wraps her hand around one of my legs and pulls me closer to her.

"Come here, cutie. Tell me what I can order you, then you can dance as much as you want."

I dip my head to try to read the menu again, but it's honestly too tedious in such a lovely moment of joy. "Whatever you're having."

"That's easy, then."

In a moment, two negronis appear, and we toast to a night out in Paris. After we take a sip, I kiss her on the cheek. "Thank you for coming with me, Florence." I rub my chest and look around the bar, taking it all in. "I didn't think I could feel this free or this happy. Not after this last year. And frankly, not even before that. You helped me let go on this trip and embrace life again. Whatever it brings."

As I say the words, I know just how deeply I believe them. It's not about if Florence and I end up together or not, it's about the support she's given me as a friend. And even if I leave this trip alone, I leave a whole person who is more ready to face everyday life and everyday joy. She helped me on my path. Thanks to her, I'll be a better partner to whomever I end up with. I only hope she's gotten even a hint of the same thing from me.

She looks up at me and smiles, her dimples deep and her crow's feet tender. "It's something special, isn't it? The things that we bring to each other, expecting nothing in return. Just love and respect."

"It is." I raise my glass again. "Moon and tide."

"Moon and tide," she says as she clinks her drink to mine.

She takes a sip and spins around on her stool, taking in the festivities with me. "So, are you ready to hear about the game I want to play?"

"Um." I take a nervous sip. "I suppose so."

She rubs my lower back and grins. "Great. You're going to love it. Consider it another gift in embracing life and freedom."

"Oh shit," I mumble.

"Oh shit, indeed. The name of the game is, fill Eaden's cast!" She whips out the silver Sharpie from her dress pocket and grins. "You have to fill your cast with signatures tonight, and in order to get a signature, you have to get a kiss."

"Is a kiss on the cheek okay? Because the thing about me that you seem to be forgetting is that I have absolutely *zero* game."

"I'll allow it, but not because I'm agreeing with you."

I shoot her a sharp glance. "Why then?"

"Because I know myself, and if I had to watch other women kiss you on the lips, I'd be sulking in jealousy all night. And trust me, it's not a good look on me. Or anyone."

"Okay. Deal. But I think you owe me a kiss, then." I wave my cast, flashing her signature back at her.

"I'm pretty sure you kissed me outside the hospital for your payment." She stands and curls her hand behind my neck. "But I guess I can refresh your memory." Her lips press softly to mine, her kiss bittersweet from the negroni.

I wrap my arm around her waist and pull her against my chest. Feels so good without the sling keeping space between us. Her lips on mine, her body against mine, is all starting to feel natural. Thrilling, but also like it was always meant to be this way. Florence in my arms feels like the most normal, extraordinary thing in the world.

The Eiffel Tower is almost six inches taller in the summer.

Thermal expansion. Normal and extraordinary.

Her fingers play with the hair at the base of my neck before she pulls away.

"Don't," I say, pulling her back. "Don't go. Just stay here, close to me, for a while longer. We have all night to fill my cast."

She gives me another soft kiss and spins in my arms so I'm holding her from behind. We lean against the bar, watching people dance and sing and drink as we finish our first round. Her hips fit so perfectly against mine, and she moves them to the beat just enough to build a deep ache in me. A deep need for her. I hold her until I think I may combust from the smell of her hair, the weight of her against me, and the way she tugs my arm tighter around her every time I put my drink down.

I want to take her home so badly. Watch the Eiffel Tower glow against the dark of the night at its tallest.

"Okay." I gently extricate myself from her. "Let's fill this cast."

"I'll get us some beers!"

I survey the bar as Flo orders our next round. I don't know if this is specifically a queer bar, but from what I can see, most of its clientele seem to be somewhere on the rainbow spectrum. Men are chatting up men, and women are grinding on each other on the dance floor. Then there's me, watching them. Approaching strangers for anything more than a quick hello has never been my strong suit, especially when it comes to trying to date. Or even getting a kiss on the cheek at a bar.

In fact, I'm quite hopeless.

There's a reason I ended up working nights alone in a lab out of graduate school. And there's a reason I needed Hakim's help easing me into the fray of a classroom full of students.

Who should I even talk to?

"Dear Lord." Florence comes from behind me, hands me a beer, and drags me toward the opposite wall of the bar, planting me in front of two cute women who seem way too cool to want to talk to me. Flo introduces us, and the pair says hello in thick French accents. "My friend is trying to fill her cast with signatures by the end of the night," she explains, producing the Sharpie from her pocket. "But she's only allowed to get signatures if she gets a kiss on the cheek first."

They tilt their heads in confusion, so she speaks to them in French instead. Soon, the three of them are laughing and smiling together as I wait, clueless as to what's being said. Then the taller of the two puts down her drink and grabs my face with both hands, planting a huge kiss on my cheek. She pulls away with a smirk and takes the marker from Flo as a blush burns my cheeks.

"I need a good spot for you to remember me," the woman says as she searches my cast. "Here." She scribbles what I assume is her Instagram handle under my knuckles and finishes it with a heart. "Get better soon," she says with a wink and hands the marker to her friend.

"Hello," her friend says as she stands in front of me. "May I sign your cast?"

I glance at Florence, who sips her beer with a satisfied grin. She nods her approval.

"Yes, please," I say.

She taps the Sharpie in her palm before she leans in and gives me a swift peck on the cheek. I would think she's cute, if not a little young, if I could see anyone other than Florence in that way. But I can't. As the woman signs my cast, I hold Flo's gaze. It's heavy, besotted with want. But we play this game and flirt and smile and drink to a fun night in Paris together, all while dancing around the solidifying fact that we're falling in love.

"Thank you," I say as she pulls away and hands the Sharpie back to Flo.

We fill half my cast in the bar before we spill onto the streets to join the real party. At this point, people are kissing me and Flo, then pulling us in to dance. I keep my cast raised high in a sort of permanent fist pump to avoid spilled drinks and knocking anyone with it. It also helps Florence keep tabs on where I am in the crowd when we get separated even by a foot or two.

I haven't danced like this since college. But the beat is loud, and there are so many people that it doesn't matter if I can't dance. All I have to do is be in the moment and feel the music. And I'm *feeling* the music.

I forget about getting signatures as a cute woman with black shorts and a silk crop top starts to dance with me. The green plaster is mostly full of silver scribbles anyway. I look to my right and see this guy trying to dance with Flo. She's clearly not interested, but he seems insistent. Her face shifts from friendly to stern as she says something to him, and he disappears.

"Excuse me," I say to the woman I'm dancing with and walk through the crowd to get to Florence.

"Hey. Are you okay?" I ask.

"Oh yeah. Just an asshole guy with asshole suggestions about how maybe I'm not as gay as I think," she says, rubbing her arms.

"Ah, yes. Because surely, he could turn you!" I laugh.

"Exactly." She laughs and bumps me with her shoulder. "Look at you," she says, nodding to my cast. "You made out like a bandit."

I flip it over to look at all the signatures and drawings, making sure none of them encroaches on hers, the only one that matters to me. "Yeah. I think I accomplished the goal of the evening."

She raises a brow. "You were a little too good at it."

I scoff, hand pressed to my chest. "You made me do this. And I was shit at it. You walked me up to almost everyone who signed it."

"Yeah, in the bar. But you were knocking out signatures left and right out here," she says, and the highness of her tone hints at hurt.

"I had a fun night with you. And I really appreciate you getting me out of my comfort zone. But you have to know."

She looks up at me with vulnerable eyes. "What?"

"That these don't mean anything to me." I twist my cast back and forth. "And I'm just dying to walk you home."

She smiles and takes my arm. "Walk me home, then."

We walk quietly, our shoulders skimming as the music fades block by block. I catch her fingers in mine as we turn onto our street, the Eiffel Tower serving as a beacon. I don't think I could ever tire of this, holding her hand as we walk home. I don't think I could ever tire of her. She takes one last look at the Eiffel Tower as I hold open the door to our building.

"Don't worry. I hear there's a pretty good view from our room," I assure her. *Our room.* A quick flash of guilt hits me. It was supposed to be their room. But I let it go as quickly as it came.

"Come show me."

CHAPTER TWENTY

I lock the apartment door behind us as Florence fills two glasses of water, handing me one. We drink them in silence and discard them next to the sink as a knowing feeling tickles the back of my neck. We're letting go tonight. Of everything that we've clung to so tightly our entire lives. For me, the idea that safety and peace come from the power to please people, to keep situations under control. For Florence, it's something so similar, it's no wonder we find relief and ease in one another. I only hope that she feels loved by me, regardless of the things she can provide or accomplish for me.

I never wanted her service.

I want her.

She takes me by the hand and leads me to *our* bedroom. A perfect little room, with the perfect little view of that damn gorgeous tower. A room that has only known us this week. It hasn't seen Florence try to unpack for me or bend over backward to please me. And I'm no longer carrying any guilt past our threshold.

It's just us.

On the off chance we're not on the same page, I wrap my arm around her waist as she closes our door, the plaster of my cast catching a little on the skirt of her dress. I push her hair over her shoulder and kiss her neck, reveling in the sweet saltiness of her sweat, before I plant my hand on the door in front of her.

She takes a deep breath in my arms.

"I understand that you can't promise me forever. Or even tomorrow," I whisper on her skin, and she presses harder into me in response. "But how about tonight? I'd regret not taking this moment with you, if you want to take it with me, too."

She spins in my arms and grabs two fistfuls of my shirt, pulling me into her, and our lips connect in a deep, needy kiss. My hips pin her to the door as hers begin to move against me in their usual wanting way. My new addiction. I push the strap of her dress down her shoulder, eager for more skin, for more delicious places to lay my kisses.

"Wait," she whispers, and nudges me back. She turns and pulls her hair over one shoulder, revealing her zipper.

I take the metal tongue in my fingers and brush my lips against her ear. "You're sure?"

"Eaden. This has never felt more right than with you. Please." She turns so our lips are so close to brushing. "Take off my dress."

I pull the zipper, careful to not snag it or otherwise interrupt what has already become the most joyous moment of my life. It stops right past the curve of her hips, and I softly part the fabric that is so quintessentially Florence, it's as if I'm diving into her core. The farther I push, the more of her beauty is revealed. The dip of her muscles to meet her spine, the glorious swath of her soft pale skin, a tattoo of a bloom-covered dagger I've never seen before. The fabric falls from her shoulders, and she reaches for my hand, pulling it in front of her to place upon her heart.

We stand like that for a moment, as I hold the rhythm of her in my hand.

"Don't break my heart," she whispers.

"Break it?" I kiss her shoulder. "I cherish it."

A moment of cold reality settles on me. I know at least one very untrustworthy person in her recent sexual history, and I can't go on until I know it's safe. "Flo, I uh, don't have any STIs. Have you been tested recently?"

"Two months ago. All good." I hesitate, so she adds, "I haven't slept with her—with anyone—since before that. Do you feel okay with that?"

"Yes. Yes, thank you."

She slides my hand to cup her breast, her nipple hardening. The warm weight of her fills my palm, and I feel myself undoing. Uncoiling and untangling from my core. I drag my teeth up her shoulder to her neck, where I nip at her lightly until she moans and reaches behind her to grip the back of my neck, sinking my bite farther into her skin how she wants it.

Her deeper groan and the pressure of her ass against my groin confirms it. I pull away, and she whines at the distance, but I'm at a bit of a disadvantage with only one hand.

"Come here, love." I pull her away from the door, my breath hitching at the sight of her bare breasts, unmarked by freckles. Like a fresh snowfall. Her nipples, the sweet rose color of her deepest blush. My mouth waters to taste them.

She pushes her dress over the pronounced curve of her hips and lets it fall at her feet, the flowers of it piling on one another in a puddle of blossoms. Her eyes grow hazy as she works on the buttons of my shirt. One by one by one. Her warm breath gracing more and more of my skin as she goes. Until she breaks into an adorable, if not a little out of place, chuckle and lightly slaps me on the chest, resting her forehead on the back of her hand as she laughs.

"The fucking fanny pack," she says between laughing fits.

I let out a long groan. "Jesus Christ, it's like I can't even feel the thing on me anymore. Get it off, get it off."

She gives me another pat on the chest as she raises an eyebrow in a playfully sexy smirk. She lets her hand fall down the front of my bra, down my stomach, to the buckle of my pack. I feel my nipples harden at her grazing fingers. Though I've never been the most confident about my body or my looks, I want to be bare for her. Want her to look at me and see every pockmark, every freckle, and every scar. What does it matter what I look like when I belong to her? This body and this heart are hers.

She unclasps the buckle and tosses the pack on the chair while I race through the last couple of buttons on my shirt.

"Hey," she scolds. "Those were for me to get."

I peck her on the cheek. "Too slow."

"Fine." She reaches for the button on my shorts. "These are mine, then." She undoes my button and pulls down the zipper while I slide out of my shirt and reach to unclasp my bra. She kisses smiles to my stomach. "Eager," she whispers against my skin.

I kick off my shorts and toss my clothes on top of my pack, then I stand matching her in just my underwear. "Come here," I say, opening my arms for her. The sensation of her soft breasts against mine is unparalleled, and I thank my lucky stars for being in this gorgeously intimate moment between two women.

"If we do this, I may not be able to let you go," she murmurs against my neck.

"Isn't it already done?"

She pulls back to look in my eyes. The sight of her, nearly naked and completely vulnerable for me, is something I never dreamt I could have. The slight tug upward of her brows hints at worry.

"We're going to be okay," I say.

She nods as I back her up to the edge of the bed and guide her down, carefully balancing my weight on my elbow just above my cast as I lie over her, peppering her skin with kisses. Goose bumps form trails beneath my lips as she shivers from my touch. I slink lower, dragging soft teeth over her hip bone, until I make it to her panties. Plain navy with daisies. Simple in the sexiest way. Effortless like the woman herself. The heat of her caresses my lips before I even touch the damp cotton between her thighs. I indulge in it, rubbing my mouth over her panties, teasing her. Teasing myself. Until I truly can't stand to wait any longer. We have both been patient enough over the years. Waiting, when we weren't even aware of it, for each other.

She lifts her hips to help me rid her of her panties, and we both release puffs of laughter as they stubbornly stick to my cast when I try to toss them away.

"They seem to like me," I joke, finally flinging them to the ground.

"They're not the only thing," she says, pulling my focus back to her.

Drinking in the sight of her is a nourishment I didn't know I needed. Lying back, she smiles softly, offering her body to me. I settle between her thighs, willing myself to go slow, to memorize and savor every detail of her in case I never get to live this moment again. My mouth watering, I work my way inward, softly licking up her wetness from inner thigh, to soft crease, to silky lips I can't help but pull into my mouth and suck. A contented sigh spills from her as I slip my tongue over her smooth center and groan.

The taste of her sends me. Soaks me. I dip two fingers inside her as she pushes onto me, pulling me deep, and rocking her hips. Teaching me her favorite rhythms. Just how she wants me curled into her. I keep a constant slow lapping on her clit as she swells for me.

I never compare the women I have been with to one another, but it is impossible for me not to exalt her. To place her in a gilded spot above all. The smoothness of her skin, the delicate salinity of her come, how she throbs against my tongue and refuses to unclench my fingers. Not until the waves of aftershock subside.

Taking a deep breath, she drapes her arm over her face and relaxes. "Slowly, please," she says on staggered breaths.

I ease my fingers from her, not letting any drops of her go to waste. Careful to avoid her most sensitive areas, I kiss her glistening skin, unwilling to leave my perch just yet.

"Fucking hell," she groans. "Get up here."

I kiss her one more time and shimmy up her body, careful to avoid scratching her with my cast.

"Hi," I say through what I'm positive is the world's biggest grin.

"Hi, honey." She pulls me into a deep kiss, her needy hands gripping my face. "So this may sound a little weird, but I really want to try something with you. Think you can receive it?"

I settle on my side next to her, brushing the underside of her breasts with my knuckles. "Of course I can. This is our sex life. It's safe here. And free here."

"Okay. I trust you." She catches my fingers and raises them to her mouth, running her tongue over my fingertips before softly sucking them clean. "I really like the way I taste on your tongue. And how my come tastes on your fingers."

"Yeah?" My voice is shaky with want, I'm so fucking turned on.

"Yeah. I really want to know what we taste like together."

I roll on my back and let her pull off my destroyed underwear in one quick tug, too absorbed in her and in us to feel any shred of the standard self-consciousness that normally distracts me with a new partner. Florence doesn't feel like a new partner at all. Making love to her is innate. Comfortable and exhilarating.

She lies alongside me. "You're fucking gorgeous, Eaden."

"Thank you," I say. She makes me believe it with how she scans my body, her lip slipping between her teeth.

She drags her hand down my stomach, and I instinctively spread my legs for her. Her fingers are slow and curious as she explores me, making lazy strokes and delicious circles. She takes one of my nipples into her mouth as she slides into me, making me buck in pleasure. I try not to come too quickly, wanting to savor this. Enjoy it. But I'm already so on edge, I don't know how long I can last.

She pulls out of me, her fingers glistening in the glow of the streetlamps through our window. I can't help but touch myself as I watch her taste me from her middle finger. She groans and reaches between her thighs, coating herself again. She dips her lips to my ear. "Can I fuck you with my come?"

I make a noise that sounds vaguely like a *fuck* and *yeah* but is more primal than phonetic and push her hand between my thighs, needing her now. She covers my mouth with a kiss and drapes a leg over my thigh as she slides inside, fucking me softly. Under the safety of her body and with her fingers hitting the perfect deep, slow strokes, I come hard, shaking in her embrace.

She kisses my temple and whispers, "I've got you, baby. Easy."

My chest rises and falls in hard breaths, my heartbeat skipping away, unwilling to calm while my limbs melt where they lie.

"Can I pull out?" she asks, pressing another kiss to my forehead.

I nod, unable to form words yet. I feel a warm trickle follow her fingers.

"You're fucking incredible," she whispers, musing at her soaking fingers. "Do you want to taste us?"

I nod again. She brings her hand to my mouth, and I open for her, ready to take her in, but she holds a finger to still me. "Mm-mm. Not like that." I drop my head back as she runs her fingers across my lips. She nods. "Okay."

I lick my lips of us.

Fully understanding for the first time what sex and connection is supposed to feel like.

My heart rate calms. I wiggle my fingers in my cast. A smile spreads across my face.

"Ecstasy and peace," I murmur.

❖

Florence stirs in my arms and wakes me. The room is dark, save the orange glow spilling through the blinds. I brush a piece of her tickling hair off my face and wiggle my fingers in the cast. Only my pinkie responds. The rest are numb from the weight of her head on my arm. It's hard to care about blood flow when I feel every breath she takes.

"I hope you choose me," I whisper.

Hoping maybe she hears me in her dreams.

She scoots her hips a little tighter into me. "It's you," she says, her words barely audible over the whir of the fan and her deep sleepy breaths.

I hope she means it.

CHAPTER TWENTY-ONE

The plane lands in Dublin with a skip and a thud. We gather our belongings as we taxi to the gate, our fellow passengers seemingly anxious to get off what was an admittedly bumpy flight. Even Florence turned a bit pale with the final jolt of turbulence. I closed my eyes and focused on my Aunt Mary. Tried to imagine what it will be like to meet her tomorrow. If she'll resemble my mom at all or say a million times how the last time she saw me, I was just a baby. Mostly, I wonder if she'll let me read the letter from my mom.

Though I would never ask.

I shoot her a quick message saying we've landed safely and resend confirmation of our train arrival in Cobh for tomorrow afternoon. Our time in Paris was lovely in more ways than I could have imagined, but I'm excited for the final leg of the trip and to deliver this letter.

On our last day in Paris, we spent the afternoon walking through our neighborhood, recounting our highs and lows of the trip so far. We bought a bottle of red wine, a baguette, fresh butter, and some sliced fruit from the market and brought it back to the apartment for a snacky dinner.

"Do you remember what you said last night?" I asked, pouring her a glass.

She buttered me a piece of the baguette and handed it to me on a plate. "Well, it depends on what you're referring to. We said a lot last night." Her cheeks flushed with an adorable pink blush.

"It doesn't matter. As long as we're okay."

She sipped her wine and grinned. "Yeah. We're more than okay."

I trusted her words, though the number of texts she was receiving that night and the frowns she paid them had me anxious. We washed the dishes and packed our bags, wanting to get an early jump on our day of travel the next morning. Though we didn't explicitly talk about the night before or what it meant or what was next, the evening was casual and comfortable, filled with little touches and easy laughter until we fell asleep in each other's arms.

The passengers in front of us grab their luggage from the overhead storage and clear the aisle for us to do the same. Florence grabs my bag for me and helps me slide into its straps, then I follow her off the plane.

"Any idea how you want to spend our one night in Dublin?" she asks as we navigate toward the exit of the airport.

I have an idea. Given my Aunt Mary lives alone in a three-bedroom house, I know this is probably the last night Florence and I get to spend in the same room, and when we get back to Atlanta, there's no telling what we'll be. If we'll be anything. As far as Dublin goes, I just want to cherish her company and our last moments alone in this haven we've built.

"Drinking a Guinness, of course," I say.

She grins. "I think I can make that dream come true for you. Let's check in at the hotel and then find you a pub?"

"Deal."

❖

The pub we end up at is the most standard Irish pub I can imagine, with dark wooden booths and peeling walls littered with Guinness posters and Redbreast advertisements. A few TVs play soccer and rugby, though I can't tell if they're live or replays. Irish rock flows through the speaker system. It's perfect, really.

I order a Guinness and the fish and chips, and Flo orders the same. The food arrives in a flash, smelling like deep-fried heaven. We shake malt vinegar over everything and toast to Ireland before we dig in.

"So can I ask, how's the Riley situation?"

She rolls her eyes and wipes her fingers on an already greasy napkin. "Diving right in, are we?"

I shrug. "I guess. I just want to be aware of what's going on. It's obviously close to home for me."

"I was just joking. I totally get it." She takes a swig of beer. "She's livid. Sees it as me cheating on her with you." She pauses, her chest rising with a deep sigh. "Basically, she wants me to cut you off, or she'll cut me off."

"Cut you off?"

"Yeah. Tell her mom she's uncomfortable with me living in the family home, dissolve our friendship, that type of thing."

"Shit." I drop the fry I was holding. "What did you say?"

"I told her I needed time to process everything and that we could talk when I got back." She shrugs. "Eaden, you mean so much to me, and Paris"—she shakes her head, her eyes shining with unshed tears—"well, I didn't think I'd get to experience something like that in my life. But I meant what I told Riley. I have to process this before rushing into something. This is already causing so much fallout. I've been searching for new places to live or even just to crash for a while, but I need a little time to sort it out when we get home. And so do you, Eaden."

I clear my throat and push the half-eaten fish and chips to the edge of the table. "I have had a lot to process. But how I feel about you isn't one of those things. I get that you're not ready to let go of her. But I know what I want, so I hope you let me know when you decide what you want, too."

She looks away and wipes under her eye where a tear has slipped over the edge. "I want you," she whispers.

I know she's not lying. Florence doesn't lie. "But you want her, too."

"Not the way that I want you. But I don't want to lose her," she says.

It would be easier to believe that Florence is just scared of change. Given her scars and the abandonment she's already suffered, it is beyond reasonable for her to be afraid of losing the stability she has carved out for herself. A home tucked in the basement of a family who loves her. An ex who is, for better or worse, a constant in her life. Familiar things.

But I know it's not just that. I know she still loves Riley in a way. Though it may be in a different way than she used to, their connection is strong enough to pull her from me, and there's nothing I can do about that.

Florence loves me enough to choose me.

Or she doesn't.

And if she doesn't, then we aren't what I thought. I'll take the things I've learned and strength I've built in myself and move on.

Because I can't fight for someone who won't fight for me.

She excuses herself to use the restroom, and I watch her dress flow about her knees as she walks. My chest aches at the possibility of losing her. I would be okay. I'm a stronger person than I was when I left for this trip, but damn. I'm pretty sure it would go against the principles of physics for me and Florence to be apart.

We fill our walk back to the hotel with light chatter about where we hope to visit next, neither of us hinting at traveling together or any other part of our futures we may share. I think we're both unsure about how to navigate this evening and where we stand with one another. We wait to cross the street, and she lets her head rest on my shoulder. I don't shrug away. I'm not mad at her. I adore her. But I don't make any moves to further close the distance between us.

When we make it back to the room, I plug in my phone and reply to a text from my dad. It feels nice to check in with him, to know that someone has my back and is rooting for me. Florence lays out her outfit for tomorrow and tucks her bag back in the closet. It's another standard hotel room. Nice and clean, with tall ceilings and crisp white bedding on the two queen beds.

"There's a museum just down the road that's open for another two hours if you want to check it out with me," she says.

I lay my phone on the nightstand and turn to respond. "I think I'm going to have an early night. Just want to recharge before we get to Aunt Mary's tomorrow. I'm a little travel weary."

"Totally."

"But you should go. I don't want to hold you back," I add.

A look of hurt passes over her face, but she recovers quickly. "Okay. You sure you've got everything you need? Anything I can grab you while I'm out?"

I flop on my bed and wave the TV remote. "I'm set. Just going to watch a bad movie and chill."

"Okay. I have my phone. I'll be back in a bit. Just be safe," she says.

"Of course. You too."

She smiles with one side of her face as she slips out the door. It feels wrong to not go with her. To be acting so distant. I'm not trying to be cold. I'm just trying to respect how she feels and meet her where she's at. Plus, it's hard to continue to be wildly vulnerable with someone when I don't know if she's about to break my heart or not.

I scroll through the channels until I strike gold. *Legally Blonde.* My eyes grow heavy as I snuggle into the covers. Sure, part of me wanted her tonight. Part of me wanted to say *fuck it* and indulge in the chemistry between us for one more night. Even if it was the last time. But I can't.

In the past, I wasn't so sure what I deserved. But now I know.

I'm pretty great. A normal human amount of messy. Some think I'm cute, too. And I deserve to be chosen.

I drift off to sleep, feeling good about taking some space. I hope it will help her gain some clarity, too. Whether that clarity brings her closer to me or not. I truly want her to choose whatever will make her happiest. Me, Riley, neither of us. I need her happy.

❖

The room door opens, and I crack an eye to make sure it's Florence. Her back is to me as she quietly guides the door back into its frame, trying not to wake me.

"Hey," I mutter, my voice heavy with sleep. "How was it?"

She stoops by the side of my bed and kisses my brow. "Shh. Go back to sleep."

I nod and close my eyes, letting the quiet sounds of her getting ready for bed lull me back to sleep. I hear her get under the covers of the other bed, disappointed and relieved. She's respecting my need for space tonight. But even in my dreamlike state, I ache for her.

Morning seems to arrive quickly, my alarm taking me off guard. I hit snooze and wipe my face, feeling groggy, though I must've slept around ten hours. I can't remember the last time I slept for so long. But the body needs what it needs. Florence is still asleep as I creep past her to the bathroom and indulge in a much-needed hot shower.

Today is the big day.

In about six hours, we will be pulling into the Cobh train station and taking a bus to my Aunt Mary's house. She offered to meet us at the station, but I refused. She may be in great shape, but she's still an eighty-year-old who shouldn't be going out of her way even more than she already is for us. I rinse the hotel shampoo from my hair, the zesty lemon scent rejuvenating my senses. Though Aunt Mary is Riley's relative, too, I'm glad she's not here to overpower every conversation and make everything about her.

I want to learn about my mom and our family and Aunt Mary. What her life has been like in Cobh. What our family history in the city contains. Riley has a way of filling every square inch of a space with herself. Like a gas.

I shudder as I turn off the water and think about getting home to Atlanta and what—or who—waits for me there. Nothing will be the same no matter what happens with me and Florence. The consequences will catch up to me either way.

Riley will be in a fit of rage no matter what.

It will be something I'll have to face. But I've faced worse.

Florence sleeps peacefully as we pull into Cobh, her head on my shoulder and knees drawn up to her chest. I don't know how she folds into a pretzel so comfortably, and I briefly consider doing yoga when I get back to Atlanta. The train continues to slow, and I savor every second of her cuddled up to me before we're in a new place that doesn't allow for this type of intimacy anymore. It makes me regret taking space last night.

Facing a week of not being able to touch her makes my stomach sink.

I take a deep breath as the train comes to a stop and she stirs awake. This time in Cobh isn't about her; it isn't about us. It's about spending time with Aunt Mary and learning about my family and my mom.

"We're here?" Flo asks as she sits up and wipes her eyes, her cheek pink from lying on me.

Damn. She's adorable.

"Yep. We're here." I grab her bag from the seat across from us before I carefully fish my cast through the strap of mine.

"Don't be nervous," she says.

I tighten my straps and clip the buckle across my chest, patting my pockets to ensure I have my phone and wallet. "How do you know I'm nervous?"

She grins and gives me a little shake by the straps. "I know you. You sway from side to side when you're anxious."

"I do?"

"You do."

She stares at me for a moment before she pulls my straps hard, and I stumble into her kiss. I didn't know how badly I needed her until her warm mouth is on mine. Just as my tongue brushes over hers, she pulls away and wipes her lips with her thumb, a devious grin where my kiss used to be.

"Now I'm ready," she says.

I stare, speechless.

"Come on." She takes my good hand and leads me off the train to find our bus.

I follow, pressing the back of my hand to my hot cheek, bracing myself for whatever is to come this week.

CHAPTER TWENTY-TWO

"We're doing shots at the pub for every time Aunt Mary mentions how big I am or how the last time she saw me, I was just a baby," I mutter as we turn the corner to her house.

"Oh, so we're partying in Cobh, eh?" She laughs.

"Odds are high, yes."

The train ride into Cobh is filled with beautiful rolling hills and plentiful countryside, but to me, the town itself is the real showstopper. I didn't expect how colorful and vibrant the architecture would be. Or how the harbor shimmers under the warm sunlight and wafts a briny scent that beckons people to want to board a boat for the day. The small, charming town is a welcome respite from the bustling cities we've stayed in before.

"Wow. It's beautiful," Florence says as we start down the main drive that leads into the small community of homes.

"It's gorgeous."

The homes are almost identical, only varying minimally in size and shape or the flowers planted in their front yards. The stark white of the houses pops against the deep green of the field they were built in. It's hard to judge the distance to the shimmering water in the background, but I imagine we could walk to the beach in a half hour or so.

"I didn't know it was so close to the water," I say.

She shrugs as we navigate to the right house. "I guess if a coastal town is small enough, everyone is close to the water."

"That's fair." We wave to an older gentleman picking weeds in his yard. "I think it's that one on the right." I turn my phone to make sure we're going the right way.

She peeks over my shoulder. "Yeah. Number fourteen. That's it." She squeezes my shoulder when we stop walking. "Come on. You've got this. It's going to be great."

I nod. "Yeah. You're right."

I take her hand and walk to number fourteen, needing the strength that being connected to her gives me. The yard is small but precisely managed, with crisply lined garden beds and wind chimes that sing a deep rich tone in the breeze. It's at once professional and homey. I know she used to run a bed and breakfast, so it makes sense she'd be used to its upkeep.

I squeeze Flo's hand before I drop it and knock on the dark wooden door.

It opens in a flash, and I jump back, momentarily stunned.

Aunt Mary beams at me, her cloudy blue eyes wide with excitement and her thick, knotted hands clasped over her heart. I don't know what I was expecting, but it wasn't this. She wears her silver hair pulled back in a bun, and chunky purple glasses balance precariously on the tip of her nose. She isn't in a boring beige sweater but a colorful dress of burnt oranges and mossy greens. A stark difference to the all-white of her house.

Aunt Mary seems to be the epitome of a youthful soul.

"Oh, girls!" She grabs my face with both hands and plants a fat kiss right on my cheek, then turns to Flo and does the same thing. "I'm so glad you made it safely." She claps in obvious delight. "And that you decided to spend some of your vacation with me, well, I just can't tell you how much it means to me." She beckons us inside, barely taking a breath between words. "I hoped that one of my nieces or nephews would come visit one day, and here you are."

"Thank you for having us," I manage to say.

She whirls around on me. "Oh, Eaden. Look at you." Her hands grab my cheeks again as she observes me. "Look how grown you are! And what happened here?" She shoots a concerned look to my cast.

"Oh, I tripped in Paris and broke my wrist. But it's healing fine, I think." I give it a waggle. "Just itchy and annoying, but it doesn't hurt."

"I like the green." She winks. "Last time I saw you was when your parents came to visit before Sean started preschool, and you were just in nappies, barely crawling at that point. And now you're a beautiful grown woman. And a smart one, I hear."

I manage to sneak a side glance to Florence. *You owe me a shot.*

She drops my face and turns her attention to Flo. "And Florence. Welcome, welcome. I know you've been close to our family for a while. You're dating wily Riley, is that right?"

"Um." Flo clears her throat in obvious discomfort. "I used to date Riley. We're just friends now, but Aunt Susan has been kind enough to rent me their basement while I'm in grad school."

Aunt Mary rubs her chest in affection. "Susan always had the biggest heart." She turns to me. "And don't get me started on Eileen. Your mother was my favorite. So spirited and full of curiosity. It was no wonder she became a science teacher." A soft smile overtakes her. "Eileen had this uncanny ability to connect with people, put them at ease, make them feel loved." She shakes her head. "I'm so very sorry, Eaden."

I swallow, still trying to adjust to the whiplash of Aunt Mary. "Thank you. She always spoke so fondly of you. When she gave me the letter with your name on it, I knew I wanted to deliver it in person and meet you." I run my hand through my hair. "Well, meet you again since I was too young the first time."

"And I'm so very glad you did." She turns and walks through the living area, barely giving us time to take in the warmth of the decor.

I try to look around as we follow closely behind her. The couches are a worn navy, with big fluffy cushions that give the impression of coziness. Paintings with soft brushstrokes depicting different landscapes hang on hunter green walls. A small fire crackles lazily in the woodstove, though the house already feels toasty. Her space is as inviting and warm as she is.

"As you know, this used to be a bed and breakfast, but I can't be bothered to keep up with the business anymore. Connor, a boy from town who's in university, helps me maintain the yard and any small fixes the house needs. He's a good boy. But for you two, we're in full operation."

She opens the door to the first room. It's fully *Titanic* themed, with giant steamships printed on every surface and a quote stenciled on the wall that says, "It's just the tip of the iceberg." A battered original movie poster hangs on the far wall next to a shadow box of museum tickets.

When Aunt Mary isn't looking, I mouth to Florence, "Oh my God."

She chuckles quietly into her hand.

"This is incredible, Aunt Mary," I say.

"Well, as you know, the *Titanic* set sail from Cobh in 1912. And the tourists who used to stayed here loved, loved, loved this room." She turns to me and smiles. "This is your room, Eaden."

I drop my bag on the bed and thank her.

She walks into the hallway and points to a closed door. "That's the guest bathroom that you two will share." She pushes open another door on the other side of the bathroom. "And this is your room, Florence. The Guinness room."

Just as the *Titanic* room was dripping in ship paraphernalia, the Guinness room is dripping in the beer equivalent. Old-school advertisements for the local legend of beer covers the walls floor to ceiling, and the bed even sports a plush, creamy-looking pillow pint of beer.

"This is *amazing*." Florence spins, taking it all in. "Thank you so much for hosting us. Your home is lovely and so welcoming."

"Any time. I love having the company," Aunt Mary says. She squeezes our shoulders. "I'll leave you to it to unpack and settle in. Take your time, and when you're ready, I have some snacks and tea prepared in the garden for us."

"Thank you," we say together, and Aunt Mary leaves us.

I close the door so there's only a sliver of open space between the door and the jamb. "Holy shit," I whisper, my eyes wide. "This place is insane."

Florence chuckles as she unzips her pack. "Yeah, insanely awesome."

"That's easy for you to say. You got the Guinness room." I roll my eyes and plop on the bed next to her bag. "You don't have to be constantly reminded of one of the most infamous maritime tragedies of all time. It's all fun and good vibes in here."

"Oh, don't be so dramatic." She throws a sock at my head. "You know, if you're scared, you can always sneak into my room after your aunt goes to sleep."

I can't help but grin. After sleeping apart last night, I miss her. "You'd like that, wouldn't you?" I tease.

She bends close to my ear, the smell of her shampoo teasing me right back. "Why don't you give it a try and find out?"

Her words sit low and heavy, building an incessant need inside me. Before she pulls away, I wrap my hand behind her neck and kiss her. Slow and deep. A needy kiss from a needy woman. Her lips are full and soft, slightly salty from our sweaty journey into town. I love when she tastes like this, when I can taste the adventure and life on her. I don't care to taste her toothpaste or mouthwash. I want *her*.

Her fingers tug my hair as she slips her tongue in my mouth. I'm instantly wet for her. Pushing her bag out of the way with my cast, I gather her into my lap with my good arm, and she straddles me, settling her weight right atop all my need for her. We grind into each other with desperation, and I can feel the heat from between her legs. I momentarily worry about getting caught, but I heard a door close after Aunt Mary left, and I assume she's outside already.

"Fuck," I mutter against her hot neck as she reaches under my shirt and massages my breasts. I can't fucking take it anymore. I need her. I run my hand up her thigh, under her sundress, and groan when I hit the seam of her panties.

She grips my throat lightly to pull my face back in front of her. "Yes. I need you, too," she says, kissing the words into my mouth, giving me consent without me even having to ask.

I slip my fingers under the warm cotton and glide them through her wetness, not wasting any time. Moaning at the softness, I push my fingers into her. She grips my shirt in two tight handfuls and rides me hard and fast, biting my lip until I think she may pierce it. The pain makes me even wetter for her and helps her keep quiet as we make fast and sloppy love.

She abandons my shirt and grabs a handful of my hair instead, pulling it taut as she sinks her teeth into my neck and sucks hard. I bite my lip where her teeth used to be to keep from making any noise, though I desperately want to shout her name.

"I'm gonna come," she pants in my ear. "I'm gonna come on you, baby."

I hold her tight and fuck her with deep strokes until she tightens around me, her pussy around my fingers and her grip in my hair. She groans against my neck, and I feel it everywhere as she releases and crumples in my arms.

"Fuck," she mutters, taking a moment to come back down to earth. I kiss her hard before she slides off my lap, her hand covering her mouth and her eyes wide. "Oh my God. You have to change before we go outside."

"What do you mean?" I follow her stare to my lap and grin. "Oh. I see."

"I'm sorry." She runs a shaky hand through her hair. "It's your fault, really. For getting me so wet." The adorable blush pinkens her chest. "I'm not normally so messy."

I touch the wet spot on my shorts. It turns me on even more than I could imagine, but we have to clean up and get outside. There's no more time for extracurriculars. I stand and unzip my shorts. She watches me take her hand with a glint in her eyes. I push her past my underwear so she can feel how desperately wet I am.

"Fuck, Eaden." She groans as she slips through me. "I need you in my mouth. Tonight. Please."

"Tonight." I kiss her and pull her hand away from me, zipping my shorts back up. "Let's clean up and get out there. I feel bad."

"Me too." She lightly slaps my shoulder. "You started it."

"Oh, I know." I walk past her to my room, a stupid grin on my stupid face.

I can see why Aunt Mary is easy to adore. She has this effortless way of making us feel seen and loved for all the quirky little things that make us different. Her positive demeanor is infectious, as evident by my cheeks growing sore from smiling. We sit in the back garden chatting with Mary among the roses and sunflowers, bees happily buzzing around us, for hours. Until tea turns into a pint, and snacks turn into the most delicious summer stew I've ever had.

We pile our empty bowls in the sink, and Florence and I wash the dishes as Mary lights the stove in the family room again.

"She may be the coolest person I've ever met," Florence whispers as I hand her a bowl to dry.

I peek over my shoulder to watch Aunt Mary stoke the fire and settle into her mustard-colored armchair. She waves at me and smiles. I turn back to the sink and scrub the spoons. "She's amazing. I didn't know what to expect, but it wasn't this."

We fall into one of our comfortable quiets as we work together to clean up. I can't help but think that if Riley was here, she would've left the dishes to our aunt, accepting the hospitality and a chance to be lazy over helping the woman who's putting us up and cooking for us. But she's not here. I catch Flo's eye and grin. It just feels right, being here with her. How she treats people and interacts with them makes me proud. Asking questions, getting to know them, exhibiting true curiosity about a place and a life that isn't her own.

It's refreshing.

We finish drying the final dishes, and I follow her to the comfy sofa next to the armchair. She sits close enough to touch my knee with hers but not too close to arouse suspicion from Aunt Mary. Or "Mary," as she likes to be called.

"Do you have any more stories of my mom when she was little?"

Mary looks to the ceiling in consideration, tapping her chin. It's random moments like these when I see Mom in her. It kind of takes my breath away.

"Oh, I have so many stories of Eileen." A grin deepens her wrinkles. "The question is if you want to hear them. She was a spirited one, your mum."

I look to Florence—I don't know why—but she squeezes my knee briefly and nods.

"Tell us one," I say.

She chuckles and pulls the chunky knit throw over her legs. "Well, she was head over heels for your father and brought him to meet me the second they graduated college. I remember the letter she wrote me, asking if they could stay for a week in June. Of course, I said yes." Her chuckles overtake her again, and she wipes her lips with her knuckles. "Your father was so charming, I could easily see why Eileen had fallen as hard as she had. The moment they walked through the door, they couldn't keep their hands off each other."

Flo and I exchange a quick grin, and she puts an extra inch of space between us. It's refreshing, hearing about my parents' love story without the stifling feeling of guilt or rage tightening around my throat. All I feel is gratitude for the chance to hear about it more.

"It was cute, really," she continues, "until one night after dinner, they excused themselves to the garden." She rolls her eyes, hands tossed in the sky.

"Uh-oh," I say, peeking through my fingers. "I feel like I know where this is going."

She tosses her head back and laughs a deep belly laugh. "Well, I walked by the window, and clear as day, saw Eileen giving your dad a handy on my antique bench!"

Florence and I roar in laughter, hands over bellies, tears welling in our eyes.

"I walked straight to the garage and grabbed the blowhorn I have from managing the summer solstice 5k. I cracked the window overlooking the garden from the *Titanic* room, and I laid on that blowhorn loud and hard. Your mum jumped so high, she almost took your dad's willy with her!" She takes a break to laugh just as hard as we are. "He came limping in the kitchen, holding his willy, asking for an ice pack. I gave it to him under the condition he acted with respect under my roof. Even though I knew damn well it was your mum's idea, I said, 'Damn it, Andrew. It's not like I'm making you sleep in separate rooms. You keep those shenanigans to the bedroom, do you understand me?' He was hopping from foot to foot, his face all twisted in pain."

"What'd he say?" I ask, tears streaming down my face from laughter.

"He promised to be a gentleman and to never allow something like that to happen again." She shrugs. "So I rewarded him with an ice pack for his penis and my blessing to marry my favorite niece." She shoots me a sharp look. "Don't you go telling folks I said that. If anyone asks, I love all my nieces and nephews equally."

"Your secret is safe with me," I say.

Mary makes us a cup of mint tea, and we continue chatting for another couple of hours. She tells us about my grandfather, her brother, and how he used to take Mary and whoever her current boyfriend was sailing so he could gauge if the guy was a good fit or not. They were really close growing up, until Mary married the one guy who was a better sailor than Grandpa, Uncle Julien, and Grandpa emigrated to the United States to go to the school of architecture at Notre Dame, where he met my grandma.

Once the conversation slows and we all become a little more

horizontal than vertical, we say good night and make our way to our own bedrooms. When Mary closes her door and turns off her bedroom light, I join Florence in the bathroom to brush my teeth.

She grins at me in the mirror as she brushes, toothpaste foaming between her lips. I return her mischievous smile and grab my toothbrush, gently nudging her for some space in front of the sink. Rolling her eyes, she spits a ferocious stream of toothpaste and water down the drain and tosses her brush into the cup, bumping me on her way out. I watch myself in the mirror, hardly recognizing this new version of myself. I'm on the precipice of having my heart broken, and yet, I'm heralding in that terrifying moment with something akin to glee.

I can't tell if I'm unafraid because I'm so confident that me and Florence are meant to be or if it's because I feel so complete now. I'm no longer flailing, desperately searching for something to cling to so I don't drown in my dark.

Maybe it's both.

I splash a handful of water over my face and wipe it on the hand towel. I'm not sleeping alone tonight. Aunt Mary basically gave us permission to do whatever we wanted behind closed doors, and I intend to take full advantage of that this week.

Tiptoeing down the hallway, I pause to make sure I don't hear any noises from Aunt Mary's room. Though I don't feel as though I'm breaking the rules, I don't want to deal with the questions from her about Riley if she were to find out. I make it to Flo's door and knock as softly I can. She opens it quickly and ushers me in, looking adorable in her linen sleep set.

"Can I sleep with you tonight?" I whisper, but she's already pulled down the covers to invite me in.

I crawl in after her, opening my arms for her to back into me. She lays her head on my bicep, and I hold her tight with the other arm. Not tightly enough, apparently, as she pulls my hand across her chest and kisses my knuckles.

"Good night, my tide," she whispers.

I kiss her hair. "Good night, my moon."

CHAPTER TWENTY-THREE

I startle awake in the middle of the night, not knowing what time it is but sensing it must be around two or three in the morning. It isn't a nightmare that wakes me—thankfully, I don't have those anymore—but the sound of Aunt Mary flushing her toilet. I guess the walls are thin enough to hear that two rooms away. Good to know.

I close my eyes and indulge in how it feels to hold Florence as she sleeps, her chest rising and falling against my arm, her hips tucked tightly into mine, nothing but thin sleep clothes between us. Pushing her hair away from her neck, I lean in and press a gentle kiss to her skin. She stirs and scoots in tighter to me.

"That feels nice," she whispers.

So I kiss her again, this time letting my tongue trace down to her collarbone, where I lightly suck until she gives me a sleepy moan, and her ass begins to move against me. She takes my hand and slips it inside her shirt, letting me play with her hardening nipples as she reaches between her own thighs to stroke herself.

"I'm already soaked," she whispers.

"Good. That makes two of us."

She pulls my hand away and turns in my arms, pushing me back against the mattress before she climbs on top of me. Pushing up my shirt, she bows to take one of my nipples into her mouth and gently sucks as she grinds her wetness against my thigh. I want to explode already. As if reading my mind, she clamps a hand over my mouth as she sits up and reaches behind her with the other hand. I give her a quick nod, and she slips under my waistband, wasting no time diving into me.

I nip at her fingers, the lingering taste of her pussy driving me mad for her.

"Shh," she chides, removing her hand. "Be good and quiet, and I'll make you come in my mouth. Deal?"

"Fuck," I groan and nod, clamping my own hand over my mouth as she slides down my body and slips off my shorts.

She spreads my thighs and devours me, licking, sucking, and fucking until my entire body shakes in her grip and I come with her tongue deep in my pussy. It has never been so easy for me to let go. To give into pleasure. I'm in awe as she wipes her mouth on my thighs and climbs back up to lay her head on my chest, tapping the rhythm of my racing heart on my stomach. I stroke her hair and ponder how I could have gone my entire life without experiencing sex like this.

"I meant it," she whispers and turns to face me, her eyes still shining, even in the dark. "It's you. I know it in my gut and my heart. I still need some time to sort through things and get myself in a position for this to work while respecting the people who have supported me."

My heart soars at her words. "I understand. Of course."

"We'll figure it out though, together? When we get home?"

"We will."

She closes her eyes and rests her head back on my chest. It only takes a moment for her breathing to deepen and for me to fall asleep with her.

I wake up alone to the sound of birds chirping in the garden. I look around for Florence, but she must have snuck out without a sound. Or I just slept incredibly hard, which is more likely since she isn't very stealthy, and I was incredibly wiped after our middle-of-the-night lovemaking. Okay. Maybe she is stealthy. I wipe my eyes and slip out of bed, checking the coast is clear before I run across the hall to the bathroom to brush my teeth and freshen up.

Aunt Mary and Florence are chatting away like old friends in the kitchen, making coffee and plating breakfast on a serving tray to bring out to the garden, I assume. Taking a moment to enjoy the scene before I announce my presence, I watch them with a smile, my heart full.

"Good morning," I finally say.

Aunt Mary crosses the small kitchen to wrap me in a big hug. "Good morning, my love. Did you sleep okay?"

I smooth my hair after she pulls away. "The best I've slept in ages." Florence shoots me a self-satisfied smirk, and I wink in return.

"Good. I'm so glad." She grabs a mug of hot coffee and hands it to me. "Just a splash of fresh cream. Florence was a dear and told me how you take your coffee."

"Smells delicious. Thank you." I take a sip and drop my head back in pleasure. It's actually so fucking good. "Is there anything I can help with?"

"Oh, no, sleepyhead. We got it all sorted." She hands me a cup of orange juice, and I take it awkwardly in my casted hand. "Pick a seat outside, then why don't you grab me that letter of your mother's, and we'll have breakfast, then open it."

My blood avalanches through my veins at the prospect of getting to be there when Aunt Mary opens the letter. "Okay," I say, obviously eager. I slip through the cracked patio door and place my drinks on the picnic table, then rush to my room to grab the letter. Carefully, I unzip the laptop compartment and slide it free, pleased with the crisp clean look of it.

I present it to Aunt Mary, and she smiles as she reads her name in Mom's cursive. "Thank you, Eaden. Thank you so very much. It's extra special knowing you came all this way to deliver it to me." She tucks it under the serving tray. "Now, let's eat before it gets cold, then we'll see what Eileen has to say."

I fill my plate with sausage and eggs and potatoes and fresh fruit. Mary's home-cooked breakfast is so much better than all the hotel breakfasts we've had lately, and I eat my fill unabashedly, especially seeing how pleased my aunt is with how much we're both eating. I'm sure last night had something to do with it, but Aunt Mary doesn't need to know that.

She takes the last sip of her orange juice. "Florence, would you mind fetching me another carafe of juice from the extra fridge in the utility room? My old joints are aching this morning."

She stands immediately. "Of course. Anything else I can get anyone?"

I shake my head, and Aunt Mary says, "No, love. Thank you so much." Once Florence is inside, Aunt Mary piles her empty plate by the serving tray and looks at me. "You know, Eaden, I've always had a pretty good sense of people. When couples came to stay at the bed and breakfast, I could always tell when they were fighting or if one wasn't happy or not feeling well. There was one time when two couples came, and I knew in my gut that the shorter fellow and his mate's wife were having an affair." She shakes her head and chuckles.

"Yikes," I say.

"Now, I'm not in the business of judging. Just loving." She points to the door leading to the kitchen. "But that Florence is a lovely woman, and I urge you to not let her go, Eaden."

My cheeks heat with blush. "We…we're not—"

"I know where you slept last night, love."

The mortification consumes me whole. "Aunt Mary, I'm so sorry. I didn't mean to be disrespectful or break any rules. It means everything to me that you're letting us spend time with you."

She waves me off with a scoff. "I think you two are fantastic together. That's all I'm saying. Does your cousin know?"

I grimace. "Florence and I aren't technically together. And, yeah, Riley knows there's something going on." I look at Aunt Mary, who's nodding thoughtfully. "She's so angry," I add.

"I can see why. It must be hard to lose a Florence." She gathers her hair into a bun and rubber bands it in place. "Sometimes, you can't control who you're meant to be with, but you can always control how you conduct yourself. You can always act with respect. And don't forget, you and Riley are family, and you love each other."

I stay quiet for a beat, considering her words.

"Hey," she says, capturing my attention again. "It'll be just fine. I promise."

Florence appears in the doorway, looking a little frazzled. "I'm sorry, Mary. I looked in every nook and cranny twice, and I couldn't find more orange juice anywhere."

Aunt Mary throws her hands in the air and scoffs. "Oh. I'm sorry, love. Must've forgotten to replace it last week." She shoots me a wink.

"No worries at all," Florence says and sits back down with us.

I have the last bite of my potatoes as we fall back into natural conversation. About the flowers my aunt has planted, the strangest bed and breakfast guests she's ever hosted, and about Florence's artwork and the watercolors she likes to paint. As I watch the two of them interact so effortlessly, I think about the things Aunt Mary said to me when she sent Flo on her fool's errand. For the millionth time, it hits me why my mom loved her so much. She's a force of warmth and support.

I can't help but wonder what my mom would think about me and Florence. In my heart, I know she'd have the same reaction as Aunt Mary and my dad. I have so many people supporting me, even when I'm walking a thin line. My heart aches at the realization that Florence doesn't have that same army behind her. She's going it alone. Especially if she loses Riley and Aunt Susan and Uncle Bob.

"Okay," Aunt Mary says, clapping. "Let's open the letter."

I sit straighter in my chair. This is it. The moment.

She pulls the envelope out from under the tray and carefully runs her finger under the seal, breaking open the ivory paper. From it, she pulls out my mom's stationery. Though I can't see it, I know her initials adorn the header in gold cursive. I wait as Aunt Mary reads, a small smile on her lips and her eyes misty.

When she finishes, she smiles and pulls a small card that I hadn't noticed was tucked inside the letter.

"She was paying me back," Aunt Mary says. She shows us the small cardstock, no bigger than a wallet. It's a beautiful watercolor of the famous row of houses in Cobh called the "Deck of Cards Houses." They're row houses of all different colors that Florence and I got to see on our way into town. The small brush strokes depict them gorgeously.

"Paying you back?" I ask. I take the watercolor and admire it. "I didn't know she painted."

"Eaden." Florence squeezes my knee under the table, seemingly not caring if Aunt Mary sees. "I helped your mom paint that," she says, her eyes watering.

I whip around to face her. "You what? When?"

"When she was in the hospital early on. I visited her a few times, and she was bored out of her mind before things got really bad. So one day, I brought her my travel set of watercolors. She told me what she wanted to paint, and I set it up for her. Gave her some tips. And she painted this little beauty."

"Why didn't you tell me when we walked by the houses?" I ask.

"I wanted to. But I've had your dad looking everywhere trying to find it. I thought she must have given it to him to bring home, and he must not have remembered where he put it. I've been hoping he'd find it so he could give it to you."

I didn't know Florence visited my mom alone. I assumed it was just with Riley. The knowledge only solidifies everything I know her to be. Tears well heavy in my eyes as I look at my mom's painting. A feeling of connection I've been so desperate for fills my chest. Being here with Aunt Mary and Florence, people who loved her, people who love me, holding one of the last things my mom did as her full self. It's everything to me.

"She was paying me back for a pocket-sized watercolor from a very beloved local artist she stole from my desk drawer when she was about eight," Aunt Mary says with a grin. She holds up the letter to read, "'Though I cannot part with the one I stole so many years ago, and yes, I know mine pales in comparison, please accept my watercolor as repayment. I know you know it was me. Is it silly, I want to keep it in death? Right there on my nightstand where it's always been. Next to the family photo of the four of us in Boston and the one of you and Dad in the sailboat.'"

She folds the letter along the creases and wipes the couple of tears that slide down her delicate cheek. "I did always know it was her," she says through a sniffle. "And I waited and waited and waited for her to come clean." She waves the letter and smiles. "I'll put this painting on my nightstand and cherish it for the rest of my days, too."

I wipe my cheek, unaware I'm crying until salt hits my tongue. I know that little watercolor on my mom's nightstand so well, the one of the sea at night and the big golden moon, with three red roses growing on the bank. Maybe Florence could paint me a replica because as long as my dad is alive, no matter if he stays single or finds a partner, that little painting is his to keep for her.

"Thank you for sharing that with me," I say, my words as sniffly as Aunt Mary's. "I've missed her so much, and I haven't felt close to her in so long. Until now. Thank you."

"You're welcome. We're family," Aunt Mary says. "All of us." She pats Flo's shoulder as Flo dabs her watery eyes with a napkin.

Three loud knocks on the front door interrupt us. I stand and hand Aunt Mary my mom's painting, giving my face a quick wipe. "You guys stay. I'll answer it."

"Thank you, love. It's probably just fresh eggs from the neighbor girl."

"No problem." I need a minute to recalibrate anyway; my emotions are overflowing. Walking through the family room, I feel calm and peaceful. Coming to Cobh was exactly what I needed. I unlock the big oak door and swing it open.

"Hey, Dildo."

I blink, struggling to comprehend what's right in front of my face. "Riley?"

CHAPTER TWENTY-FOUR

Riley stands in front of me with a sleek black suitcase and a cheap-looking bouquet of wilting flowers. Her hair is perfectly in place, and she tucks her sunglasses in her shirt, revealing a fresh face, annoyingly unscathed by travel and jet lag. She stares at me quietly for an uncomfortable minute, and I wonder if she's debating knocking my teeth out or not. She's seemingly on a mission and thankfully chooses not to. Though I do have a secret weapon now. I wiggle my fingers in my hard cast, daydreaming about how it would feel to smack her with it. Totally worth the reinjury.

"Move." She shoulders past me, leaving her giant suitcase for me to carry in.

And just like that, the trip is over.

I tug her case over the threshold and lock the door, looking around disoriented and confused. *What is she doing here?*

Riley wanders through the family room and into the kitchen, finding the door to the garden by following Flo's voice. I follow cautiously, keeping my distance. She yanks open the door and, completely ignoring Aunt Mary, whom she has also never met, gets down on one knee in front of Florence.

I watch from the doorway as her cheeks and chest turn a crimson I've never seen before. Aunt Mary scratches her throat.

"Riley? What are you—"

"Florence. I understand why you fucked Eaden. I get it." Florence covers her face in her hands, obviously mortified. "Trust me, I know sometimes, we just gotta scratch that itch and get it out of our system. But I forgive you, and I'm ready to take you back."

Flo shakes her head, her mouth hanging half-open. "I didn't ask for you to take me back."

"I know you want marriage and kids and the whole package, and I can give that to you now. We could have little Flos and Ryes running around. Why not?"

"What?" She keeps shaking her head.

"Florence Davis, marry me." She pulls a ring box from her pocket and opens it.

I'm too far to see the actual ring, but I catch a glare from what I assume is a huge diamond. My heart cracks in my chest as I watch my cousin offer the woman I'm falling in love with everything she's ever wanted, with the person she's always wanted it with. Flo looks up and catches my eye, something like pain and sorrow in her eyes. Is this the look of someone who's about to break my heart?

Riley looks over her shoulder and groans in disgust. "Don't look at Dildo. She doesn't matter. It's us. I'm your home. I keep you safe. I give you what you need. My parents took you in. It's where you belong. With me." She runs a hand through her hair, clearly getting frustrated with the lack of a quick *yes*. "You're about to start school, Flo. I know you don't want to lose all that support. You don't do well on your own, we all know that."

Flo picks at her fingers in her lap, soft tears falling down her face. Aunt Mary shoots me a worried glance, like she wants to put an end to this horrible moment. But she stays seated. I wonder if she wants Florence to stand up for herself. To be the one to say *no*.

"Is she the reason you're crying?" Riley throws a thumb over her shoulder at me. Leave it to Riley to berate someone to tears and try to blame someone else. "She's weak, Florence. She can't handle you. You belong to me."

"No. Enough," Florence says, meeting Riley's glare. She scoots her chair a few more inches away, the scraping of the wrought iron legs against the brick like an exclamation point to her answer.

"No?" Riley asks, more a taunt than a question.

"Not only did you show up unannounced and ignore Mary, but you just delivered a proposal that felt more like a threat than anything." She straightens in her chair. "Maybe there was a time I would have said yes, but you coming here with your 'grand gesture' to falsely appeal to everything I've wanted from you in the past and my insecurities?" She shakes her head, eyes wide. "I see you clearly now, Riley. I see who you are and the control games you play. But I will no longer let you control me. I'm strong as hell, and I'll be just fine on my own."

Riley puts the ring back in her pocket and stands. Florence stands, too, seemingly unwilling to let Riley take a stance of power over her. "And it wasn't just a hookup. I love Eaden."

Her words hit me hard in the chest, knocking me back a foot. I rub my chest with my hard cast. I love her, too. So much.

"I'll never talk to you again," Riley threatens.

Florence shrugs. "You're free to do what you want. You're a grown woman. And don't worry, I'll move out next week. But right now, I'm on this trip with Eaden and Aunt Mary, who is the loveliest host." She looks at Aunt Mary. "Mary, I'm so sorry. I clearly had no idea we were going to be interrupted."

Mary squeezes her wrist and nods to me. "It's okay, love. Why don't you and Eaden take the bikes in the utility room and ride to town? Check out the shops. Oh, and bring me back some orange juice, please. I'm going to stay with Riley, and we're going to get to know each other a little better."

We wordlessly bring the bikes to the front of the house. Then we ride.

Wind in our hair, freedom among the rolling green grass, and the salt of the harbor licking our skin, we don't have to speak. We just pedal. To me, the moment is cathartic, and it isn't too hard to imagine that Florence is feeling the same way.

When we make it to the coffee shop, we chain our bikes and walk inside. Florence grabs us a table in a quiet corner, and I order us two fruity smoothies, figuring we've had enough caffeine already. I wait by the counter as the blenders whir to give her a little space to process what just happened. She was proposed to, if one could really call it that.

"Thanks," I say and carry the smoothies to our table.

I place the more delicious-sounding one in front of Flo. It's her favorite color, pink, and I'm hoping it will help to ease her, bring back her normal blood pressure. She smiles at me and takes a small sip.

"It's good. Thank you," she says.

I take a sip of mine and make a face. "Fuck, that's tart. In a nice way."

She cracks a smile, bringing me some relief. "So that was fucking wild," she finally says.

"Yeah. It was. I don't really know what to say. I'm so sorry you were put in that position. And I'm so sorry you have to navigate the fallout with Riley."

She shrugs. "So do you."

I have no idea what lies ahead for me and Riley, and it may be wrong, but I'm struggling to care. My new mantra is, if something is meant for me, it will come to me. That doesn't mean I won't put effort into mending our relationship. I just won't bend over backward to win the approval of someone who has frankly never treated me kindly anyway. I'm done with that.

"We'll figure it out," I say.

Her laugh is sardonic and sharp. "I have a *lot* to figure out. I wonder if those nurses found a roommate yet. Maybe I can still move in with them when I get back."

"Even if they've filled the spot, there are so many great options around SCAD. You're going to be okay. I promise." Maybe I'm supposed to offer her a place to stay, but I don't think she wants that. I think she wants the time and space that comes from not living under a partner's roof in whatever shape or form.

"Yeah." She nods, assuring herself. "Yeah, you're right." She looks at me, her eyes narrowed in worry. "And us?"

"Well, I think we've made it pretty clear how we feel about each other. Florence, I love you. I don't want to see any other women. Just you."

Her features relax, and a smile spreads over her lips. "Same."

I wipe my brow dramatically. "Phew. Good."

"Shut up." She laughs.

I hold her hand over the table. "In all seriousness, I know things are going to be a little chaotic when we get home. Hell, they're a little chaotic now that Riley is here, but we can go slow. I can help you move, and you can take all the time and space you need. I'll be ready when you are." I pull her hand to my mouth and kiss her fingers. "I'm yours."

"After this trip, I don't think I can keep away from you." She looks away, blushing. "I may be slightly obsessed."

I smile, too pleased with myself. "The feeling is mutual."

"But I hear you, and I promise to let you know my needs."

"Deal."

We drink the rest of our smoothies and muse about what Aunt Mary and Riley are talking about or if she is currently smacking Riley with a rolled-up newspaper for being so cocky and cruel. I hope that's exactly what's happening. Whatever they're talking about, I find some solace in the fact that Aunt Mary is unbiased when dealing with me and Rye. She only knows us from our mothers and can hopefully share some impartial observations and advice with Riley. Doubtful she'd be able to hear any of Aunt Mary's words in her agitated state, but it's something.

On our bike ride home, we stop at a particularly gorgeous vista of the dramatic lush hills clashing against the sharp blue water. A singular red farmhouse stands between them on the horizon, captivating us.

"We have to come back every year while we still have Mary," Flo says.

I drop my bike, take her face in my hand, and kiss her deeply, sweetly, with all the love and strength and freedom that is newly a part of me. She kisses me back, her hands in my hair, her tongue in my mouth. Florence and I are everything.

"We will," I say when we finally break away. I pull my bike off the grass. "Are you ready to face whatever is back at the house?"

She straddles her seat, red hair gleaming in the sun. "I'm ready. Just stay close to me."

"Always."

The house is eerily quiet when we get back. No sign of Riley. No shouting in the garden or her giant suitcase. Nothing but Aunt Mary sitting alone among the flowers. We spot her through the kitchen window and join her, presenting her a cup of the orange juice she'd wanted.

"Thank you. You girls are the sweetest."

We sit on either side of the table, Flo to her left and me in front of them. "Where's Riley?" I ask.

She grimaces. "See, the thing about people who are in a rage is, they can't hear reason. They can't hear concern. And most of all, they can't hear love." She takes a small sip of juice and wipes her brow. "I wanted to help her—she's got a battered soul, that one—but it was fruitless. She agreed that it was best for her to leave, so I called my friend Kieran, and he gave her a ride to town. She'll stay at an inn for the night and travel to Dublin tomorrow to sort her travel back to the States."

"So that's it?" Florence asks.

Mary shrugs. "Well, I assume that's not it for you two and Riley, but it's certainly it for me and Riley. I told her she could come back, but as it is, she couldn't stay."

"Thank you. I'm so sorry, Mary. This is all my fault," I say.

"Oh, quiet now. It's no one's fault. It's just life." She looks between us. "You girls okay? I know that was quite the scene."

"Yeah, we're okay," Florence says.

Aunt Mary gives her a warm hug. "Now, be honest with me. Are you going to save me some laundry this week and tell me I don't have to wash the *Titanic* room sheets?"

We all break into a soothing laughter, releasing all the tension from the day.

"I think it's safe to say yes," Flo says.

"Well, good. I hate washing sheets." Aunt Mary stands abruptly. "Let's get this Cobh vacation back on track! Who fancies a pint?"

And with that, everything returns to normal. Ireland normal. We have yet to discover the new Atlanta normal.

CHAPTER TWENTY-FIVE

I file onto the plane with everyone else, extra careful not to knock into anyone or anything with my cast. For their sake and for mine. It now feels so strange to travel without Florence, but maybe it's a small blessing we didn't book our tickets together. Why would we have back then?

Back then feels like a different world.

Maybe we both need this time alone to process the trip. To process us.

There's one spot left in the overhead bin above my seat, and I wiggle my bag against a black roller bag and the panel. Perfect fit. I've become quite emotionally attached to that bag, and as I buckle my seat belt, I wonder if I could buy it off Sean. Passengers are still boarding, so I put in my earphones and play a Spotify playlist that Florence made for me before we left Aunt Mary's. I think we both knew it would sting, separating for the flights home, so she had the idea to swap playlists.

Sweet lyrics fill me as I think about our trip, our last days together in Cobh with Aunt Mary. She showed us all over town. The cemetery in the back of the small Catholic church where our family is buried, the spot where my mom broke her toe on an abandoned anchor in the shallow water of Cork Harbor, and the local pub that my uncle used to own. We had *many* pints and swapped many tales there. Aunt Mary even took us to a local craft market to find a frame for my mom's watercolor. I picked out a blue wooden one, hand-carved, with a delicate pattern around its edges. Not too busy or bright. Nothing that would take away from the painting itself. I bought it for Aunt Mary as a small thank-you gift for hosting us.

I gnaw on my lip as I remember waiting for our train. Aunt Mary is a hard person to say good-bye to. A hard person to let go of when her soft warm arms are wrapped around me and she's kissing me all over my face.

But she gave me something I'll cherish forever. She and Florence. They gave me ties back to this earth and taught me that even when they loosen, I have the strength to tighten them up. And if I need help, I have people I can lean on.

I'm going back to Atlanta changed.

I hope that Florence is listening to my playlist, looking out the window, and processing the last few weeks. I hope she's feeling changed, too. I hope she knows that no matter what mess is waiting for us in Atlanta, she's strong enough to handle it. And if she needs help, she has people she can lean on. People who love her.

That's what I hope the most.

That she feels wildly loved.

CHAPTER TWENTY-SIX

Being back in my townhouse feels strange. Unfamiliar in the best way. Before I left for Europe, my home was filled with anger, pain, and depression. But now it's so much lighter here. No more mug cakes. In fact, I bake a damn good chocolate mousse cake with the help of Florence for my dad's birthday. We're having a small party for him later tonight at his place. My TV has been quiet recently as I'm busy going to faculty meetings to gear up for the start of the school year and meeting up with friends like Hakim. Though, there is a new season of Great British Bake Off dropping next week, and Florence and I are going to watch every episode together.

It's been a quiet morning of reminiscing on my adventure with Flo. Though I've only been home for two weeks, it feels like ages ago that we were traveling. My cast is growing grimier by the day, but I adore looking at all the signatures—one in particular—and remembering the first night we made love.

Alas, work calls. I open my laptop and log in to the Zoom meeting with my camera off. My phone pings with a notification from Instagram, and I grin, knowing exactly who it is.

@**Gowithflo33:** *Hey loser. Don't forget to wrap your dad's present.*

Flo and I pass the time chatting during my pointless meeting. I sip my cold coffee and groan, unwilling to microwave it again. Once the meeting ends, it hits me.

The electric mug.

I race upstairs and pull the small box from under my bed, excited to wash the new mug and set it up for tomorrow. It comes with a warming coaster I can set next to my laptop while I work. It really is the perfect mug for me. I run downstairs with my gift in hand and sit at my desk. The sparkly green bow still sits plump on top of the original box. It's silly that I haven't opened this yet, given how much I hate microwaving my coffee. But I couldn't let go of my pain enough to do it.

I peel the bow from the cardboard, trying not to rip it in the hope that Flo can turn it into a magnet for me so I can keep it. *Success.* I notice the circular tape that had closed the box has been cut. When I open it, a small blue envelope pokes out from the side of the mug. My heart skips at the sight of my mom's handwriting.

It's the thing I've been dying for, a little piece of her just for me. Carefully, I open the note.

Happy birthday, Babygirl!

I can't believe both my babies are well into their thirties now. That about makes me old as dirt. And therefore, less able to put up with your crying every time you have to microwave your tea or coffee! Just kidding. But really, use the damn electric mug.

You light me up, sweet girl. And I can't tell you how proud of you I am for following your dreams and doing what's right for you. Even if it isn't what you expected. This next year is going to be magic. I can just feel it.

All my love.

Always.

Mom

My tears are a constant stream down my face, and I hold the card away from me to avoid dripping on it. I push it to the side and sob. Everything I needed from her she had already given me. Everything I needed from me I already had. She *loved* me. She loved me so fucking much. And that is a superpower I will carry with me forever.

I wipe my face in my shirt and try to calm my breathing, but my crying turns to laughter, and the hysterical wet mess of me continues. And it feels like flying. Feels like home.

❖

My parents' house slowly fills with family friends, and though I am cool with my dad now, I find myself pacing around the kitchen. It's not because when I look up and see the laundry room, I think of my dead mom from my nightmares. No, when I look at the laundry room, all I see is her singing along to a song she barely knows, smiling, living. I'm pacing because I know that any minute, Riley is going to walk through that door, and I haven't heard from her since I helped Florence move into her new place. And even then, it was rough.

Flo kisses me on the cheek and rubs my back. "It's going to be okay. We know the worst is over."

I try for a smile. "You're right. I'm not holding on to this anxiety."

"Exactly. The people here love and support us."

I nod slowly. "Exactly."

The door to the garage opens, and Riley walks in with a bottle of wine and a card. We all pause and stare at one another. Of course it's just the three of us in the kitchen. Finally, she walks in and places the gift on the counter.

"Hey, Rye," I say.

She walks to my side of the island. "I need to say something to you."

I swallow, and Florence takes a protective step closer to me. "Okay."

"Aunt Eileen didn't write me a letter. I lied. I don't know why." She shakes her head, clearly frustrated. "To hurt you. I guess to hurt you. And the funeral...*fuck*." She wipes her hands down her face. "Just want you to know that I was operating with a lot of pain and a lot of alcohol in my system. Not an excuse. Just the reality."

"Thank you for telling me," I say softly.

I'm shocked to see tears welling in her eyes. "And I'm so fucking mad at you." Her voice cracks, and it seems to enrage her even more. "I'm so fucking mad at you, Eaden. I always have been but never more than now."

I stand, speechless.

She knocks her fist on the counter. "I don't intend to make another scene at a family function, so I'm going to rein this in. But if you could pull your head out of your ass, maybe you could see you weren't the only one desperate to be chosen."

It hits me: all the times Riley cried through the night, sleeping in my room as a kid. How she'd do anything to get the attention of my mom or the approval of my dad. How she ran and lifted and trained every day to become the best athlete she could and to date all the women she could. Like there was always a void she was trying to fill.

I grab her hand and squeeze. "I think I can see that."

She nods. "Okay. Then maybe we can meet up sometime and talk about it." She jerks her hand away from me. "Later. I can barely look at you still."

"Okay. I hear you. Later."

She walks around the island toward the back deck. "Hope the new spot is treating you well, Flo."

"Thanks, Rye," she says.

"See y'all out there," Rye says and disappears outside.

We stare at each other, digesting what just happened. Flo's eyes are wide. "I'd call that a step in the right direction," she says.

"Yeah." I grimace. "That was hard to hear, but I think you're right. A step in the right direction."

She rubs my shoulder. "You guys are going to figure it out."

"I know we will. Just not today." I kiss her and grab her hand. "Let's go join everyone outside."

The night is a wild success in my book. Sean asks more questions about our trip and Aunt Mary than I ever expected him to, even hinting at wanting to plan his own trip with the new girl he's dating. Flo and I really like her, especially how she seems to mellow him out. My dad says his birthday cake is the best cake he's ever eaten. Jury is out on if he is lying or not. And when I give him his gift, he cries. To be fair, it is the best gift in the entire world. Aunt Mary let me take an old Polaroid of my parents in Ireland from when they were only twenty-two. She even gave me the letter my mom wrote her after meeting my dad. Being able to give that to him with the photo inside wasn't just a gift to him. It was a gift to me, too.

And now Dad has them.

I don't know exactly where they were in their marriage when my mom died. It's not my business, really. But I do know and trust that my dad adored her. He loved her. No matter his mistakes. Being in Ireland allowed me to bring back this piece of her for him. It allowed me to reconnect him to that time when they were twenty-two and so deeply in love. They gave each other so much. At least, that's how I'll remember their marriage.

I know that's how he'll remember it.

Later, I hold Florence in my arms and close my eyes, ready for bed and exhausted from the party. I kiss her hair and whisper that I love her before I drift into sleep. And when I sleep, I see her.

Eileen Knight Bilbo. And she's smiling.

About the Author

Ana is an award-winning author of sapphic romance. She worked in the Pacific Northwest wine industry for eight years and now lives in her hometown of Atlanta. She loves all things fermented or distilled, walking the local trails, and eating pastries...so many pastries. She is currently working on her next book and dreaming of a beach trip.

Books Available From Bold Strokes Books

The Moon to Me by Ana Hartnett. Sometimes it takes traveling thousands of miles to discover what's been yours all along. (978-1-63679-918-6)

Royal Rush: 75 Days to Fall in Love by Lissandra Rowe. When a royal matchmaking scheme leads to a chance encounter with Isabella Acosta-Ramon, a slow burn sparks that neither can deny. (978-1-63679-965-0)

To Love Violets for Their Thorns by Rachel Sullivan. Forced to face the heartbreak they never quite got over, Elly and Sonia must decide: breathe fresh life into an old love or try again with someone new? (978-1-63679-928-5)

Virtually Perfect by Melissa Sky. If your AI flirts better, listens harder, and never ghosts you...does that count as love? (979-8-90035-005-9)

Brooke Takes Queen by Alaina Erdell. Brooke Staley faces personal and professional upheaval when Elizabeth Bettancourt, the emotionally scarred new owner of the resort she works for, considers selling. (978-1-63679-886-8)

Coda by Anna Gram. Parker is intriguing, magnetic, impossible to ignore—and completely wrong for Hannah. But sometimes love's melody refuses to end. (978-1-63679-926-1)

The Debutante Dilemma by Jane Walsh. Two debutantes are engaged to wealthy and titled brothers...but discover they only have eyes for each other. (978-1-63679-896-7)

The Love Book by Gun Brooke. When literary agent Rowan Cross receives an anonymous manuscript that deeply resonates with her, Verity realizes she has accidentally sent her own manuscript, complete with her very real feelings for her boss! (978-1-63679-850-9)

Secrets Under the Junipers by Suzie Clarke. Who killed Hallie Lynn Peeples? Cecilia McConnel needs to know. Bitsy Hanover holds the key. Can love uncover secrets? (978-1-63679-845-5)

Traveling Toward Forever by Erin Dutton. When almost-strangers take a road trip through America's national parks, love may be the final destination. (978-1-63679-894-3)

Beautiful Things by Emma L McGeown. A warmhearted romance of missed chances, undeniable chemistry, and a stubborn love that maybe, just maybe, can find its way back. (978-1-63679-934-6)

The Great Popcorn Romance by Georgia Beers. Opposites attract, and Riley Shaw stands no chance of resisting Hannah Kramer's magnetic pull. But opposites know just how to drive each other crazy... (978-1-63679-910-0)

Love Takes a Village by Karis Walsh. As Lena Preiss struggles to manage a busy restaurant in the Bavarian Christmas village of Leavenworth, Washington, chocolatier Devin Meyer brings an unexpected richness into her life, along with her delicious desserts. (978-1-63679-902-5)

Secrets of the Heart by Jenny Frame. When a beautiful stranger starts asking questions about Nikki Sharkey, head of an infamous crime syndicate, Nikki will stop at nothing to protect her daughter Isla. (978-1-63679-653-6)

Talon and the Songbird by Julia Underwood. In a world where survival depends on strategic alliances, Makayla and Talon must navigate not only complex politics but also the dangerous territory of their hearts. (978-1-63679-970-4)

Three Blissful Days by Dena Blake. Kendall Jackson attempts to make her ex regret dumping her by announcing she's dating beautiful park ranger Ivy Patterson. But there's nothing fake about how attracted Ivy is to Kendall. (978-1-63679-707-6)

The Art of Love by Ali Vali. When Mimi and Bianca both set their sights on Jolly, sparks fly, loyalties are tested, and hearts collide as they navigate the unpredictable nature of their hearts. (978-1-63679-719-9)

Chasing Her Scent by MJ Williamz. When Sheridan Rousseau walks into Lisette Mouton's charming little bookstore in Quebec City, she unknowingly holds the key to a mysterious box hidden in a secret room. (978-1-63679-900-1)

Heart's Run by D. Jackson Leigh. Hoping to recover an escaped racing mare, stock transporter Tobie Mason locks horns with local wild horse advocate Maggie Wilkes. (978-1-63679-825-7)

Scandalous by Kris Bryant. When a Hollywood actress trades places with her twin sister, everyone's in an uproar about getting duped, but Lindsay's more concerned about finding out which twin she made out with. (978-1-63679-874-5)

The Secrets of Rhydian Hill by Ronica Black. A doctor in need of a new start. A woman running from a killer. A love story that could end in tragedy. (978-1-63679-880-6)

Feeling Lucky by Krystina Rivers. What happens when, despite suddenly having enough money to buy almost anything, Lucy and Tanner start to discover that maybe all they need is each other? (978-1-63679-876-9)

Iceberg by Gun Brooke. When Lady Arabella hires Zandra, she never expects to find love, especially not as a disaster looms on the horizon. (978-1-63679-908-7)

It Happened One Semester by Aurora Rey. After a Pride night hookup, can eager new Assistant Professor Hudson Greene and Dean of Advising Callie Shaw overcome the odds and ace falling in love? (978-1-63679-814-1)

It's Kind of a Bad Idea by Sarah G. Levine. What happens when an emotionally unavailable serial dater meets the one woman she can't help but fall for—who happens to be the one woman who told her not to? (978-1-63679-920-9)

Thankful for You by Tagan Shepard. Everyone deserves to find their person. Maybe Karen has finally found hers? (978-1-63679-884-4)

What Happens On Location by Nan Campbell. How can Helen produce a successful movie when its director is the woman responsible for the demise of her marriage? (978-1-63679-904-9)

When Love Comes Around by Radclyffe & Ronica Black. Can Maya Sanchez and Nolan Wright trust each other enough to build something real, or will the past tear them apart? (978-1-63679-930-8)

www.ingramcontent.com/pod-product-compliance
Lightning Source LLC
Chambersburg PA
CBHW030520020726
47494CB00004B/1166